Praise for *Passages of Hope*

What a beautiful story! *Passages of Hope* not only illuminates the fascinating and dangerous work of the Underground Railroad but tells of the longing for family and home. Separated by time, Gracie and Olivia are both intriguing heroines, strong but vulnerable. Terri J. Haynes's writing brings these women and their trials to life, using a poignant ribbon of the search for belonging to tie it all together. I couldn't put this novel down!

—Sarah Sundin, bestselling and award-winning
author of *Until Leaves Fall in Paris*

Terri Haynes has written an extraordinary story of family, freedom, and forgiveness in her newest novel, *Passages of Hope*. The painful aspects of what it means to become family are beautifully knit together with a liberation story from the Underground Railroad in Philadelphia. Haynes ensures that her main heroine, Gracie, must learn what it means to be knit in her mother's womb and that God has fearfully and wonderfully made her to learn about her heritage and love. Well done!

—Piper Huguley, author of *By Her Own Design*

Doors to the Past

PASSAGES OF HOPE

TERRI J. HAYNES

BARBOUR
PUBLISHING

Passages of Hope ©2022 by Terri J. Haynes

Print ISBN 978-1-63609-406-9

Adobe Digital Edition (.epub) 978-1-63609-407-6

All scripture quotations are taken from the King James Version of the Bible.

This book is a work of fiction. Names, characters, places, and incidents are either products of the author's imagination or used fictitiously. Any similarity to actual people, organizations, and/or events is purely coincidental.

Cover Model photograph: © Shelley Richmond / Trevillion Images

Published by Barbour Publishing, Inc., 1810 Barbour Drive, Uhrichsville, Ohio 44683, www.barbourbooks.com

See the series lineup and get bonus content at DoorsToThePastSeries.com

Our mission is to inspire the world with the life-changing message of the Bible.

ecpa Member of the
Evangelical Christian
Publishers Association

Printed in the United States of America.

For Maxine

You lived on your own terms, and I love you for it.

CHAPTER ONE

GRACIE

Philadelphia, present day

$\mathcal{G}$racie McNeil stood in front of her gran's three-story row house. She tipped her head back to see all the way to the roof, the red brick warm in the September sun.

No, not Gran's house anymore. My house.

Her gaze dropped to the front door, and the world seemed to tip toward her, giving her a moment of vertigo. How many times had she stood here? Walked through the front door? She closed her eyes, reorienting herself. This would not be like any other visit she'd had before.

She reached into her bag and sighed when her fingers closed around a key ring holding four keys. Not until this second had she dared touch it for fear it would slip from her grasp and be lost. Now she flipped to the front door key. It glowed like amber in her hand. Standard rounded-head door key. One that shouldn't be in her possession. But somehow this key and this house had made their way to her.

Two shuffling steps and she was at the foot of the stairs. The house looked much the same as it did the last time she'd seen it. Almost four months ago, two weeks after Gran died. The family had gathered here after the funeral at Gran's church, Mother Bethel AME, for a repast that ended with a fight. If Gran knew how she had acted then. . . She could still see that frown. One she never wanted to see on Gran's face but one she knew she deserved a thousand times over.

No one was inside now. No one and nothing but memories, good and bad.

She climbed the three gray concrete steps and slid the key into the lock. It clicked, muffled, like the whole world was wrapped in wool. She gripped the doorknob. All she had to do was turn. Turn and open a door into the unknown future.

Palm sweating, she glanced at the window next to the door. The opaque image of herself stared back, her black hair in two strand twists, a little fuzzy from the humidity of a city near a body of water. Her eyes ladened and puffy with dark bags against her brown skin. Her reflection was tense, shoulders raised. Like it was taking all her strength to open the door. All of it, what little she had left.

Do it for Gran. She stood a little taller. Gran was the strongest woman she knew. Even to the end. Gracie took a big breath, as much air as her lungs allowed, and mimicked Gran's fortitude. She turned the doorknob and pushed the door open. Gran's empty house greeted her, both familiar and foreign. It was the same house, but it wasn't the same as before.

The house had been shut up for months. The movers came to haul in her meager belongings a few days ago, but other than that, this door had remained locked. But instead of stuffiness, the house smelled of nothing. No cake baking. No sharp twang of vinegar in collard greens. No rosewater candles, smoky and sweet.

No signs of Gran.

Tears blurred the rooms before her as she stepped inside and closed the door. The sound echoed through the empty space.

Most of Gran's furniture had been divided among Gracie's uncle and cousins. A cheap consolation prize for Gran's most valuable possession going to Gracie. Her uncle's anger had boiled hot. Gracie's disbelief had chilled her to numbness. Gran had given no clue that she was going to leave the house to Gracie. Maybe if Gran had told her, she would have had time to prepare for all that came with the house. All the memories and heartbreak.

Gracie had received one additional item from Gran: an ornate wooden keepsake box. Apparently Gran kept a box of mementos for each of her children and grandchildren. There was a similar one at her father's house that belonged to Gracie's mother. Gracie had never seen what was inside hers or her mother's. Now it would be too painful to look.

She wiped the tears from her cheeks with the back of her hand. The house had an open floor plan, except for the staircase. Most houses were built with the staircases against a wall, but not this one. The foot of the stairs sat in the middle of the house, shielding the back of the house from people coming in the front door. How many times had she come in the door and heard Gran call out to her from the kitchen behind the staircase? Hundreds. *Oh, to hear it one more time.*

She walked through the living room, past the fireplace that covered one wall, and set her bag next to the staircase. She did a quick check of the kitchen and laundry room. Then the half bath. Everything was clean and sterile. Like no one had ever been there. No evidence of the joy and pain that had once been. Her circuit complete, she picked up her bag and started upstairs.

At the landing, she studied the rooms below. Her mind overlaid an image that had often been in her thoughts in the past months: couches and armchairs full of knitters and crocheters, laughing, drinking tea, and perusing the yarn selection Gracie had curated. The brick-and-mortar home for her yarn shop, Stitch Wishes. With the cream walls and all the natural light through the long windows in front of the house, the room would be a cozy, luminous place. Warm and welcoming, like it was when she would come to see Gran.

A bittersweet plan. One that was likely to fail.

At the top of the stairs, she went through another door, one fitted with a lock like the one on the front door. At some point in the house's history, the second and third floors had been for rent. There was another door on this level that led outside, down a set of wooden steps. She walked down the hall. This floor also held a full bath attached to two of the bedrooms, and the third had been converted to a small kitchen. At the end of Gran's life, having a kitchen on the second floor had been invaluable. Gracie had never wanted to be away from her grandmother's bedside for long.

As she requested of the movers, her bed sat in the larger of the two bedrooms, surrounded by bins and boxes. The rest of her furniture was in the other bedroom. It wasn't much. A nearly threadbare couch she'd gotten at a thrift store. A TV, a scuffed plywood TV stand with a right-hand door that no longer closed all the way, and a coffee table that wasn't strong enough to hold more than a plate of food or a ball of yarn. After kicking off her shoes, she unwrapped the couch from the heavy blankets it had been swathed in to make the move. Her old couch in her new space. Pulling the blankets away grounded her and helped her believe this was real.

When she was done, she sat, closed her eyes, and took a few deep inhalations. *Lord, help me to see this as my home.*

When she opened her eyes, the room around her was still Gran's spare bedroom. For a second, the weight on her heart felt almost unbearable and threatened to sink her so deep into grief that she couldn't climb out.

"Be strong," she said to herself. Her voice warbled.

Stuffing her sadness into the back of her mind as she had done for months, she took out her phone. She needed to live despite how she felt. She ordered groceries to be delivered later that night, checked to see what the hours at the library were, and then tracked the shipping on a rug she had ordered. That done, she set the phone next to her.

Her attention was drawn to the windows and the view they gave her. The house faced a sports field, its grass still a little green. Gran used to take her over there to play when she was young. At the end, when Gran was still strong enough to go down the stairs, they sat on the benches, Gracie knitting and Gran crocheting.

Her phone rang and jarred her away from the memory. She glanced down at it. The display read UNKNOWN CALLER, but she well knew who it was. The lender for her student loans had called nearly every day since she left Richmond. She tossed the phone to the other end of the couch, anger coiling through her stomach. Why couldn't they leave her alone? She told them the first twenty times they called that she had no job, no money. She told them that she was grieving a lost loved one. None of that mattered. They still called.

She let out a huff and grabbed the phone. Maybe this time they would listen. As she moved her finger to press the answer button, she was reminded of another phone call, a call that had lit her anger like a bonfire. She dropped the phone again. What was anger then had morphed into shame now. If she'd had any idea the journey that call from Gran would set her on, she would have checked her anger. But she hadn't known.

She put her hands over her eyes. The memory remained clear, undimmed by time. *Oh, Gran.*

⁂

Gracie spent the next hour unpacking boxes and bins of her things. The TV was one of the last items she put in place. Beads of sweat dotted her forehead as she lifted it to the stand. It was almost too heavy to lift alone, but she was alone, so she had to do it alone like everything else in her life.

The doorbell rang as loud as church bells, echoing through the empty house. Gracie jumped up, walked to the windows, and looked down. Because of the angle of the house, she couldn't see who stood on the stairs. It was too early for her grocery delivery. She rushed down to the door. The window next to the door framed her visitor. Ms. Lila Brown stood, looking straight ahead, hands resting on her cane. Weathered, rich brown, veined hands. She stood upright and proud, her silver hair in an afro halo around her head.

Gracie swung the door open, smiling. "Ms. Lila." She bounded out the door and embraced her grandmother's closest friend.

Ms. Lila returned the hug, and although she was shorter and thinner than Gracie, it felt like being enveloped in a cashmere shawl lined with steel fibers. "Gracie. You're here. I hope you don't mind me stopping by. I thought you'd be here soon when you asked me to let the movers in."

"Just arrived." She stepped aside to allow Ms. Lila to enter. "I'm sorry I don't have chairs down here yet. . . ." Ms. Lila was quiet behind her as Gracie closed the door. A weighted quiet.

When she turned, Ms. Lila was standing still in the middle of the living room. Gracie stood as tall as she could, pushing back against the sadness welling in her chest. But when she moved to Ms. Lila's side and saw tears in the older woman's eyes, Gracie's shoulders slumped. Hadn't she stood here and cried earlier today? The emptiness, the sting of loss, had stopped Ms. Lila in the same spot.

"It doesn't seem real that she's gone. Keep half expecting her to come out of the kitchen with two cups of tea." Ms. Lila let out a soft laugh that ended with a sniffle. "Or with a whole meal she just 'threw together.'" She made air quotes with her fingers.

Gracie laughed, swiping her own eyes. "Like she always had a roasted chicken with all the fixin's just lying around waiting for company to arrive."

"That's right." Ms. Lila turned to her. "How are you doing?"

"I'm okay." She tried to smile and prove her words. "Never thought any of this would happen. That I would be living here after. . ." She swallowed back tears.

Ms. Lila looked at her, brows furrowed. "Maybe you didn't know how fast the cancer would progress, but how could you not know that she wanted you to live here after she was gone? This house meant a lot to her. She thought of it as her legacy."

Gracie nodded. That was all Gran would talk about. How the house was family history. *But why leave it to me and not her children?* Wouldn't it have been better to leave it to someone whose life didn't look like a patchwork quilt of mismatched jobs, an incomplete degree program, and hopscotching housing situations? How could she be trusted with something so important?

Ms. Lila reached out and touched Gracie on the shoulder. "You meant as much to her as a daughter. As much as your mother did. This was important to her. You were important to her."

Gracie squirmed at the mention of her mother. A mother who had died in childbirth and one Gracie didn't know. There was no way she could fill her mother's place. "Would you like to go upstairs?"

Ms. Lila gave her soft pat on the shoulder. "No, baby. My grandson is waitin' outside for me. I just stopped in to see if you needed anything."

Gracie took Ms. Lila's hand and held it, her heart lifting. "I'm fine. Thank you for asking, but you didn't have to."

Ms. Lila took her hand from Gracie's and placed it on the side of Gracie's face. "You were important to her and you are important to me. You're going to carry on Marian's memory and this family's legacy."

Gracie smiled at her, trying for all the world to hold back tears but failing. Standing here in Gran's house with someone who loved Gran as much as she did both comforted and pained her. The two women couldn't be separated.

Ms. Lila wiped her own eyes, and they returned to the door in silence. "You still got my number?" Ms. Lila asked.

"Yes, ma'am."

"Call me if you need something. Or need to talk." She beamed at Gracie. "Consider me your first friend in the city."

Gracie giggled. "I think we were already something like friends."

"We are officially friends now. Besides, I have a knitting project I need help with."

Gran and Ms. Lila had become friends in their church's prayer shawl ministry. "Of course I will help you."

Ms. Lila nodded. "I'll be talking to you," she said and made her way down the front steps and the half block to her car. Gracie watched as a tall young man opened the passenger door and assisted her in. The grandson. He looked Gracie's age from the distance. But the way he helped Ms. Lila into the car brought the sting of tears. *The same way I helped Gran.*

Ms. Lila's words still echoed in her mind as she returned upstairs. *"You're going to carry on Marian's memory and this family's legacy."* Could she even do that? Gran and Ms. Lila's expectations for her had always been high. Too high and misplaced. Too easy to fail to reach them. But she had given Gran her word.

She returned to her place on the couch, and her eyes fell on one of the few boxes she hadn't unpacked yet. She slid the box closer, rummaged through it, and pulled out a folder.

Before she died, Gran had told her to live her dream. Had told her that her dreams would make the world a better place. Gracie had thought she meant her dream to go back to school to finish her business degree. She didn't think Gran meant her dream to open a yarn shop. But as it became more evident that Gran's time was winding down, the older woman took to asking Gracie every day about her yarn shop plans.

Gracie opened the folder to the wrinkled papers inside. On top lay a rough sketch of the layout of her yarn store, one she had had commissioned years ago. When she thought she could possibly afford a space in a strip mall. The dimensions had to be adjusted a little to fit Gran's house, but they still worked. This was her real dream. One she had had for so long that she didn't know how she came to want it. A space with walls of yarn. A refuge like knitting had become for her. A solace and a balm.

She wanted that for herself and for other knitters and crocheters. And Gran wanted that for her.

She moved the drawing aside and lifted the page beneath. It was a financial breakdown of how much it would cost her to open the shop. The first item listed was *Rent/Lease*. She had written a figure down that she thought she could afford. Another rush of tears flooded her eyes, surprising her. Still crying like she did when Gran died, then when she learned she had inherited her house and an annuity.

She wiped her face and set the financial breakdown to the side with the sketch. The new budget set a few pages down, and it included something the first didn't: how much money she would have to make to pay herself. With the need for rent gone, she could possibly do that and still be able to bring in all the yarn brands she loved.

All because Gran made her promise to open the shop in her house. Because Gran believed in her dream more than Gracie did. The house around her was quiet. In this bubble, with Ms. Lila's words and Gran's gift to her, she could almost believe this could work. But even if it didn't, she would give it her best effort. She'd promised Gran that she would.

CHAPTER TWO

*G*racie sat in her car in front of her Uncle Rand's house. The pep talk she had given herself on the drive over had run out. Her fingers refused to let go of the steering wheel. Tonight she would moderate the first family meeting. The meetings served to update the heirs of the progress she'd made on closing Gran's estate. Or lack of progress. That would be obvious the minute she started talking.

She inhaled, stretching the breath as far as she could before she released it and the steering wheel. She grabbed the door handle and used her shoulder to push the door open. After climbing out of the car, she gave herself a once-over. The night was cool enough for her lined blue pants and cashmere sweater. She let her fingers glide over the sweater's softness, and pride swelled in her heart. No one would guess it used to be an ugly one that she'd found at a thrift store, unraveled, and repurposed the yarn. It made her feel happy and accomplished. She would need both feelings to get through this meeting.

She walked around to the other side of the car and retrieved a folder of documents. Tucking it under her arm, she made a straight line to the front door with only a slight wobble of nervousness. She knocked and waited. A square of light from the front window fell on the porch just next to her foot. Just one step away. She moved her foot toward it, but the front door opened, flooding the porch with light. She squinted to see Uncle Rand standing in the doorway with a scowl on his face.

"Are you coming in?" he asked, his words clipped.

"Hello, Uncle Rand." She gritted her teeth into a smile.

His eyes narrowed. "Come inside." Not a request this time.

She pulled her shoulders back, stepped inside, took off her coat, and hung it in the hall closet as she'd done hundreds of times before. Uncle Rand closed the door and moved past her and down the hall so that she was following him. She held in the sigh that almost escaped.

The hall led into an open-floor-plan living room and dining room. The décor was tasteful and expensive, but not in a welcoming way. These were rooms to look at, not live in. The furniture was a little more modern than you would expect. Once her cousins Ada and Bernard had moved out, Aunt Elle had upgraded. Next to Gran's house, where they normally gathered as a family, it was the next option for Thanksgiving and Christmas dinner. Now this was the only house available to host the holidays.

Aunt Elle, Bernard, and Ada sat on the couch. In the armchair sat Natalia, Gracie's much older second cousin. All of them looked up when she stepped into the room. Gracie gripped her folder tighter to keep from adjusting her clothes again. "Hello, everyone."

They all returned her greeting, which was more than she expected. She took the nearest seat and placed the folder in her lap. Uncle Rand took the other seat.

"You're here," Natalia said. "When did you arrive?" Natalia had always lived on the fringe of the family. Gran had told Gracie that Natalia and Gracie's mother were close like Gracie and Ada had been.

Gracie balanced the folder on her lap and tried to give off a casual air. "Last week."

Bernard's eyebrows rose. "That long. I didn't know."

Gracie rubbed the back of her hand with her thumb. "I didn't really tell anyone." Her eyes caught Ada's gaze and the unreadable expression on her cousin's face.

"Shall we get started? I'm sure everyone wants to go home after a long day," Uncle Rand said. He narrowed his brown eyes, making the wrinkles around them even more pronounced.

Gracie cleared her throat. "Well—um, this should be a short

meeting. Unfortunately, not much has changed with Gran's estate since. . ." She looked down at the folder and took two steadying breaths. If she cried now, she would look like she was falling apart, and most of the people in front of her probably already believed that. "I filed my Letters Testamentary, publicly announced the estate, opened an estate bank account, and paid all the most recent bills out of that account."

As she continued, everyone nodded while she talked, most of them wearing open or neutral expressions. A flicker of hope formed in her heart. If the meeting continued to go like this—

"And what about the house?" Uncle Rand asked.

Gracie trembled as the sharpness of his words extinguished that hope. "I'm sorry, but because Gran had a living trust, the house isn't included in the estate."

"I think you mentioned that before," Ada said quietly. She moved her hand to grip her upper arm.

Stop repeating yourself. "I don't have anything else to report."

Uncle Rand leaned forward in his chair. "Pennsylvania law gives children rights as next of kin."

Gracie gave Ada a quick glance before repeating herself. "As I said, a living trust along with a will allows assets to pass directly to beneficiaries. The estate is no longer responsible for the house. I am."

His gaze narrowed. "So you're still going through with your plan?"

"Yes." She brightened her voice to sound cheerful and excited. "I will eventually need a contractor who is going to do some upgrades."

Uncle Rand was on his feet, his face contorted in a sneer. "What kind of upgrades?"

Someone sighed, but Gracie didn't know who. She instinctively leaned back in her chair. "For the shop."

"With what money?" His tone held a thread of disapproval.

"Uncle Rand, let's not do this." *Not again.* He was always concerned with her finances. He'd loaned her money once. Once. It had taken longer than she wanted to repay the loan. He had made sure she understood it was a loan when he gave it. Now he felt that he had a personal stake in her bank account. She closed the folder with trembling fingers. "If there aren't any more questions—"

"I am not done talking."

She held her face in a mostly pleasant expression with some difficulty. "I have explained my plan multiple times. I don't think there is anything else to say."

He glowered at her. "If you ruin the house—"

Gracie clenched her jaw, closing off the urge to tell him he was right. That she shouldn't have this house and he should. Instead, she rose. "If that's all, good night."

After a few mumbled goodbyes from the rest of the family, she let herself out. Her shoulders were tense with the dread that he would start yelling down the hall at her. But he said nothing more. If only it were that simple. If only she could silence all his grumblings. The only way that was happening was if she signed over the deed to the house and went back to dreaming about opening her yarn shop. And she'd be homeless.

Time to keep her word and convert her plans from paper to reality.

Gracie woke early, had breakfast, and went to her "office," the old laundry room. Her stomach knotted as she sat at the small desk set against the wall. The folder with her shop plans lay next to her laptop. She placed her hand on it. It had grown soft like fabric from years of her taking the papers out of it and reading them. Now it was time to do more than read them.

She slowly flipped open the folder. She had rearranged the papers inside, so now the list of things she needed to do to open the shop was on top. The first item was to announce that the shop had changed addresses. She opened her laptop and logged in to her website's e-commerce dashboard. Renting a PO box like she had when she was in Richmond was an unnecessary expense now.

The next task was to announce that her shop was moving from online only to a brick-and-mortar location as well. That wasn't as easy as changing the address. Her face felt flushed as she looked at her projected opening date, January 3. That was only twelve weeks from now. Approximately four months to get the fixtures installed, order product, advertise in the community, create the layout, and do a million other little things. A dot of pain pricked above her eyebrow. Was that enough time?

Instead of a date, she typed "coming soon" into the text box on her website.

She had already secured a contractor, Preston Dawkins. Ms. Lila had recommended him, and Gracie had been impressed with what she saw on his website. He had come by last week to look at the space and get measurements. He was friendly. He had listened to her and taken her seriously. More than that, he seemed excited about her ideas. By the time they were done with the consultation, she was grinning. He said he would be back in a few days with some options for a counter she could use for a checkout. Soon the house would be transformed into a shop.

The next item on her list was setting up classes. When she was in Richmond, she taught classes in a shared space at the local art center. Those classes provided a little revenue outside of yarn sales. Besides, she enjoyed teaching knitting and crocheting. Someone had taught her to knit and changed her life. She liked to think she was doing the same by teaching the classes. Changing someone's life.

After going through all the plans, it seemed best that she offer one adult knitting class, a kids' class, and a crochet class, each meeting once a week. The classes would start once the shop opened. The kids' class was a last addition and the one she was least sure about. She'd been around children before. One of her many jobs had been a hostess at a children's entertainment business and pizza restaurant. If she could handle twenty-five screaming boys and girls and sorting out tickets and prizes, she could teach knitting.

It couldn't hurt to open class enrollment now. She created the registration form and added the classes, all on Saturdays, to the website. She limited the kids' knitting class to five. It would be a test run to see how well she could handle it. The whole opening of the shop felt like a test run. And it had great potential to fail since she would be doing almost everything herself at the beginning. But hadn't she lived most of her life like that? Doing everything by herself?

After saving the class listings, she went to her next task: assembling shelving for the shop. The contractor had offered to put them together for her, but she wasn't going to pay for something she could do herself. Besides, if she was going to meet the deadline she planned to open the shop, those fixtures would have to be full of yarn as soon as possible. She closed her laptop and went to the living room where the boxes of shelving sat against the wall. She slid one to the floor, opened it, and with a sigh, removed all the pieces. They clattered on the floor, echoing through the emptiness, making her feel like she wasn't in her beloved gran's house.

An hour later, someone knocked on the front door. Gracie rose slowly, her back protesting all the way up. Half a shelving unit sat in front of her. *Maybe I should let Preston put these things together.* She rolled her shoulders and went to the door. If it was Preston, she would ask how much he would charge and save her back.

The person knocked again just as she reached the door. "I'm coming. I'm coming," she said as she opened it.

On the doorstep stood her cousin Ada. She was a little taller than Gracie but about the same size. She had the same cocoa-brown skin and brown eyes as Gracie, but her mother's genes had given her thinner lips. People often told them that they could pass for sisters. Gracie never thought so until now. But why was she here?

Gracie straightened her posture. "Ada. Uh, hi. I—" She swallowed.

Ada gave her a small but genuine smile. "Hi, Gracie."

Neither of them spoke for a moment, then both spoke at the same time.

"If this is a bad time, I can come back later," Ada said.

Gracie stepped back. "Come in."

Ada smiled and stepped inside. As her cousin took in the space, Gracie closed the door and inhaled. Ada, a few years older than Gracie, was the person who most felt like real family besides Gran. When she and Ada were younger, Gran had regularly arranged to have Ada over at the same time as Gracie. But when Ada went away for college, they only saw each other for the holidays. Then Gracie moved to Richmond, and whatever connection they seemed to have evaporated. Ada had been very quiet during the settlement of Gran's estate. Her father had all the bluster, and Ada had said almost nothing.

"I hope you don't mind me stopping by," she said, fingering the collar of her coat.

"No. I was just—" Gracie waved her hand at the pieces of shelving.

"Ah, good ole IKEA. You'd think after all these years, they'd make these things a little easier to assemble."

"Yeah, I know."

"When do you plan to open?"

Gracie steeled herself. Did Uncle Rand send Ada over here to berate her some more? "A few months from now. So I'm very busy."

Ada smiled. "That's great."

Gracie relaxed her shoulders. "Thanks."

Ada shifted from one foot to the other. "I wanted to talk to you about the shop more at the meeting, but my father. . ." She looked at the shelving again. "I'm surprised he let you talk as much as he did."

"Which wasn't much. Besides, there's only one subject he wants to talk about, and there is nothing to be said about it. It's almost like he's obsessed—" The fact that she was discussing Ada's father dawned on her. Gracie covered her mouth. "Sorry," she said through her fingers.

"It's okay. I think we all know how displeased my father is with all this." Ada gave her a wry smile. "But he's displeased about lots of things, so don't worry yourself too much about it."

Gracie shook her head. "This is kind of a big thing to be displeased about."

Ada looked around. "He shouldn't be. If he'd been paying attention, he would have known what Gran was going to do."

"Did you know?"

Ada shrugged. "Not for sure, but I suspected. At the end, your yarn shop was one of the few things she talked about with excitement. I even thought she was hanging on long enough to see it."

Tears stung Gracie's eyes, and she bit her lip. Uncle Rand wasn't the only one who didn't see this coming.

Ada saw and took a step forward, then paused. "I'm so sorry. I shouldn't—"

Gracie swiped her tears. "Sometimes it's so hard to believe she's gone."

"I know," Ada said, her own eyes shimmering. "I still expect her to call me to talk about how my classes are going and when's the next time I'm coming over."

A whisper of guilt floated through Gracie's thoughts. Ada had lost her grandmother too. But because the battle lines were drawn and Ada hadn't made it clear which side she was on, Gracie had assumed that losing Gran hadn't affected her deeply. Obviously it had.

"I'm between terms now, so if you need some help putting together shelves, I'm mostly free," Ada said, making brief eye contact before looking away.

Gracie grinned. "You may regret that offer."

"Probably." Ada laughed. "But the offer still stands."

CHAPTER THREE

The computer screen in front of Gracie seemed to pulse in time with her headache. How could she think with all the racket the contractors were making?

Two hours ago, Preston and Jo, one of his employees, had arrived with her counter wrapped in so much plastic, it seemed to shimmer. Gracie's heart had swelled. She'd watched for them all morning, her dread rising with each hour. But they had come on time, and things were moving forward.

Then the noise started. Gracie had suggested mounting one end of the counter to the wall to keep it in place if her customers leaned on it. Preston had laughed at the idea. It was too heavy to be moved. When she pushed the issue again, he huffed and said nothing more. Now she regretted it. She rubbed the bridge of her nose. Returning her gaze to the computer screen, she scrolled through the site of a yarn dyer. She needed to place an order soon if she was going to receive it before January.

A drill screeched, jolting her thoughts.

Sighing, she gave up. Preston had said they would be done before four o'clock. At this rate, probably not. She and Ada would have to work around them to hang artwork tonight. She frowned. Why was Ada being so helpful now? Unfortunately, Gracie couldn't afford to question or refuse the help.

She went upstairs for the pair of socks she was knitting. As she came back down, she assessed the space. The sofa she'd bought at a closeout sale sat near the fireplace. Two armchairs she'd found at a thrift store were being cleaned and reupholstered and would flank the sofa. Once they arrived. The delivery date kept getting delayed. Gracie couldn't complain. She'd paid almost nothing for them. Along the walls were three white storage cubes she had assembled while sitting on the floor for long hours. She rubbed her sore lower back. She wasn't looking forward to assembling the other three.

The space was starting to come together. Now could she fill it with crafters? She sat down on the couch and began knitting the sock. The circle of the stitches soothed her, and her thoughts drifted to other things she needed to do for the shop. Her shop. One she'd wanted to open since she was young. The dream began shortly after some women had come into her middle school and started a knitting group. Although not their intention, it became the place to dump troubled students.

Gracie had landed there soon after the group began, just back in school after a suspension. Her teacher had escorted her down to the small classroom where the knitting group was held, pulled the leader of the knitting group aside, and whispered, "Gracie doesn't have a mother."

Gracie had dropped her gaze to her shoes to miss the pitying look on the leader's face. It was always that way. The *poor, broken little thing* look. How could a kid whose mother had died in childbirth and whose father was distant not be broken? Her knitting slowed. She didn't have parents, and now she didn't have Gran. The weight of loneliness weighted her shoulders, and she slouched. That's the way it was now without Gran.

Behind her, a sharp trill cut through the air. The throbbing in her head intensified. She turned to find Preston looking sheepish. She massaged her temples. Laying aside her sock, she walked over to the counter.

"Sorry about that," Preston said, "but there's something back there."

"Maybe a crawl space beneath the stairs?"

That earned her another frown from Preston. He motioned to the hole they'd cut in the drywall. "Looks like brick."

Gracie tilted her head. Although the house was a typical townhouse with brick on the outside, there was very little inside. "Are you sure?"

"Yup. I could cut a bigger hole so we can see."

Uncle Rand's words rang in her mind like an alarm. *Don't ruin the house.* She fiddled with the hem of her shirt. "Okay, but can you make the smallest hole possible?"

Preston stooped and put his hand on a space next to where the counter would be mounted. "We'll cut it here. That will make it a little less noticeable." He pulled out a saber saw and went to work cutting a bigger hole, a perfect square. He removed the cut like a slice of cake. "More brick."

Gracie let out a sigh. "Do you think the whole thing is bricked?"

Preston looked at her, eyes questioning. "Yes, but the only way to find out is takin' down almost all this drywall."

Her stomach sank like a stone. "I guessed that."

Her nerves jangling, she returned to her sock. But after a few mistakes, she stopped. Gran never did renovations to the house, only needed repairs. Gracie had been here for less than two weeks, and she was tearing down a wall. Did Gran even know what was there?

"Ms. Gracie?" a voice asked from very close. She turned her head to find Preston next to the couch.

She jolted. "Yes?"

He cast a worried look over his shoulder. "Uh, you need to look at this."

She followed him back to the wall, but her steps slowed when she saw the door. Her heart tripped as she took a step closer. *What in the world?*

It stood about five feet tall and was made of wood. The key plate and doorknob looked to be brass dulled by age.

"Does this house have a basement?" Preston asked.

Gracie shook her head. "Just a root cellar."

"You sure? The old houses in this area are full of secrets."

A trill of curiosity traveled along her spine. This door led somewhere. Gracie stepped to the door, grasped the knob, and turned it. She pulled, and the door opened with a loud squeak fit for a horror movie. Preston took a step back.

Behind the door the air smelled wet, like earth and soil.

She peered down into the darkness. "Do you have a light?"

Preston handed her a flashlight and grimaced. "Are you sure you want to do that? I've seen some things in my line of work."

Someone will have to. She flicked on the flashlight and shone it in the opening to reveal that the whole enclosure was brick, like an elevator shaft. There were also stairs, the open, wooden kind. They looked pretty much intact.

Preston peered over her shoulder. "Huh," he said, the sound of his voice echoing down the stairs.

"Do those steps look like they'll hold me?"

His look of curiosity turned to horror. "Ms. Gracie, I don't think this is a good idea."

"They look sturdy enough."

He sighed and took the flashlight from her. "If you're determined to go down there, we should test them first." He gripped the side of the doorway and gave the top stair a hard stomp. "Oh."

Gracie jumped at the sound. The echo of the stomp floated up to her ears. "What?"

"They are pretty sturdy." He stomped a few more times, shining the light on the stairs. "Nails look almost new."

Gracie took the flashlight back. Her hand trembled a little as she stomped each stair as she went down like Preston had. She focused all her concentration on each step below her and reached the bottom before she knew it. She looked up and gasped.

The light revealed a small room with brick walls. It was about ten feet by ten feet with a dirt floor.

"Ms. Gracie?" Preston called from above.

"You can come down. The stairs are safe."

She stepped away from the stairs and shone the light around the empty room. One end of the wall opposite the stairs had a different look to it. She shone the light on it. It was a wooden panel, about four feet wide, that reached almost to the top of the ceiling. A slice of light lined the top edge.

Preston reached the bottom of the stairs and let out a whistle. He moved past her toward the panel. "That doesn't look very secure."

He touched it, and it fell with a bang. He jumped out of the way, and Gracie yelped, nearly dropping the flashlight.

Steadying her breathing, she pointed the flashlight into the space the panel had hidden. There was a short passage. Behind that, old metal shelving with empty mason jars lined the walls of a small area. The root cellar. Why would the house have both a root cellar and a secret room?

"I know where this goes," she said.

They walked into the root cellar and past the shelves together. Three short stairs sat below a door that was almost above their heads. Preston grabbed the door's handle and, grunting, pushed the door up and open. He climbed out, and Gracie followed him. A small alley ran between where they stood and the next house.

Preston stood squinting, shielding his eyes with his hand.

"That was exciting." Gracie tried to sound light, but her voice trembled. "I knew about the root cellar, but I never knew that other room was down there."

Preston hadn't moved. He was still staring at a house on the row across the street. "Uh, Ms. Gracie. I don't think we should do anything else on the house yet."

She whipped to face him. "Why not?"

He pointed at the house across the street. "A couple of years ago they figured out that house belonged to William Still."

She frowned. "I know that name, but I can't recall where from."

"He was called 'the father of the Underground Railroad.'"

"I remember now," she said with a smile. The Underground Railroad was one of the many history lessons Gran had given her. "My gran said that people here believe there were several station houses nearby, but—"

Realization hit her hard enough to make her gasp.

Why would a house need a root cellar and a secret room?

To hide people who had escaped from slavery through the Underground Railroad.

CHAPTER FOUR

OLIVIA

Philadelphia, 1855

Olivia Kingston reached the bottom of the stairs, the darkness no hindrance to her steps, and then lit the oil lamp in her hand. The light glowed gold around the small room, creating a ring around her. The brick walls and dirt floor seemed to absorb some of the brightness, but not enough to keep the three figures huddled in a corner in complete shadow.

The frightened, wide-eyed expressions on their faces were familiar. She had seen it many times before. "All is well," she said quietly.

The two men and the woman relaxed, their shoulders slumping with the release of worry.

Olivia set the lamp down and traveled back up the steps to get the basket in the doorway at the top of the stairs. Her movements were quick. Sluggishness could be dangerous tonight. She set the basket in front of the three. "The arrangements for your departure have been made. We must go to the docks tonight."

The faces in front of her shifted, each in its own way, from alertness back to worry.

"Do not be too anxious. This will be dangerous, but you will have friends with you. There is food, warmer clothing, some blankets, and a little money for each of you." She moved the blanket atop the basket to reveal the items.

One of the men, Otto, stood and went to the opposite corner and picked up the traveling sack he had arrived with. The other two, a couple, Lula and Albert, looked dismayed. "We do not have any way to carry those things."

Olivia smiled at them. "We will fashion a sack from one of the blankets, but we must hurry. The next conductor will be waiting for you."

With Lula and Albert's help, Olivia spread one of the blankets on the floor. The four of them had all the goods and few coins distributed between them and their bundles secured with knots in less than five minutes.

"We will go out the door you came in and down to the docks," Olivia told them, noting the charge that now filled the air. Moving the "passengers," their code name, was a feat that required great care and caution. One mistake and these three would suffer worse fates than they ran away from.

She moved to lift the lamp. "I will return within the hour to accompany you to the docks."

Otto gave her a worried look. "Miss Olivia, are you sure? Won't it be dangerous?"

Olivia touched her hand to her heart. "It will be fine. There will be others there to watch out and make sure you get on the boat safely. If you do exactly as I say, you will be gone before there is any danger."

Lula smiled, tears sparkling in her eyes. "We want to thank you."

Olivia gave them a gracious smile. This was one of the great joys of being a stationmaster. Helping every living soul who passed through her room. Knowing that she had been a part of their journey to freedom. Also to give them a picture of what their lives could be like. Olivia was very often the first free Black woman her guests had ever seen.

"No thanks needed," she said, moving to the bottom of the steps. "Your freedom is enough thanks for me."

Lula swiped the tears from her eyes. "Thank you, Miss Olivia. May God bless you," she said in a low voice.

Olivia nodded. "Please try and get some rest." She steadied her breathing with each step up the stairs and extinguished the light at the top. She heard a faint shuffling from below before she moved through the short wooden door and out onto the main floor of her home.

A home she had been using to shelter fugitives for a little over a year.

The room in front of her held the lawful side of her life. Her dressmaking shop. Although the walls were an ordinary cream, the room was full of color from the bolts of fabric and half-finished dresses on mannequins. This was where she worked her other trade.

She placed the lamp on a small table by the door and lifted the wood panel that leaned against the wall. Mr. Colton, a free Black bricklayer who built her home, including the room below, had also fashioned her a lightweight piece of wood that she could secure over the door so it remained unseen. Once in place, no one looking at it would know that there was a door behind it that led down to her secret room.

Her task done, she extinguished the rest of the lamps on the bottom floor and began her trip up to her bedroom. She let out a yawn. A few customers had come through her door, but preparing her passengers to leave had taken up most of her day. She'd had to collect all the supplies, bake some bread for their journey, and plan the route to the docks. They could almost never take the quickest, most direct route. They had to go a longer way that allowed hiding places if they were followed.

It was well after dark, and her husband, Douglas, would already be in bed. Probably long asleep. She had seen him very little today. His work as one of the few Black doctors in Bella Vista exhausted him, and he retired from the table not long after dinner. Her heart craved a conversation with him, but it would not happen tonight. Maybe not tomorrow night either. Maybe it was for the best, because she couldn't talk about the topic uppermost in her mind.

Douglas and Olivia had been married for nearly three years, and they'd had only one conversation about the work she did. He had recently graduated from medical school, and they were in the process of buying this house. She had sat him down and explained that she wanted to continue the work she had done with William Still and the Underground Railroad. Her parents, free Blacks, had planted the seed in Olivia, using their modest home in Delaware as a station house. She was helping fugitives by the time she was nine.

Her parents had moved to Philadelphia and served Mr. Still for a few years and then had moved again to Ohio, where they used their new home as a station house as well. She had married Douglas and stayed near Mr. Still even though Douglas was supportive of their moving closer to her parents. Olivia had to be here. This was where she could do the most good. She would not stop until every single Black person was free like she was.

She would help the three in her secret room down to the docks without Douglas knowing much. He had agreed that she continue her work during that conversation three years ago. She'd promised that she would keep the details from him. There was a stiff penalty for helping fugitives. If questioned, he could honestly say he did not know anything about what she was doing. And he would have no need to lie.

She had honored that promise. If she was caught housing fugitives, all Douglas' hard work of becoming a doctor would be wasted. They would have to take flight themselves to keep their freedom. So she only ever told him that she had "work." It must be the tone that she used when she told him, but she never had to explain to him which of her jobs she meant. He only nodded and said, "I will pray."

As she changed into her sturdy boots and dark cloak, she wondered again what he would say if he knew just how much danger she was in.

※

Olivia sat at the head of the table in Shipper's dining room and stifled a yawn. She glanced around to see if anyone saw. It did not appear that the members of the Friends of Bella Vista had. Conversation and laughter floated around her.

The Friends monthly meeting was held at Shipper's, an inn owed by Mr. Abrams. The committee had been active for years. William Still, chairman of the Pennsylvania Society for the Abolition of Slavery, had begun it. He had also enlisted several members to be stationmasters or conductors. The Friends of Bella Vista met to find ways to help their neighbors, but it was also the safest way for them to discuss their antislavery work without raising questions.

Olivia had soon been nominated to chairwoman as she was already connected to the Bella Vista community. She had accepted the honor with all her heart, thankful for the opportunity to help.

She glanced around the room, taking account of who was in attendance. All the stationmasters and conductors, Mr. Wilson and Thea, Mr. Abrams, and Mr. Gull, a conductor who lived about ten miles north. He had been assisting many years before Olivia and was one of the first conductors she had met. Also in attendance was Henry Foley, a newly freed Black man who worked at the docks. Mrs. Steward, a widow, had sent a note to Olivia that she would not be coming. Lottie Muller, a sharp young woman, had stopped by to tell them she was working tonight. The Friends discussed community concerns while Mrs. Steward, Lottie, and Henry were present. But when they weren't, they discussed Underground Railroad business.

Rubbing the bridge of her nose, she thought her fatigue had escaped notice until Mrs. Thea Wilson sat down beside her.

"Did you sleep at all?" Olivia's friend and fellow stationmaster asked.

"Yes." She looked down at her notes. She had slept for about two hours after returning from the docks. The sun rose too soon, and she had dragged herself out of bed. Douglas required little attention, but food still needed to be cooked. And, in a quiet tone, he had asked her to mend a button on one of his favorite shirts. He had stood very near to show her which one. Did he notice how she had leaned toward him, their shoulders almost touching? She had fixed the button this morning, replaying the comfort in being close to him. Words between them were so precious. Even words asking if she could fix a button.

"How long?" Thea asked, her gaze still on Olivia's face.

"All I could."

Thea raised an eyebrow. "I am in awe at how you can do so much with so little sleep."

"Not everything. I wanted to finish repairing the tear in Franklin's coat. It will be done by tomorrow."

"Olivia, you cannot continue like this. You are not responsible for everything. I told you he has another coat. You have more important things to do than repairing a coat ripped by an energetic boy."

Olivia grimaced at Thea's words. "If I had his energy, sleep would be unnecessary."

Thea shook her head. "Not true. Franklin is so tired after a day of running errands that he nearly collapses. It is impossible to get him up in the morning, and he often sleeps late."

Sounds glorious. To get in bed and not have to be out of it before the sun rose. She nearly yawned again but took several deep breaths instead.

Mr. Abrams entered the room with a cup and saucer in his hand. He set the black coffee in front of Olivia. "Had to start prep on tomorrow's meals."

Olivia stared at it, and Thea let out a soft chuckle.

"Thank you. Shall we begin with prayer?"

The room quieted. Every single person in the room knew they were doing God's work. Each heart's conviction was as strong as the next. Several in the room had aligned themselves with the Quakers' stance against slavery. All of them believed that every person should be as free as they were in God's eyes.

Olivia said a short prayer, asking for God's help and guidance in their work, and once a hearty "Amen," sounded around the room, she lifted her notes.

The words on the page blurred, and she blinked several times to focus. The first item was Mr. Wilson's report on the funds. She sighed with relief. If Mr. Wilson had to talk first, it would give her time to have some coffee and wake up a bit. "Mr. Wilson, please share your report."

Mr. Wilson began with recounting the funds the group had dispersed. Their donations went toward three areas: the Institute for Colored Youth, the needy in the Bella Vista community, and Underground Railroad activities. Only the first two would be discussed at the official Friends meeting. The third would be addressed once Henry left.

Pride filled Olivia's heart at how their efforts had gotten more books for the institute. Mr. Wilson finished his report by stating how much was in the community fund.

"Which brings us to the next item," Olivia said. "We need to decide who in the community needs help so Mr. Wilson can disburse funds."

Mr. Abrams cleared his throat. "We already decided."

Olivia paused in the middle of lifting her cup to her mouth, alarm bringing her alert. Had she missed that discussion? She was tired but had no memory of drifting off to sleep in the meeting. "We have?"

"Well, we have a very strong candidate, and most of us were already prepared to nominate him," Mr. Abrams said. Everyone around the table nodded in agreement.

She exhaled. "With such a strong endorsement, I guess our vote is only a formality. Who is it?"

"Douglas."

Olivia blinked. "My Douglas?"

Mr. Abrams nodded. "He has treated our poorer neighbors many times without being paid, as you know."

Olivia managed to keep her surprise from her expression. *He has?*

"He is a saint for that, but still, his generosity must be creating a hardship for your family," Mr. Wilson said. "We don't have much to give, but we can at least assist with some of the unpaid bills."

Henry nodded. "You will need to convince him to accept it."

Of all the requests they could have made of her, talking to Douglas about anything would be the most difficult. "Wouldn't it be in bad form for a committee member to accept funds?"

Mr. Gull laughed. "Like when the committee helped me repair my wagon?"

"Or the repayment for the food my wife and I supplied when that large group of children arrived at the institute?" Mr. Wilson asked. His grocery had been a hub for the station houses in Bella Vista. It was one of the few places that almost all of the stationmasters could go without suspicion. Everyone needed food, so it provided the perfect cover.

The committee had done all that and more. It was one of the convictions of the group that made it work. No one stood on ceremony.

They all understood the sacrifices required to do what they did. More than that, accepting assistance meant they could do more work. Assistance that none of them would think of refusing. . .except her. "I will speak to Douglas."

The meeting continued, and Olivia's exhaustion increased. The thought of talking to Douglas had put an additional weight on her shoulders. What would he say? How could she even bring up the topic? *I found out from the committee that you have not been charging the poor residents.* No. Accusing him like that would make her a hypocrite. How many secrets was she keeping from him?

The sun had set by the time the first meeting adjourned. All of the conductors and stationmasters made the pretense of leaving, collecting their things, but began to have conversations with one another while they waited for Henry to leave. They could count on him leaving shortly after the meeting because Henry always walked Lottie and Mrs. Steward home. But tonight Henry, who was normally so reserved, began chatting with Mr. Gull, more animated than Olivia had ever seen him.

Mr. Wilson had to manufacture a reason to escort Henry out of the room. As he passed Olivia, he whispered, "Go ahead without me. Thea can tell me what you discussed."

As soon as the two men were gone, everyone returned to their seats. "We should go through the rest of the items quickly," Olivia said. "We are already behind."

"I thought that boy would never leave," Mr. Abrams said with a chuckle.

They dove right into their Underground Railroad business. Most of the discussion centered on their recent encounters with slave catchers.

"We have to be extra careful right now," Mr. Gull said. "I have seen at least two new slave patrols in the last week."

November was the worst month. Because more slaves ran in November, there were more catchers in the area. "I believe that our measures to travel in pairs as much as we can is our best course of action. We may need additional options when traveling alone is unavoidable," Olivia said. "Have we heard from Moonie?" she asked, worry heavy in her heart.

Moonie was a free Black, only twenty-two years old, who had gone missing earlier that summer. No one had heard from him since, and no matter how much they and Mr. Still had searched for him, they had not been able to find him. No one wanted to accept that he had been kidnapped and sold south, but they had few other explanations. Moonie had been working at the mill one day and gone the next. If he had been sold, it might take months for him to get word to Mr. Still. It had happened before, so they had some hope, but with each passing day, hope dwindled. Olivia shuddered at the pain he may be suffering. But Moonie was young and strong. He would not accept being a slave after being free his whole life.

When the second meeting adjourned, Mr. Gull drove Olivia and Thea home. After Olivia climbed down from the wagon, Thea placed a hand on her shoulder. "Get some rest."

Olivia nodded and watched the wagon drive off. She checked her surroundings as she rushed up the stairs with her remaining energy. The lights were still on. Douglas had not gone to bed yet. She put the key in the lock of the front door, her muscles stiff with fatigue. Stepping inside, she breathed a sigh of relief that the front room was empty.

Her relief evaporated when Douglas came around the end of the stairs with a cup of tea in his hand. "Evening. How did the meeting go?"

"Well." The desire to sleep overshadowed her discomfort. "There is something I would like to discuss with you."

He studied her. "Can it wait until the morning? You look as if you need sleep first."

She removed her hat and cloak and sat in a chair. Douglas came and sat in the chair across from her. "The committee members voted tonight to settle some of your unpaid bills with the money we raise to help members of the community."

He frowned. "Surely there must be a more worthy cause than me."

"The committee feels you are worthy, especially since you are treating patients at no charge." She said the words, waiting for him to explain why he kept his generosity secret. Not that she was surprised. Or angry. But finding out from others did needle her.

"I would rather they find another cause. Can you convince them?"

She shook her head. "They want me to convince you."

He looked down at his tea. "If you feel it is proper."

"I had little say in the selection."

He looked up at her and opened his mouth to speak but then closed it. His expression told her that he had considered saying something other than, "Very well." But that was what he said, and the matter was closed. Very closed.

CHAPTER FIVE

GRACIE

*G*racie started the day with her head buzzing with thoughts. Yesterday Preston had packed up shop and left as soon as they got back upstairs, leaving installation of the countertop and the pegboard for hanging yarn undone. He had told her that the site was probably historic and wouldn't continue work until she got it verified.

Apparently there were big penalties in Philadelphia for renovating a property that was deemed historic. Gracie knew that the whole Bella Vista district was designated historical. Practically the whole city was historical, and contractors knew not to proceed if anything looked remotely unusual. And a room underneath a house across the street from William Still's house was unusual.

Gran had never said anything about it. Maybe she didn't know.

After dragging herself out of bed, Gracie got a cup of coffee and went to the living room. As she sipped the hot liquid, her eyes focused on her keepsake box from Gran. She set the cup down, went across the room, and picked it up. It was a sturdy box, heavy and coarse against her fingers. This house was full of secrets, including whatever was in this box. Gran had never told Gracie what was inside. They had talked so much in the year she was Gran's caregiver, but Gran didn't say much about it. Gracie knew that Gran was still adding to the box. She had come into Gran's room one morning and seen Gran putting something into it.

When Gracie asked how soon she could see what was inside, Gran had said, "Soon enough."

Secrets. Now any forward progress she'd made on the house was at a standstill because of a huge one downstairs. She could use the time to order yarn and other inventory, but that wouldn't take more than a week. Her headache from yesterday hinted a return, a prick above her eyes.

She went downstairs and stood in front of the secret door. The gray day outside paled the natural light coming through the front windows. If there wasn't so much animosity between her and her family, she would call them and ask them about it. Uncle Rand would not be happy about her removing the drywall and would accuse her of ruining the house.

But there was someone she could ask. She made a phone call.

"Hey, Gracie." Ms. Lila's voice instantly lifted Gracie's mood.

"Good morning. Do you have time to talk?"

"Just a little bit. My grandson is picking me up for lunch."

A pang of jealousy pricked her. "I don't want to hold you, but I wanted to ask you about the house."

"Of course, but I'm not sure how much I can tell you," Ms. Lila said with hesitation.

"Did Gran ever tell you anything. . ." Gracie paused. "Anything secret about the house? About a secret door that leads down to a little room?"

The line went silent for a few seconds. "No. Nothing like that."

"Preston was doing work yesterday. There's brick and a door behind the drywall."

"My word."

"Then he told me that historians recently discovered that William Still lived across the street from this house."

"They sure did," Ms. Lila said. "My grandson, Clarence, was one of the ones who discovered it." The pride in her voice was unmistakable.

An idea lit up her thoughts. "You said you're having lunch with him today?"

"Yes, in a couple hours."

"Any chance you both can come by?"

"Absolutely." Ms. Lila's voice was charged with excitement. "I wanna see this room. When they found the Still house, they found a room over there too. I wanted to go see, but the owners weren't letting anyone but the researchers inside. And we thought Mother Bethel was our most significant historical location." She laughed. "Listen to me going on like this. I sound like Clarence."

"If you and he could stop by, I would really appreciate it."

"We will."

"Thank you," Gracie said, and she ended the call, her shoulders relaxing.

The rest of the morning dragged by. She blew through the day's tasks, but the clock didn't seem to move. She stopped in front of the door more than once. Had Gran said anything about the house being a part of the Underground Railroad and she just didn't remember? Not likely. Gran talked constantly about history. And not just local history. Gran had Gracie memorize the family tree four generations back. Gran was a huge history buff. That was one of the reasons she had loved living in Philly.

"Living around so much history makes you feel your importance and your insignificance," Gran had said.

One day when they were walking past the Liberty Bell, Gran had squeezed her hand and said, "It's hard to believe that we are also a part of this city. Part of all this history. Marian Leander and Gracie McNeil."

Gracie had laughed. "You may be, Gran, but not me. I don't even live here."

Gran smiled. "You are still a part of this history, because I am."

Sadness crashed over her with that memory. Gracie fought back tears. The sound of the doorbell prevented her from dissolving into a blubbering mess. She swung open the door. Ms. Lila and a very handsome man, presumably the grandson, Clarence, stood on the steps. "You're here."

"We cut our lunch short. Clarence was very excited about your room and wanted to see it sooner rather than later," Ms. Lila said, motioning to him.

Clarence smiled. "I hope you don't mind." His hair was dark, cut in a fade with coarse curls on top. He had a thin mustache and beard on a face the same rich brown as Ms. Lila's. He wore glasses that seemed to magnify the kindness twinkling in his eyes.

Gracie blinked, sure she was gawking. "No, I don't."

He offered her a handshake. "It's nice to finally meet you. My grandmother talks about you all the time."

Gracie glanced at Ms. Lila, who had the nerve to be wearing an innocent expression, eyes on the room behind Gracie.

"Does she?" Gracie asked.

"She said that you might need a friend."

"Thank you." *Can a girl have friends as handsome as you?*

"Is that it?" Ms. Lila asked, bringing a welcome shift in the conversation.

Gracie led them to the door. "Yes. And I don't know what to do."

Clarence stopped in front of the exposed brick wall. He ran his hand over it but didn't speak. After he was done examining the wall, Gracie picked up the flashlight she'd left nearby, flicked it on, and opened the door.

Clarence sucked in a breath behind her.

"Be careful, Ms. Lila," Gracie said.

Ms. Lila waved her hand. "I ain't that old. And I wouldn't miss this for the world."

They traversed the stairs with Gracie leading the way. Clarence descended, stepping sideways, supporting Ms. Lila. His eyes grew wide as they reached the bottom of the stairs.

Gracie shone the light around the room. "This is it. It's not a root cellar. That's right behind that wood panel on the other side." She and Preston had replaced the panel before exiting the secret room.

Clarence walked the area of the small space, still not speaking. He came to a stop in the middle of the room. When he turned, he wore the biggest grin. "I think you have found yourself a secret Underground Railroad room."

Gracie gaped. "Really?"

"Really." Clarence's excitement practically had the air humming.

Back at the top of the stairs, Clarence watched Gracie close the door. "I can't believe it."

"But what are the chances that there would be two station houses this close together?" Gracie asked.

"It's not unheard of." Clarence led Ms. Lila to the sofa. "Documents show that the Underground Railroad was very active in Bella Vista. It was a vibrant free Black community in the 1800s. There was probably a network of houses in the area."

Ms. Lila nodded. "That's what the curator of the museum at Mother Bethel said. She said that there were a couple of row houses around here that were probably station houses, but the rooms were destroyed when they were renovated. That the homeowners didn't have any idea what they were demolishing."

"Good thing your contractor knew about William Still's house." Clarence shifted from side to side. "Ms. Gracie, if you don't mind, I would like to do some research. With your permission."

Gracie smiled at him. "Of course. And call me Gracie."

"Okay. . .Gracie." His eyes sparkled, and his energy made him even more handsome.

"I wish I could help you, but I don't know much about the house," Gracie said.

He glanced over her shoulder at the door again. "This could be huge."

Ms. Lila rose. "Don't worry, Gracie. If anyone can find information about your house, it's Clarence."

Clarence dropped his gaze, and it looked like the tips of his ears turned pink. "I will do my best. I'll get in contact with you as soon as I know something."

"You'll need Gracie's number." Ms. Lila smiled the most suspicious grin Gracie had ever seen on the woman's face. "I'll give it to him."

Clarence didn't seem to notice. "Great. I'll call you."

"Thank you so much for this," Gracie said.

He cleared his throat, adjusted his glasses, and rubbed his palms on his pants. "Let me do something before you thank me."

"He'll find something," Ms. Lila said, smiling.

"Thanks again," Gracie said.

She stood in the doorway, watching their progress up the street. Her heart thumped. *Oh, Gran. Did you know what you were doing when you gave me this house?*

Gracie put her hands on her hips and smiled. In front of her stood her third completed cube shelving unit. To keep herself from obsessing about the door and the secret room, she had thrown herself into the remaining items on her list. Removing the drywall was the messiest renovation. Preston had cleaned up almost all the white powder, and a good sweep and mop took care of the rest. That done, she could begin setting up the shop.

She had moved the two armchairs that had finally arrived, to flank the sofa. The racks for knitting needles were on the other side of the staircase near the kitchen. She could probably open the boxes of yarn next. After a long search, she purchased the perfect shades for the front windows. Her next purchase was a sign. Yesterday she had taken a stroll, studying the signage of other businesses on her block. It would be an unwelcome eyesore if her sign was too gaudy.

As she had walked, she couldn't help wondering how many other houses on the street were hiding secrets.

With a little effort, she pushed the unit against the wall just as movement in the front window caught her eye. From where she stood, she could see Clarence standing on the front step, but he couldn't see her. As she approached the door, she watched him do a quick check of his clothes and run his hand through his hair. She slowed. He couldn't be primping for her.

"Hi, Clarence. Come in," she said, swinging the door wide before he could ring the bell.

He stepped inside with a draft of cold wind. "I hope I'm not interrupting."

"Nothing but shop prep."

He looked around the room. "This is really coming together."

She smiled at him, although her expression was probably closer to amazement. "Thank you."

He unbuttoned his coat and unwound the scarf from his neck. "I probably should have called, but I was at my grandma's house and she said it was okay if I just stopped by."

"It's fine. What can I do for you?"

"I talked to my colleagues at the Philadelphia Historical Commission, and they asked me to come by and talk to you about the house." He grinned. "And I wanted to see the room again. I couldn't stop thinking about it. It seems so unbelievable."

She couldn't help but return his smile. "I can't believe it myself."

"And if it's not too much trouble, can I see the rest of the house? I need to see if there are any other features that might give us clues about its age."

"Of course. Especially if it will help move this process forward."

For the next thirty minutes, she gave Clarence a tour of the house. They started from the secret room and the root cellar and went all the way to the attic. Clarence was quiet the same way he was when she first took him into the room, studying door hardware and windows. The only time he spoke was when he saw the little wooden box Gran had given her.

He stepped to where she had set it on the TV stand. "That's very nice."

"My gran gave it to me. She had a box for each of her children and grandchildren."

"That's really thoughtful. Must be some amazing memories inside," he said, stooping down to study the box more closely.

Gracie sighed. "I wouldn't know. I don't have to the key to open it. And I'm too afraid of damaging the lock to try and pick it."

"Smart idea."

As they made their way through the rest of the rooms, she couldn't help but notice the sparkle in his eyes.

They returned to the sitting room. "Can we talk?" he asked.

She nodded, motioned him to a chair, and took the seat across from him.

"First, I wanted to ask a difficult question." He leaned forward in his seat. "About your grandmother."

Although he spoke softly, his words knocked the wind out of her. She stiffened. "Yes?"

He moved his hand like he wanted to grasp hers but then rested it on his knee. "Did she say anything about the history of this house?"

Gracie shook her head. "Not to me."

"Is there anyone in the family you can ask?"

The family meeting flashed through her mind. She scowled and then tried to quickly smooth out her expression.

Clarence let out a soft chuckle. "I'll take that as a no."

A big no. If Uncle Rand knew. . . Her stomach soured. "I'd rather use other means than family."

"I understand," he said. "Now for another question. Would you like to nominate this house to be classified as a historic site?"

Gracie raised her eyebrows. "Should I?"

"Based on what I've seen, I think you should. This house is too close to William Still's house for your room to have been used for storage."

She looked down at her hands in her lap. "How long would the process take?"

"Months. But sometimes years."

Her gaze snapped up to him. "Years? I can't wait years before I open my shop."

Clarence held up his hands. "It's okay. I think you can still open your shop while you wait for the process to finish. The biggest thing would be that you couldn't do any renovations until the process was finished."

She turned and motioned to the wall behind her. "I've already started."

"No, no. Not things like removing drywall. I mean structural changes. Like knocking out a wall or extending the back of the house."

"Oh," Gracie's mind whirred. It could be a real boon to have the shop in a historic location. Then she thought of Gran. It would be an honor to have this house designated as an Underground Railroad Station. Bittersweet. "I guess. Yes."

Clarence grinned. "Great. Don't worry. I'll walk you through the whole process. And I can direct you to some people who can help."

His excitement lifted her spirits a little. "Okay. What do we do first?"

"Research. We need to learn as much as we can about the history of the house. We live in the most historic city in the country, so it shouldn't be hard to find information."

Gracie laughed. "Gran used to say something similar."

"Are you free tomorrow? I would like to have you come down to the Historical Commission headquarters. There are a lot of records there." He suddenly became interested in lint on his coat. "Maybe we could have lunch."

"Lunch?" she squeaked.

"A working lunch. We can start filling out the paperwork." He clasped his hands together.

Gracie fought the urge to squirm. People had lunch while working together all the time. That was what this was. Just lunch. "Okay."

"Great," he said. He popped up from the chair and pulled a business card from the holder he took from his pocket. "You can look at the forms on the website."

"I'll do that tonight."

He buttoned his coat. "All right. Good. Uh—I should go then. Thank you for letting me look at the house again."

"You're welcome."

They walked to the door together. "See you tomorrow," Gracie said, opening the door.

He stepped out then stopped. "One more thing. Tell as few people about the house as you can. The situation could grow volatile if people suspected this site has a secret Underground Railroad room. I could tell you some horror stories. And I would hate for you to be put in danger."

She held his gaze for a second, and warmth started at the tips of her ears and flushed her whole face. "I'll keep it to myself."

He nodded. "See you tomorrow."

She closed the door and leaned against it. This house was turning out to be quite an adventure.

CHAPTER SIX

OLIVIA

*M*rs. Catherine Mason turned slowly on the crate Olivia had provided for her to stand on, admiring herself in a tall mirror. Standing behind her, Olivia let her eyes travel over the nearly finished dress. Though done when Olivia was so tired her eyes drooped, the stitches in the lace were neat and nearly invisible. The quality of the work had cost her some sleep, but it was worth it.

"Lovely," Mrs. Mason murmured, running her hand over the silk skirt. Her pale hand stood out against the blue fabric beneath her fingers. "This is quite exquisite."

Olivia held the woman's gaze and watched Mrs. Mason's expression morph into a scowl. Mrs. Mason had not said outright that she would prefer that Olivia be meek, that she avert her gaze, but the woman's actions, like so many of Olivia's other customers, announced it. Nevertheless, Olivia carried herself like she was their equal. Because she was. After all, they were in her house, requesting her services.

Olivia bit the inside of her cheek. "Thank you."

Mrs. Mason's frown deepened as she turned once more before stepping down off the box. "You will be done by next week?" Although a question, it sounded like a command.

"Yes." Olivia moved to undo the two pearl buttons on the back of the dress' collar. "As soon as it is done, I will have my delivery boy bring it to your house."

Mrs. Mason nodded curtly and stepped behind the screen to

change back into the nearly new dress she had worn into the shop this morning. The dress Olivia was finishing, Mrs. Mason told her, was for a special occasion. Just like the last one a month ago. Soon Mrs. Mason's entire wardrobe would be filled with Olivia's dresses. That was fine with Olivia.

The front door opened, and her delivery boy, a lad named Franklin Wilson, Thea's son, stepped inside, rubbing his hands together and shivering. "Cold out."

"Close the door, then," Olivia said with a laugh.

Franklin turned and stared at the door like it had not been there a moment ago. "Oh, sorry."

Olivia motioned for him to follow her. "I have some tea in the kitchen. That should warm you."

Franklin grinned and trotted behind her. "Thank you, Ms. 'Livia."

In the kitchen, Olivia poured a cup of tea, added a splash of milk and a generous amount of sugar, and handed it to him. She had brewed it for Mrs. Mason even though the woman never took tea from her.

Olivia was tempted to take a cup for herself. The heat might clear her mind. Because, looking down at the boy, she had no idea why he was there. "My memory fails me. Did I say I had deliveries for you today?"

Franklin took a big gulp, ending with a sigh, and wiped his mouth with the back of his hand. "I have one for you." He reached inside his jacket and pulled out an envelope.

A letter from Mr. Still. "Thank you. Finish your tea, and you can go out the back door."

The boy nodded, and she left him in the kitchen.

She rounded the stairs to the front room. Mrs. Mason was still behind the screen, soft swishing telling Olivia that she was putting on her own clothes. Olivia quickly opened the letter:

> *Mrs. Kingston,*
> *I am writing to request assistance from you. Two*
> *friends have arrived recently and need lodging for a short*
> *time. If you can assist them, they will be at your house*

tonight after eight. They may require special attention
until they have left your care.

Thank you,
W. Still

Olivia read the note again, decoding the message. "Two friends" were two fugitives. "Special attention" meant that these two friends likely had had a particularly difficult trip from their former slave master's house. They might even be sick. She would need a little time to prepare the room and some food.

She returned to the kitchen, placed the note in the sink, and with the matches she kept to light her lamps, set the note on fire. Every Bella Vista stationmaster and conductor did the same. All correspondence between them and Mr. Still had to be destroyed even though Mr. Still kept meticulous records of every runaway who passed through his care. He took that risk on himself but did not want to pass the risk on to the rest of the free Black community assisting him.

When Olivia returned to the room, Mrs. Mason stood waiting, her expression thunderous. "Where have you been?"

Olivia, mind still whirring with the preparations she would have to make, waved a hand. "Taking care of some important business."

"Important business other than me?" The woman's voice ended on a high, incredulous note. "I have been standing here for a full minute."

Olivia looked up, giving the woman a steady gaze. "Oh no. It could not have been that long." She made her expression as sweet as Franklin liked his tea. She walked briskly over to the woman and ushered her to the front door. "And I hate to have you waiting a minute longer."

Mrs. Mason blinked as Olivia carried her along. "Well. I expect my dress to be finished next week."

"Next week," Olivia repeated.

Mrs. Mason huffed and shuffled out the door, which Olivia kept open just long enough to be polite. Then she closed it and went to work.

The rest of her day was spent getting the room ready for the passengers. If Mr. Still sent the note, they were probably going to his house first and then coming to hers. While they were at his house, he would take down details about them, like what plantation they had run from, what their escape was like, and if they had any family remaining in slavery. Those records had been used to reunite many families.

She had another quiet dinner with Douglas. Once they had talked about his workday and her fitting with Mrs. Mason, silence settled between them, an unwanted guest. Anytime she shifted in her chair, he looked up at her expectantly. She found herself doing the same, not knowing why. She longed to pour out her heart about Moonie and Henry and the fact that Lottie would make a wonderful addition to their Underground Railroad group. But all those topics were not to be mentioned. Was stopping her work the only way they could bring conversation back?

As they rose from the table and headed to the stairs, he glanced over at Mrs. Mason's unfinished dress. "Are you working tonight?"

She followed the direction of his gaze. "Yes—no." Then she paused. "Yes."

He looked back at her, understanding in his eyes. "Late?"

"I am not certain," she said softly.

He held her gaze for a little longer then gave her a quick peck on the cheek. "Good night."

Even in that short time he was close to her, she could feel the warmth from his body. "Good night," she said with some effort.

Once she could no longer hear Douglas moving around upstairs, Olivia went down to the room, lamp in hand. The two friends would be arriving soon. She again checked the basket of items she'd assembled. Food, water, tea, both men's and women's clothing—she never knew who was coming ahead of time—and blankets. She had dressed the small cot with some clean blankets and given the room a quick sweep. There was only so much she could do with the dirt floor, but she did try to make it as comfortable as possible.

She thought of Douglas. She should have known he would see Black patients without requiring them to pay. He and his family had run from Maryland when he was young. Although he had no real memories of being enslaved, he was passionate about antislavery work. He sat on the board for the Institute for the Improvement of Colored Youth, an amazing example of what the students could become. He had overcome hardships, apprenticing with an abolitionist doctor before finally being accepted into medical school in Maine. The students saw in him the hope of overcoming their hardships as well.

The guilt of keeping things from him sometimes became too much to bear, but she would do everything in her power to protect him. He was one of the few Black doctors in the state to hold a medical degree. He must be allowed to continue to do the work that he was doing. He helped as much as she did, just in a different way.

A soft knock sounded at the root cellar door, and Olivia rushed across the little room. Opening the door, she found two people standing in the cold night. One was Mr. Wilson. Behind him stood a young woman. The fugitive. Just one then. Olivia's heart sank. Did the other one not make it?

She stepped aside and ushered them into the room. When she lifted the light, she saw the truth of the situation.

There were two runaways.

The woman was holding a small child.

Olivia resisted the urge to gasp. The child, wrapped in nothing more than strips of fabric, lay limp in the mother's arms.

"She is sick," the woman said, concern making her voice hoarse.

"We met with some trouble but thought this was the best place for her to be," Mr. Wilson said quietly.

Because of Douglas. Even though all the stationmasters and conductors knew she shielded Douglas from her work, they still factored his being a doctor into their plans, sending the sickest fugitives to her house. *God, help this child.* "Please sit."

The woman shuffled, pain evident in every step. Amazing that she had run with a child. The courage that took. She went to the woman's side as she sank down on the cot. "What is your name?"

"Beulah. And my baby is Hope."

Olivia smiled. "Beautiful name." She helped Beulah undo the thin blankets and took stock of the child's condition as she did. Hope was hot to the touch, confirming Olivia's suspicions. The child was thin, too thin, like her mother. Even in the dim light, her brown skin held a grayish pallor. "There is some food in the basket," Olivia told Beulah. "I have some broth upstairs for the child."

"I will wait until you get back," Mr. Wilson said, removing the food from the basket while Beulah cradled Hope.

Olivia rushed up the stairs. Turning toward the kitchen, she froze. Douglas stood in the doorway, holding a cup of tea. When did he become so fond of tea before bed?

"Is everything all right?" he asked.

She opened her mouth to tell him about Hope, then, remembering herself, snapped her mouth shut. She nodded.

"I am going to read for a bit before I go to bed. In case you need me. . ." Douglas was still studying her.

"Thank you," was all she managed to say.

Oh, how she wished she could take Douglas down the stairs and let him examine Hope. For all their sakes, she would have to do as she had always done. Handle it alone.

CHAPTER SEVEN

GRACIE

*G*racie donned her coat, wrapped one of her hand-knitted cowls around her shoulders, and headed out into the crisp October air. That was something she needed to adjust to. Winters in Philly were much colder than Richmond. Depending on how warm it was, it wasn't unusual for her to head to Virginia Beach in October.

She walked to her car, letting the air cool her anxiety for the task ahead of her.

Clarence had asked her if there was anyone in the family she could ask about the house. She had said no, but in fact there was someone. It would take a bit of sneaking, but Ada might know something. She had spent as much time with Gran as Gracie had, especially since she only lived twenty minutes away from Gran. Ada was also three years older than Gracie. That meant she was sitting at the grown-up table at Thanksgiving long before Gracie was.

The problem was that Ada still lived at home with Uncle Rand.

She had texted Ada earlier to see if she was home. . .and to see if Uncle Rand wasn't. He'd retired a few years ago and spent much more time at home. Ada had told her that he'd gone out to a doctor's appointment, and Gracie had hurried to get to her car.

After pulling up in front of Uncle Rand's, Gracie hopped out of the car and rushed to the door. She tried to regulate her breathing and still her thoughts, but each step sent her nerves jangling. Ada must have seen her hurrying up the walk, because she opened the door before Gracie reached it.

Once inside, Ada helped Gracie take off her coat. "What's wrong?"

"Nothing. It's just that. . .well, it's better that we have this conversation in private."

Ada nodded. "Let's go up to my room."

Ada's room was as large as a master bedroom and was neatly decorated with a bed with a padded headboard and a comfy-looking armchair surrounded by books.

She steered Gracie toward the chair and sat on the end of the bed. "What's up?"

Gracie took a deep breath. "I need to ask you some questions about Gran's house."

Ada tipped her head in surprise. "Me?"

"Yes, and I need you to keep this conversation to yourself," Gracie said slowly.

"You don't have to worry about me talking to my dad. I'm on his bad side right now. He's not happy that my mother let me move back home."

Gracie resisted the urge to reach over and grasp her hand. Ada's relationship with her father ranged from cool to problematic. They went through seasons of not speaking to each other. "Aw, Ada."

Ada gave her a weak smile. "You know how it is. Now tell me about Gran's house."

Gracie looked at the door. "I found something at the house."

"Something like what?" Ada asked.

Gracie gripped the arms of the chair. "A secret room."

Ada leaned forward. "What kind of secret room?"

"Well, I've been talking to someone from the Philadelphia Historical Commission, and he thinks it may have been a station house on the Underground Railroad."

Ada eyes widened. "For real?"

Gracie nodded. "I found the room when the contractors came. There was a little door under the stairs next to the bathroom."

"What?" She shook her head as if to clear her shock. "You know there's a root cellar down there. Could it be that?"

"No," Gracie said. "It's hidden behind the root cellar."

"That's incredible."

"Did Gran say anything to you about it? Did she. . .did she know it was there?"

"She never said anything to me about it. But Gran loved her history."

"I know," Gracie said. "It seems odd that she wouldn't say anything about it. That's a pretty big secret to keep."

Ada stood and began to pace. "Why would she keep it a secret? To think that Gran and Paw-Paw lived in that house all those years—" Ada stopped pacing.

"What is it?" Gracie asked.

Her expression changed to wonder. "Oh. Do you remember the Christmas Paw-Paw disappeared? You were young, so you might not remember."

Gracie frowned. She had spent a lot of Christmases at Gran's house, especially when she was younger. Her father insisted that she stay connected to her mother's side of the family. Gracie had always believed it was because he didn't want the reminder that he was spending the holidays without his wife. "How old were you?"

"Twelve. So you would have been nine." Ada was bouncing on her toes now. "Paw-Paw was trying to convince us that Santa had brought our gifts. Then he said he could prove that Santa could get in and out of the house without us seeing him."

In a flash, the memory rose in Gracie's mind in full color. Paw-Paw had made her and Ada cover their eyes and count to thirty and then he "disappeared." They had searched the whole house. Gran, with a sneaky smile on her face, had even let them peer into the root cellar. Paw-Paw wasn't in the house. They returned to the living room and covered their eyes again, and he reappeared.

"I do remember!" Gracie said with a laugh.

"We searched that house top to bottom and couldn't find him. He was probably in the secret room."

"I thought he had simply gone outside, but we didn't hear a door open." Gracie felt tears prickling in her eyes. "They knew."

Ada sat down on the bed again. "But they never said anything. That makes the house even more special."

"What makes the house more special?"

Both Gracie and Ada jumped at the sound of Uncle Rand's voice. He stood in the doorway, arms across his chest. He was still wearing the black fedora he always wore when he went out. On his face was a scowl.

"Dad!" Ada gave him a stern look. "Why are you lurking?"

He looked from Ada to Gracie. "What are you doing here, and what are y'all talking about?"

Gracie opened her mouth to respond, but Ada beat her to it. "My cousin is visiting me, and what we are talking about is our business."

"Do I have to remind you that you are living in my house?" he asked.

"You remind me every day. I will remind you that just because I'm living here doesn't mean you can eavesdrop on my conversations."

He faced Gracie. "Is this about the house? What have you done?"

Ada sprang from the bed. "Out, Dad." She grasped the doorknob. "I don't come into your room uninvited, and I don't think you should do that to me."

He looked past Ada at Gracie. "I will find out what's going on."

"Dad, please," Ada said as she began closing the door.

"We'll discuss this later."

Ada closed the door and listened for a few seconds to make sure her father had walked away. Then she let out a loud sigh. "He can be so difficult sometimes. I wish I could afford to move out. I normally went to Gran's to get away—" She wrung her hands. "Actually, I have something to talk to you about too."

"Okay."

"Can I move in with you"

Gracie froze. "Are you serious?"

"I can help with the bills." She took a step forward. "I'm not asking to live there for free."

Gracie looked down at her hands in her lap. When she had moved into the house, her expectation was that she would always live there alone, especially with Gran gone. But having Ada there. . . Hope flickered in her heart, but she tamped it down.

"Your dad is going to be furious."

Ada rolled her eyes. "He already is."

Gracie laughed. "You're right about that."

"I can move myself, and I'll take the small bedroom on the second floor."

"I'm already in that room."

Ada frowned then brightened. "Then I'll help you move to the big one on the third floor."

Move into Gran's room? She swallowed. The urge to say no was strong. She and Ada had been estranged from one another for a long time. And Gracie had wrongly assumed that Ada was just as angry at her as the rest of the family was.

"Unless you don't want me to move in. I understand if you hate me for—"

Gracie's head snapped up. "I don't hate you."

Ada flinched like she had been stung. "I—I thought you would with the way my father has been treating you. And I didn't exactly stand up for you when all the drama was going down with Gran."

"That was a whole mess." Gracie shook her head. "Losing Gran hurt so bad, and then being accused of conning her out of the house by everyone. I didn't know who to trust."

Ada came across the room and knelt in front of her. "I'm sorry. I should have spoken up sooner and not left you to be eaten by the wolves." She pulled Gracie out of the chair and hugged her.

A flood broke in Gracie. This was one of the few genuine hugs she'd received since Gran died. She cried big ugly sobs. Ada rubbed her back until the tears subsided.

When she pulled back from the embrace, she saw that Ada had tears in her eyes too. "All better, baby cousin?" Ada asked.

Gracie laughed at the nickname Ada had given her years ago. "Yes. And I think I would like for you to move in with me, on one condition.

You cannot call me baby cousin."

They laughed, and Gracie could just imagine what Gran would say if she saw them now.

"Family should stick together." Gran had repeated that to both her and Ada. Yes. Gran would approve of this togetherness.

❧

Gracie woke and sat up in bed. The morning sun brightened her room, saturating the colors of her things. Her thoughts seemed lighter since she had talked with Ada, even though some of their conversation had been hard, especially when Ada asked how she was coping with Gran's death. How to answer that question? Tell Ada that everything reminded her that Gran wasn't there anymore? Tell her about the cold of loneliness she fought off the longer she stayed in the house? How it felt to realize that the two women who loved her the most had left her in a soup of emotions? Ada wouldn't understand that.

She'd told Ada that it was hard but she was handling it. Still, it cheered Gracie to be able to talk to someone who loved Gran as much as she did. And now she was on her way to the Philadelphia Historical Commission to look for proof that this house that Gran loved played a role in history.

Cool air prickled her face as she walked to her car. The last day of fall was fast approaching, but the chill felt closer to Christmas. She picked up her pace, focusing on walking and not thinking about spending the holidays alone. Not completely alone. Ada would be at the house by then.

Enough of that. She climbed into her car and started her drive. If she didn't stop thinking about it, she would be in tears when she reached Clarence. She sighed as she took Penn Square around City Hall. Her grip on the steering wheel increased with every inch closer she drew to the commission's headquarters.

She parked in a lot that put her a block away from her destination. She strolled, looking up at the buildings. As she passed Love Park, she stopped, staring. How many times had she, Ada, and Gran come here for the Christmas market? Or for an outdoor concert? Grief blurred the memories and sharpened the pain.

She plunged ahead and spotted a man standing in front of the building. As she got closer, she recognized Clarence—standing outside in the cold waiting for her. That revelation warmed her more than her coat had done since she left the house.

He glanced up from his phone, met her gaze, and smiled. *Very warm.*

"Hi, Gracie," he said.

She adjusted her bag on her shoulder. "You didn't have to stand outside to wait for me."

He turned and opened the door of the building behind him. "It's okay. I needed the air."

Clarence led her to an elevator bank. "You've created quite a buzz in the office."

She turned to look at him—rather, up at him. Way up. Every other time she'd talked to him they had been farther away from each other. Or sitting. She hadn't noticed his height compared to hers—or how good his cologne smelled. "I have?" she asked with a squeak.

The elevator door opened, and he motioned for her to enter first. "Yes. My colleagues are excited there may be another site so close to William Still's house. It would be a huge find and give us more insight into how the station houses might have worked."

"Don't you have records?"

Clarence shrugged. "Some. William Still had the most extensive collection of notes, but that was because he went to great lengths to hide them. He didn't keep them in his house but in a crypt in a cemetery. The other conductors and stationmasters would have been taking a dangerous risk to keep records."

She looked at the LED lights displaying the floors as they rose. "I hope your colleagues aren't too disappointed if my room is just extra storage." Might as well manage expectations early on. Given her track record in life, the room wasn't something special. Simply a cleverly hidden cellar.

The elevator door opened, and Clarence led her down the hall to a wooden door that held a placard with Philadelphia Historical

COMMISSION on it. He opened the door and led her into a small reception area. The man at the desk looked up and smiled. "Is this her?"

Clarence leaned close to her and whispered, "Told you." Then he turned to the man at the desk. "Yes, this is Gracie McNeil. Gracie, this is my boss, Arthur Winston."

Arthur moved around the desk to shake her hand. "You have no idea how excited we were when Clarence told us about your house. I'm assuming you're here to nominate it?"

"Yes, I am," Gracie said, accepting the handshake, her scalp tingling with nervousness.

"But you didn't have to come in to do that. You could have filled the forms out online. Clarence, why didn't you have her do that?"

To Gracie's surprised, Clarence flushed. "Well, uh, we were going to look at some records while she's here, and I wanted to—uh—show her around."

Arthur seemed not to notice Clarence's reddened ears and beamed at Gracie. "In that case, welcome."

"Thank you," Gracie said, her own face heating.

Clarence smoothed the front of his jacket. "Shall we go to my office?"

He led her down a short hallway. Gracie covered her smile with her hand as she entered the room. If she hadn't met him, his office would have given her a clear glimpse into his personality. An armchair was perfectly positioned in the small space. A small bookshelf sat behind his desk, the books on it shelved by height. A slightly disorganized pile of papers in an open folder and an empty paper cup on his desk were the only evidence that someone worked here.

He moved to his desk and tossed the cup into the trash. "Are you ready?"

"Yes." Gracie sat in the chair and took out the sock she had been knitting. "What are we looking for?"

When he looked up, his expression was mildly confused. "I thought we would start with finding out how old your house is." He stared at the sock and then back up at her. "Uh, you can't sit there."

She popped out of the seat. "I'm sorry."

"No, I mean, you can't sit there if you want to see. Sit here." He motioned to his desk chair.

"Oh," was all she could manage. She kept a tight grip on her knitting as she moved around the desk and sat.

He leaned over and slid the keyboard closer. He typed her address into a search bar. "Let's look the house up on the Office of Property Assessment website. It's easier to start with public records."

"Okay," she said, sliding the stitches on her needles back and forth.

The screen changed to show the details of her house. Clarence leaned closer, eyes narrowing. "This says your house was built in 1930."

Gracie exhaled, her shoulders slumping. So her room was just a cellar. "Oh well," she said quietly.

"That doesn't seem right." Clarence tapped the desk with his finger. "The rest of the properties in this area were built much earlier. Let me check our records of nominations."

He clicked into a different window on his computer and typed her address again. He hit Search, and the screen changed almost immediately: No Results Found.

Gracie let out a sigh.

Clarence looked down at her. "Don't give up just yet. William Still's house was listed as built in 1930 and wasn't nominated right away either."

"What's next?"

Clarence moved around his desk and sat in the armchair Gracie had vacated. "You need to submit an application to the commission. That includes an essay and photos of the house. Most of all, you need to prove why the house is historic."

Gracie lifted her knitting again, her fingers threatening to cramp by how tightly her hands had been clasped in her lap. "But we can't prove that yet."

Clarence smiled. "Not yet. But we will. Once we do, you can submit the application."

"You are so confident," she said softly.

He leaned forward. "After what I saw at your house, I am."

Gracie stared at him for a moment. If anyone could determine the chances of her house being an Underground Railroad station, Clarence seemed to be the one. "How exactly do we do research on the house?"

Clarence's smile was so wide his glasses seemed to go up with it. "That's where I come in. It will involve a lot of reading and a lot of dust inhalation."

She laughed. "That makes sense."

"And we can start right away, if you like."

Before she could respond, there was a knock at the door and Arthur popped his head through the doorway. "Hate to interrupt, but, Clarence, can I speak to you?"

Clarence stood and, before he stepped into the hallway, gave her a nod.

Gracie sat in the chair, her thoughts a tangled ball of yarn. As much as she wanted to nominate her house, what if this was a big waste of time? She already had enough to do. Close Gran's estate. Get all the zoning permits and licenses to open a business. She let out a weary sigh. Maybe she should wait until she had the other things done. The room wasn't going anywhere.

But Gran would have been so excited about this. She would have plunged right into the research or whatever else she needed to do. Gracie would have to do what Gran couldn't.

Clearance returned, wearing a slight frown. "I know I said we could start right away, but something has come up that I have to deal with."

Gracie rose, putting her sock back into her project bag. "That's okay. You've done a lot already."

He escorted her back down the hall. "I can't work on it today, but that doesn't mean forever." He looked down at her. "I'll call you to reschedule."

"Great. I'll talk to you then."

Walking back to her car, Gracie wondered more than once if this meant he was also rescheduling the lunch date.

CHAPTER EIGHT

OLIVIA

Olivia ran the thread through the hem on a cotton dress. As she pushed the needle back through the opposite side, she jabbed her finger.

"Ouch!" A bubble of blood formed.

Douglas looked up from his book. "Did you stick yourself again?"

Olivia replied with a grumble. Yes, she had. Again. She had just stopped the bleeding from the last poke.

To her surprise, Douglas put his book down and crossed the room to her. He gently took her finger, produced his handkerchief, and applied pressure. Stunned, she sat and stared up at him. When he pulled the handkerchief away, he studied her finger. "There." His palm was warm against the back of her hand.

"Thank you, Dr. Kingston," she said with a small smile. She slipped her hand from his. "Maybe I should finish this tomorrow." Her focus was on the little girl downstairs.

At her last check, Beulah and Hope were bundled in every blanket Olivia had brought down for them. The basement, because of its location in the center of the house, was not as cold as the root cellar. But Olivia suspected that Beulah was suffering from the same ailment as Hope. Maybe just a chill, but with the long stretch of time they were on the run and without proper nourishment, it could grow worse quickly.

"How about a cup of tea?" Douglas asked.

Olivia let out a laugh. "Not sure I can be trusted with fire."

Douglas chuckled, a sound that warmed her straight through. "Then let me get it."

She let out a long sigh. This was one of the hardest parts about having passengers in her room. She had to leave them unattended for long hours. She tried not to open the secret door before Douglas was upstairs. He knew where it was, of course. Douglas' knowledge of the room did not concern her. It was the unexpected visits from patrols. The Friends had determined that all the Bella Vista stationmasters and conductors must be under suspicion.

Several of the stationmasters regularly received surprise visits from the local patrol headed by a man named Archibald Saunders. It would not be a leap for them to think she was involved with the Underground Railroad, given how closely she worked with Mr. Still. And his house was only across the way. Because of this, she normally gave her passengers everything they could want before she closed the door and put the panel up to hide it.

She always prayed the supplies would be enough until the next time she went down. But most of her passengers had already proven their resilience. They had gone through much worse than a slightly damp basement, traveling miles and miles through swamps, creeks, woods, and open field. They went days without food and water. All for freedom. Freedom they had as soon as they crossed into Pennsylvania.

What had Beulah gone through to get to Olivia's room? And with a child?

Olivia reached for the dress, then pushed it away again and placed her hand on her stomach. What would it be like to run with a child? Although she and Douglas had not been blessed with children yet, Olivia knew they would do everything they could to give their child freedom. There was great danger in what Beulah did, but she'd decided that her daughter's freedom was worth the risk.

Douglas returned with the tea and set the cup in front of her but slowed as he straightened. "You are well?" He looked down at her hand on her stomach.

Her face flushed, and she snatched her hand away. She would not give Douglas false hope. "Oh yes. I am well."

His expression turned pensive. "You seem distracted this evening."

"I have been thinking about a baby," she said before she realized the words were on her tongue.

Douglas' eyebrows shot up. "You have?"

Her stomach soured. Months without real conversation, and she had to bring up the most painful subject. If there was one thing she could give her husband. . . "What it will be like when we finally have a child."

He remained still, just continuing to look at her.

"If we ever—" she began.

"We will. I am certain God will bless us."

She looked up at him, soaking in every word of this conversation. He had shown his heart more in these few words than he had in months. "I know He will. It is very hard to wait."

The smile he gave her was grim. "But we must wait. It is likely for the best that it has not happened yet. Consider how hard it would be for both of us to work if we had a child."

She looked up at him, his expression making it clear what he was talking about. That sobered her. Both a mother and a stationmaster? "It would be difficult," was all she could say.

"Do you need to work?"

She let out a sigh. "Only to prick my finger again?"

"Not that work." He held her gaze.

She jolted. "I—"

"You have been fretting over something, and it is not that dress."

She clamped her mouth shut and only nodded.

He collected his book and climbed the stairs. "Good night." But the tone of his voice contradicted his words.

Oh, Douglas.

When she heard their bedroom door close, she raced across the room and removed the panel that hid the door to the stairs. She lit the lamp after three tries. She rushed down the stairs to find Beulah staring at her. Hope lay across the woman's lap, beads of perspiration on her forehead.

"I believe the fever is breaking, ma'am."

Olivia crossed the room and touched the child's forehead. She was indeed clammy, not hot. "Thank God."

Beulah nodded in agreement, her face weary.

"Have you rested?"

"I was worried 'bout Hope." Beulah's words were slurred with exhaustion.

"How about I hold her for an hour and let you sleep?"

Beulah's eyes widened. "Oh no, ma'am. You done so much for us already."

"You need to rest for the next stage of your journey." She leaned over and lifted Hope from Beulah's lap. "It will be easier from here, but you will still need your strength."

Beulah eyed her for a moment before she lay down on the cot. Olivia moved to the end of the cot and cradled Hope close.

The longing for a baby welled in her. Douglas was right, but the desire was still strong. She wanted this for Douglas. To make them a family. But sitting here with Hope in her lap, she wondered again about how a baby would change her life. There would be no more late-night trips to the docks. Douglas would probably not agree to that. The stairs and carrying baskets might become too much for her. But after the baby came, she could return to being a stationmaster.

Beulah's heavy breathing told Olivia that the woman had drifted off to sleep. Hope took a deep breath and shifted to snuggle her face against Olivia.

Lord, heal Hope so she and her mother can truly be free.

CHAPTER NINE

GRACIE

*A*s Gracie stood at the door and waited for Ada to arrive, absurdity sent darts into her psyche and threatened to upend what peace she had. How wild was it to invite Ada to move into the house before Gracie was settled herself? How careless to jeopardize Ada's housing situation? Letting Ada move in before Gracie was established was reckless. She had been reckless enough with her own life. Now she was pulling Ada into the madness.

But it was too late now. Around noon, Ada pulled up, her car packed full of her things.

Ada had waited until after her midterms to tell Uncle Rand that she was moving and where. Gracie had offered to be moral support when she told him, but Ada had turned down the offer. That answer dissolved the knot in Gracie's stomach because she didn't want any more anger from Uncle Rand. She had stolen his mother's house, and now she was stealing his daughter.

In under thirty minutes, they had unpacked Ada's car and carried everything upstairs to the other bedroom on the second floor. Ada brought a few pieces of furniture, and Gracie was glad to add a few newer pieces to her mismatched stuff.

Gracie's wooden box caught Ada's eye as she was setting down a three-legged wooden table.

"Hey," she said with a grin, "I have one of those too. The stuff Gran kept. . ." She shook her head. "Maybe we should go through our boxes together and compare notes."

Gracie fought back the prick of tears. "I would love to, but I don't have the key."

Ada eyes softened. "It wasn't with the house stuff?"

"No. And Gran never gave it to me. I guess she figured I knew it was mine, and I was living here at the end."

"And you went through everything?" Ada asked quietly.

"I did, and I don't know where else it could be."

Ada looked at the box a minute longer. "I'm sure it'll turn up."

Once they moved in all the things Ada wanted in her bedroom, everything else went up to the third floor.

On one of their trips, Ada asked, "Why didn't you move up here? It's the biggest bedroom in the house."

Gracie looked into the empty room where Gran had quickly declined until she went into hospice. "I'm not ready."

Instead of speaking, Ada just nodded in agreement.

In her room once again, Ada began to unpack. "I need to have this place in some sort of order when it's time to go back to school. At least get my desk set up."

"Then let me help you," Gracie said and began hanging Ada's clothes in the closet. "What did Uncle Rand say?"

Ada let out a huff. "You would've thought I was moving in with the world's most notorious criminal."

Gracie laughed. "In his mind, you are. I'm a thief."

She gave Gracie a lopsided grin. "You said it right. In his mind, you are. But you are not, and hopefully he'll recognize that."

"I don't know. We were never close."

"No, but you could have been if he wasn't always so difficult." She began unloading a box of her college textbooks. "Gran didn't have much to do with him either."

Gracie lifted a dress from the pile of clothes she was working through. "This is nice."

"You can borrow it if you like. It should fit you. Maybe for your lunch date with Clarence."

Gracie scowled and hung the dress up with more force than necessary. She was getting very close to regretting telling Ada about Clarence. She hadn't meant to tell her about him at all, but having family again, family she could confide in, had loosened her tongue. "It isn't a date. It's supposed to be a working lunch."

"Any food with a cute man is a date." Ada came over and removed the dress from the closet and held it up to Gracie. "It'll fit. You'll look great in it."

Gracie pushed the dress away with a smirk. "Clarence's interest in me is this house."

"He could be interested in you," Ada said, shaking the dress at Gracie.

"Why would he be?" She pulled the dress from Ada's hands and dropped the hook of the hanger back on the bar.

Ada gaped at her. "Because you're smart, successful, and pretty."

"I am not successful," Gracie said, lifting another dress from the box. It was cottony soft under her fingers.

"Why aren't you?" Ada grasped her shoulders and turned her so she could look in her eyes.

"Do you know how close I was to being homeless?"

"But you aren't. And that isn't a measure of success."

"I couldn't pay my bills." *I still can't pay my student loans.* Her voice warbled and her vision blurred with tears. "If I hadn't come to take care of Gran, I would have been living out of my car."

"Your father wouldn't have allowed that. Gran wouldn't have either." Ada sat her down on the end of the bed and stood in front of Gracie with her hands on her hips. "Did you know that Gran asked me what I thought about you coming to stay with her?"

The memory of that phone call flashed in her mind. Gran had called sounding completely normal, until she asked Gracie to come and stay with her as a caregiver. Gracie, the least responsible member of the family. She had bit her tongue to stop from asking why Uncle Rand wasn't coming to care for her. Or even Natalia. People who were in Philly who could come without having to uproot their whole lives.

Gracie had been angry that somehow this unpleasant task had passed to her because people felt she wasn't doing anything else important.

Which she wasn't. Nothing more than bouncing from job to job and avoiding bill collectors. *Oh, to take that anger back.* "Gran knew about my money problems?"

"I think she suspected. But she asked you because she wanted you here. And that's another thing that makes you successful. Gran wanted you around. You know she didn't deal with foolish people. Hence her relationship with my father."

"I never understood how that relationship broke down. How I inherited the house and not Uncle Rand, her oldest child." The words came out in a rush after having held them in for so long.

Ada stilled for a moment before she sat next to Gracie. "It makes me sad that you're missing so much of this story. Your story."

"It was so hard being a part of this family. With my mother gone."

Ada nodded, her eyes soft. "My dad kinda went off the rails when your mother died. At least that's what Gran said."

Gracie looked up at her. "Really?"

"They were very close. He took his job as big brother seriously. He had even planned to come down to Richmond when you were born."

Gracie shook her head. Uncle Rand grieving? But he disliked her so much. "That's hard to believe."

"Gran said he stopped talking about your mother after the funeral. Like it hurt too much. He still doesn't talk about her."

"I can imagine." Being an only child, she had no concept of losing a beloved sibling. But she did understand loss. Gran's death nearly crushed her.

"I heard him and Gran arguing about you one day," Ada said quietly.

"Me? Why?"

"Gran was trying to get him to acknowledge that you were Auntie's daughter. That you were a piece of her. My father yelled at Gran."

Gracie pressed her hand over her mouth.

Ada chuckled. "I was hiding behind the door, wondering if Gran was going to wallop him. Instead, she just said, 'She's a part of Rochelle, and she needs you.'"

"Did Uncle Rand say anything?"

Ada shook her head. "He started crying."

They sat there for a moment, Gracie too overwhelmed to speak. Could Uncle Rand's behavior be the same as her father's? Both of them distancing themselves from her because of her mother, not because they didn't like her?

Gracie's phone rang, bringing them both back to the present. She glanced at it. "Clarence."

Ada grinned. "Reschedule your date, and then try on the dress."

It wasn't until the clerk at the city's Permit and License Center told Gracie that she would be notified by mail about the status of her rezoning application that Gracie realized she wasn't getting any mail. Not even her own, which wasn't more than bills that had followed her from Richmond. She needed to find out why as soon as possible in case one of Gran's creditors was trying to contact her estate. While the clerk entered her information into the computer, Gracie googled the nearest post office. When the application was submitted, she texted Ada and told her that she was going to the post office before she got home. Ada texted back and asked Gracie to grab a change-of-address form.

The post office, a two-story brown brick building, looked like it used to be a historical mansion. Gracie chuckled as she stepped inside the quiet lobby. Now she was thinking that every building had undiscovered history. The floor was tiled with large black-and-white tiles. She resisted the temptation to try to get to the counter by only stepping on black squares, and walked to the counter.

A cheerful man greeted her. "How can I help you?"

"I recently moved, and I'm not getting mail at my house. I'm not sure how I didn't realize that sooner."

The man nodded. "What's your address?"

She handed him her ID. "The house used to be my grandmother's before she passed, so she may be listed as the addressee."

The man gave her a sad smile. "I'm sorry for your loss. I recently lost a family member too. Grieving is rough. That's probably why you didn't notice you weren't getting mail. Let me check on this."

"Thank you," Gracie said. Grief did erase one's logical thoughts. There were days after Gran died that the world could have burned down around her and she wouldn't have known it. It had gotten better over time. Better in the sense that the grief wasn't continuously in her thoughts. The pain was still as sharp as when Gran first passed.

The man returned with an armful of mail. It was in bundles secured with rubber bands. Gracie gasped. "Is that all mine?"

"Yes, ma'am. It appears someone put a hold on your mail delivery. But you were correct that you are not the addressee. I just need you to prove that you are authorized to pick up this mail."

Gracie reached into the folder she had taken to the Permit and License Center. "I do have proof." She handed him the document that named her as the executor of Gran's estate.

The man slid the bundles across to her. "Here you go."

Gracie thanked him and lifted them from the counter. She managed to get back to her car without dropping any of it. She dumped the bundles on the front passenger seat and stared at them. There was at least nine months' worth of mail there. She bit her lip. It might take her that long to go through it all.

Ada gaped when Gracie carried all the mail inside. "What's all that?"

"Mail," Gracie grunted. "Apparently Gran put it on hold. Probably before she—" Gracie swallowed. As Gran declined, Gracie had lost track of time. Days were a blur. Their routine continued to grow narrower as months passed. First it was church, the doctor's office, Ms. Lila's house, and the park across the street. Then it narrowed to the doctor's office and the park. Ms. Lila started coming to them. Then it was nothing. Gran was too weak to come down the stairs.

One day stood out in Gracie's memory: the day she and Gran went to the lawyer's office to add Gracie to the deed.

Pushing the pain aside, she carried the mail upstairs and gingerly placed it on her feeble coffee table. She stood over the pile for a second, expecting the table to collapse under the weight.

Ada followed her up the stairs. She peered over Gracie's shoulder. "Need some help?"

"No. I'll take care of it."

Ada frowned at her. "It'll go faster if we both work on it. A lot of it is probably junk. Let's have some food delivered and knock this out."

Gracie studied Ada. She seemed serious. But why would anyone want to help her with this if they didn't have to? "If you really don't mind."

Ada pulled out her phone. "I don't. How about I order from that Greek restaurant down the street?"

Gracie smiled. "Okay."

Ada proved to be as dedicated as she said she was. They had sorted the real mail from the junk mail before the food arrived. But by then, Gracie's nerves were so frazzled that she wasn't sure she could eat. She had seen two letters from the Office of Property Assessment in the pile of mail she had sorted.

The Office of Property Assessment handled real estate taxes. Taxes Gracie hadn't paid and didn't know when the last time they were paid. She almost opened the envelopes but decided she should fortify herself with food first.

They chatted while they ate, but the conversation was seasoned with sadness. Every single piece of mail was a pin in their hearts. A reminder that Gran wasn't there anymore. Gracie was half tempted to tell Ada not to worry about sorting through the rest. She didn't think Ada's heart could take it, and Gracie's couldn't take much more either. There was no sense in both of them being in pain.

But Ada rose and cleared away the food containers. "Okay, let's start opening these envelopes."

Gracie rose. "You don't have to help with that part. You've done so much already."

"I'm not doing anything, Gracie. I want to help you."

Gracie squirmed. People normally didn't want to help her. "Okay."

They grabbed butter knives to use as makeshift letter openers and went to work. Gracie lifted out the letters from the Office of Property Assessment and opened them.

The house's property tax for the previous year was overdue. The current year's taxes were due soon. She let out a groan.

"What is it?" Ada moved to look at the letter in Gracie's hand.

"The taxes for last year haven't been paid."

"Oh no." Ada said. "But it should be pretty easy to explain why they're late. You were kinda busy."

Gracie nodded. Maybe there was a way to plead hardship. Paying off both years would take a huge chunk out of her funds. The taxes were her responsibility, not the estate's. The estate had plenty of money from Gran's life insurance policy to cover the bill. But she couldn't see Uncle Rand agreeing to let her use it.

There were a few other bills that she had to take care of in the pile, like the small balance on Gran's filtered water delivery account. That she could handle. She could not financially, or emotionally, handle any more surprises in this pile.

Ada had grown quiet, and the silence in the room seemed to press against Gracie's skin. Like a physical presence. She looked to find Ada holding a card, with tears streaming down her face.

Gracie moved to sit beside her and took the card from her hand. It was a get-well card from one of the members of Mother Bethel.

"Gran was the best," Ada sniffled. "So many people loved her."

"She was amazing."

"Sometimes I wonder why God—" She snapped her mouth shut.

"I know. Me too," Gracie said, draping an arm around Ada's shoulder and joining her tears to her cousin's. Gran seemed so close in this moment, yet so far. But a memory of Gran rippled to the front of Gracie's mind. "Remember Gran used to say, 'God's business—'"

"'—ain't your business,'" Ada finished.

They both chuckled. "I asked God 'why' a lot during the time that

Gran was getting sicker. But Gran kept telling me that. That God has His own ways of doing things that we may not understand."

"I really don't understand this," Ada said, wiping her tears.

"Me either. And I don't like it."

CHAPTER TEN

Olivia

As soon as Douglas left to go to work in the small clinic blocks away from their house, Olivia headed for the secret room. She had gone down to give Beulah and Hope breakfast and wanted to check on them once more before she went to the Wilsons' grocery. Hope had been improving when Olivia left her and Beulah last night.

In all her years of being a stationmaster, she never could make herself comfortable with leaving passengers in the house alone. Of course, there was nothing to fear. If something happened abovestairs, like a fire, she had told all her passengers to go across the alley to Mr. Still's house if they needed help and she wasn't there.

Despite this, it took her over an hour to work up the nerve to leave Beulah and Hope. She had never had a child in her room, and a sick one no less. Beulah assured her they would be fine. Olivia's nerves still jittered. She had reluctantly left them, promising she would return as soon as possible.

Outside, the November day was chilly, but not the uncomfortable cold that Philadelphia weather could bring. She put on her coat and hat, slipped out the door, and locked it behind her. The Wilsons' grocery was located ten minutes away. Her trip took her past rows of houses, some of which she knew to be station houses as well.

They had a network of houses in the area. Mr. Still even kept passengers in his home when it was too dangerous to move them. That happened more often than any of them were comfortable with. Not only did they have to worry about patrols but also their fellow citizens who opposed the abolishment of slavery. Added to that was the risk of getting caught aiding a fugitive.

Their fellow citizens were easy to navigate around, since most of their actions happened in the day, with anti-abolition protests and speeches, newspaper articles, and such. The slave catchers, however, moved with stealth after dark. Many conductors had found themselves staring down the barrel of the gun of a slave catcher intent on recovering their quarry. The need for secrecy was paramount because the slave catchers were watching and were ruthless.

The grocery had a fair number of customers this morning. She spotted several of her neighbors and Henry mulling over some potatoes. Olivia smiled her greeting to Thea before she started her shopping. As she finished, Franklin rounded one of the shelves, carrying a crate of apples.

He grinned at her. "Ms. 'Livia."

"Hello, Franklin."

He looked over his shoulder. "I think my pa is looking for you."

"Thank you, Franklin."

The boy continued down the aisle to the section of the store that held the produce. Olivia finished her shopping, her mind picking at the mystery of Mr. Wilson needing to speak to her. Thea stood at the counter, taking notes in a ledger. "Good morning, Mrs. Kingston." Her greeting was as warm as ever, but a little louder than normal.

"Good morning." Frowning, Olivia placed her purchases on the counter.

The curtain that separated the back storage room from the front of the store parted, and Mr. Wilson stepped through. "Mrs. Kingston, I was about to send Franklin 'round. I got somethin' special in that I thought would interest you."

Her hand slowed. "Something special" was code for passengers. "Would you like me to come now?"

"Yes, and if you could step in the back. . ." His tone would have sounded light to anyone else, but Olivia heard the note of seriousness in it.

She set her basket on the counter, and Thea took ahold of it. "I can finish this."

Olivia followed Mr. Wilson through the curtain and down a row of shelves. At the back was a small room being used as an office. Mr. Wilson cracked the door. "It's all right," he said quietly.

It took a second for Olivia to realize that he was addressing someone other than her, since the room appeared empty. Then she saw a man, clothes tattered and skin pallid, ease from under the desk.

Olivia kept her mouth from gaping. "Hello."

The man eyed her. "Hello, ma'am."

Mr. Wilson moved around the edge of the desk. "Our guest is in need of attention." He turned to the man. "This lady can help you. Show her."

The man stared at Mr. Wilson for a second longer before turning his shoulder. There was a rip in his shirt, and an angry slash could be seen through the tear.

Olivia kneeled and peered at him. "Gunshot?"

"Yes, ma'am," the man said.

"Looks like the bullet grazed you, but we will need to clean it before it gets infected." She looked up at Mr. Wilson. "Do you have medical supplies?"

Mr. Wilson nodded, stepped to the door, and called for Franklin. The boy appeared seconds later, and Olivia told him what supplies she needed. When he left, she turned her attention back to the man. "I am Mrs. Kingston. What is your name?"

The man dropped his eyes. "Walker."

"Walker, can I ask you about how you got here?"

The man nodded.

"Did a conductor help you get here?" Mr. Wilson asked.

"Yes, sir. But when we was runnin', we got separated." He rubbed his face. "The slave catchers caught us while we was sleepin' in a barn, and sent the dogs in for us."

Olivia fought a shudder. "You ran with others?"

"Two more. Men from a plantation near me. We met someone

who would help us, but when the catchers came with the dogs, he didn't have time to hide us."

"How did you know to come here?"

The man looked exhausted. "Two fellas at the docks told me."

"Did they tell you their names?" Olivia asked.

"One of 'em did. Logan."

Mr. Wilson gave Olivia a puzzled look. There was no one named Logan in their network. Could he be a sympathetic dock worker?

Franklin returned, handing the supplies over without seeming to react to the injured man on the floor. Olivia turned to the man. "This may cause you pain. Can you be strong?"

The man nodded. She went to work, using alcohol to clean the wound. Then she made a poultice and applied it. "Try and keep this as clean and dry as you possibly can."

Walker smiled. "Thank you, ma'am."

"You are welcome. Unfortunately, you have to stay in your hiding place a little longer."

"Yes, ma'am." Walker scooted back under the desk. Mr. Wilson led her toward the front of the store, Franklin a few steps behind them.

"He came during the day?" Olivia asked.

"He was hidin' in some crates outside the door when I came in this mornin'."

"Thank God he made it."

"Problem is. . ." Mr. Wilson stopped at the curtain and lowered his voice. "He brought a slave catcher with him. I already sent a letter to Mr. Still."

"It is not as if there weren't slave catchers around before." Olivia tried to inject optimism into her voice.

"True. However, somethin' ain't right."

"How so?"

"Beulah and the baby. When I went to meet Mr. Lloyd, who assisted them through Maryland, he was takin' a short rest in the back of the wagon. Beulah wasn't there. When I woke him, we went lookin' for her and found her about a half mile away, hidin' in the trees."

Olivia frowned. "Did she say why she left the wagon?"

"Mr. Lloyd got her in the wagon and movin' so fast, she was gone before I could ask. Maybe you could ask her." Mr. Wilson slowed. "If I know Lloyd, he told her to stay in the wagon under the blankets. No reason for her to hide in the trees."

"I will speak to her about it."

"How is she and the baby? That one had me worried," he said, his tone fatherly.

"Still unwell from their journey. Hope is a bit better now but still too weak to move."

Mr. Wilson sighed. "We have to believe that everything will work out."

Olivia touched him on the shoulder. "Believe and pray."

Mr. Wilson opened the curtain, allowing Olivia to step through. When she did, she had to stop short to avoid running into Henry.

He stepped back in surprise. "Sorry, Mrs. Kingston."

"Did you need help with somethin'?" Mr. Wilson stepped from behind her.

"Uh. . .I. . .yes. I wanted to know if you had any more apples."

Mr. Wilson looked around. So did Olivia. Had she not just seen Franklin carrying a crate of apples? "I do. Over there."

"Thank you," Henry said, rushing away.

Olivia gave Mr. Wilson a quizzical look before lifting her basket from the counter. "I appreciate you showing me the special item. I will let you know what I think of it."

Mr. Wilson nodded.

Olivia walked as fast as she could back to her house. Helping Walker had kept her from home longer than she planned, but she had to help. She pondered who this Logan could be and how to find out who he was. She put her key in the lock. A chill swept over her neck like a breeze. She turned.

Saunders stood down the street, watching her.

Olivia's heart plummeted. How far had he followed her? Did he know what she had seen in the back of the Wilsons' grocery? He was a member of the police patrol, but most free Blacks were sure he was also working for slave catchers. Had she just given him another clue to who she was and what she was doing?

God seemed to have heard Olivia's prayers concerning Hope, because the baby seemed to be on the mend. She took some broth and a little bread the night before, and Olivia had nearly cried in relief. Hope's improvement also encouraged Beulah. The lines of worry on her face had grown deeper each day.

This morning, Beulah had asked, "How long before we have to leave?"

Olivia had said, "Soon."

Beulah had quieted, and Olivia realized what the woman was asking. She sat down beside her on the bed. "I mean, you can stay as long as you and Hope need to recover. I said soon because it appears that Hope is close to being well enough to travel."

Beulah looked down at the sleeping child. "What if she is still sick when it is time to go?"

"Then you stay here until she is better."

"I don't wanna burden you," Beulah said, her voice quiet.

Olivia grabbed her hand. "You are no burden. Knowing that you and Hope will be free to learn to read one day brings me joy."

Beulah brightened a bit. "Hard not knowing what comes next. And I am tired."

"Rest a bit. All will be well."

She had left them both asleep. Her heart ached. She would have to find a way to cheer Beulah's spirits.

Olivia had returned to her sewing table when the door opened and a cool draft chilled the room. She shivered. There was a sharpness to the air that felt like snow was coming. She turned in her seat to see who had stepped in. Thea was hastily closing the door.

Olivia tried to smile, but the cold remained and she shivered again. "Thea. What brings you by?"

Thea stepped to the table. "Do you have a customer?"

Olivia glanced at the screen that would have concealed a customer. It was still standing in the corner. "Oh no. I simply forgot to take that down from yesterday."

"Good," Thea said. "I need to tell you something."

"What is the matter?" Olivia motioned for her to sit.

Thea shook her head and glanced behind her. "Something peculiar has happened. I cannot stay. I have to go to the other stationmasters."

Olivia smoothed out the piece of fabric in front of her. "Is it about the passenger that showed up at your shop?"

"Yes and no." Thea leaned closer. "He moved on."

"Where to?" There were a few states that the stationmasters would send fugitives to if they wanted to continue further north. Some were transported all the way to Canada.

"That is the issue. No one knows."

Olivia pressed her hand to her throat. "Who moved him?"

Thea threw up her hands. "No one I have spoken with knows. I came to you to ask if he came here, seeing as he met you at the shop. Marin and I didn't think he knew where you lived but took the chance that maybe he had spotted you walking about and asked for assistance."

"He is not here, and I have not seen him. You went to look for him, and he was gone? Did he say nothing of leaving?"

"No. Nothing. There were only a few people who knew he was at our shop. We sent a note to Mr. Still. Not knowing who this Logan is, we did not know who else to contact."

"That is odd."

"Marin thought that too." Thea rubbed her hands together. "Why would a fugitive leave safety in a place where he knows no one and knows there are slave catchers about?"

"That is very odd indeed." As long as her home had been a station house, she had never heard of a stationmaster losing a fugitive. There had been a few cases where a slave catcher recovered a fugitive the stationmaster was assisting. In those cases, they knew precisely where the fugitive was. But to lose one without any idea of where he or she had gone? Olivia wrapped her arms around her middle.

"Mr. Gull and Marin believe something is amiss."

"Amiss how?"

"They are not sure yet, but they will be speaking to Mr. Still today. They thought it might be a good idea to put the other stationmasters on notice."

"Thankfully, we have extra safety measures in place."

"I will come back around to tell you about Marin's meeting with Mr. Still and—" She looked behind her and glanced out the window. "Oh no."

Olivia shuddered again but not from cold. "What?"

"Saunders is coming."

Olivia peered out the front window as Saunders started up the steps. Several of the Friends members thought Saunders had discovered some of the key players in their network. She knew he suspected Mr. Still, who was so active on the Vigilance Committee. Olivia had lost count of the days she left Mr. Still's house and found Saunders watching. But none of the Friends had given Saunders any reason that might confirm his suspicions. And she would keep it that way. Seeing her and Thea here together could help him connect them to the rest of the stationmasters Thea had already visited.

She grabbed Thea's arm. "Here, get behind the screen."

Olivia had barely stashed Thea behind the screen before Saunders opened the door.

Olivia relaxed the frown on her face. "Can I help you, sir?"

"Where is the woman I saw come in here?"

Olivia's heart raced. "What woman?"

"I saw Mrs. Wilson from the grocers come in the door not ten minutes ago. I have business to speak with her about."

Olivia motioned around the room. "As you can see—"

His face transformed into a sneer. "Where is she?" As he spoke, his eyes shifted around the room. His brows rose when he saw the screen. "Is she behind there?"

Olivia moved between him and the screen. "There is someone behind that screen. Don't you think it would be wholly improper for you to look?"

Saunders looked at her and then back at the screen. His forehead furrowed with skepticism, but he did stop. "You lie."

"She is not lying," an imperious and slightly annoyed high-pitched voice said. "Now, if you are done, I would like to get back to my business without a gentleman present."

Olivia fought back a grin. She recognized Thea's voice, but the alarm on Saunders's face told her that he did not. "My apologies."

"Don't apologize. Leave." Thea's tone perfectly mimicked many of Olivia's customers.

Saunders snapped his mouth shut, turned on his heel, and left. Olivia eased to the window, trying to look as unconcerned as possible, to check if he had actually gone. After all, the man did watch the house. She scanned the street, then pulled the shade and locked the front door.

When she turned, Thea was peeking out from behind the screen. "Is he gone?"

"From what I can see." Olivia laughed. "That was a good ploy."

"Heaven knows I've heard enough of our customers speak to me that way," Thea said with a chuckle.

"Unfortunately, he may still be out there watching the house where I cannot see him." Olivia moved to the panel covering the hidden door. "You will have to go out the back."

Thea nodded, helping her move the panel. "We will have to be extra careful with him snoopin' about."

They reached the bottom of the stairs to find Beulah huddled in a corner, clutching baby Hope to her chest. Olivia gave her a reassuring smile. "Please do not be afraid. This is Mrs. Wilson. She is a friend."

Beulah visibly relaxed and stood. "I didn't know what to think. Missus doesn't normally come down during the day."

"You don't have to call me missus." Olivia removed the panel that separated the root cellar from the secret room. "We had some company, and now Mrs. Wilson needs to slip out the back in case he is still watching."

"Company?"

Thea followed Olivia across the room. "A patrolman."

Beulah's eyes grew wide, and she trembled. "Have they come for me?"

"No, no. Please do not worry," Olivia said, pushing open the double doors of the root cellar. Watery sunlight filled the space, and Beulah shielded her eyes.

Thea hurried up the stairs. "I will send word around about the meeting. We need to solve this puzzle."

"Please be careful."

Thea nodded and was gone.

When Olivia turned from closing the door, Beulah was sitting on the cot, Hope pressed to her chest. "What if he comes back?"

"He most likely will."

Beulah gasped. She scampered onto the cot until her back was against the wall.

Olivia let out a sigh. Not the best choice of words. "What I meant to say was that there are always slave catchers in the area. They know many of the fugitives come through Philadelphia. But you do not need to worry. Our work is secret. We will keep you safe."

Beulah looked down at Hope, who was sleeping. "But will you be safe?"

Olivia only nodded. She believed she would be, but a note of worry sounded loud in her heart.

CHAPTER ELEVEN

GRACIE

*T*he calendar Gracie had hung on the wall in front of her desk caught her attention and taunted her. She glanced at it and grimaced. Two of her twelve weeks had passed. Now she had only ten weeks to get the shop ready for the grand opening. She should have been excited that she had accomplished so many things on her list. But those were the easy things. She still had the harder things to do.

Preston had called several times for an update. Grateful as she was that he was concerned, she dreaded the calls. His thoughtfulness reminded her that she was stuck. How was she supposed to move forward when the pegboards to display the yarn weren't installed yet? She also hadn't ordered the shop's sign. No sense doing that if she wasn't sure she could hang it outside. And it made no sense to hang a sign on a shop that wouldn't be open for at least a month.

But she still had to pay her bills. In her office, she reviewed her plans again. All of her income was tied up in opening the shop. The zoning permit wouldn't take long, but getting Preston to come back was going to take longer. She could find another contractor, but that would take time she didn't have. She rubbed the bridge of her nose. What was she going to do?

She heard the front door open. In a moment, Ada rounded the staircase. "Oh, hey. Working?"

Gracie leaned back in her chair. "Something like that. Trying to make some decisions about the shop."

"I thought you had put the online shop on hold while you prepared to open." Ada unbuttoned her coat.

"I did." She shook her head. This was not a conversation she wanted to have right now. "How was class?" she asked.

Ada ran through her day, letting her book bag slide off her shoulder. As she did, Gracie's laptop let off a soft ping, and she looked at the screen. She'd received a message on the shop's site.

Gracie squinted at the screen. "What is this?"

Ada looked over her shoulder. "I thought you said you put the shop on hold."

"The retail part anyways." She opened up the website's inbox. There were thirty new messages there, all dated during the days she'd been trying to figure out the secret room.

Ada laughed. "When was the last time you checked your messages?"

"Only a week. But I normally don't get this many." Most of them expressed excitement that she was opening a brick-and-mortar store in Philly. A couple were from her old customers, one asking if she would still be taking online orders since Gracie was her favorite yarn store. Gracie groaned. Why didn't she think of that? She could reopen the online shop. That would generate income.

"Oh, wow," Ada said. "Looks like people are ready to shop. That's good, right?"

"Yes, it is." Shock jumbling her thoughts, Gracie read the rest of the messages.

They were class enrollments.

"Oh! Look at this." Gracie pointed to the screen, her finger trembling. "I almost forgot I'd opened up those registrations."

"The adult class is half-full, and the kids' class is completely full," Ada said, her grin growing wider.

Gracie covered her mouth with her hand. She didn't know what to expect when it came to registration, but she didn't expect this. She looked through the kids' class registrations first. The listing had said that the class would be suitable for children ages ten to twelve. Most of the students were twelve. One of the registrations had a note saying that the student, Mia Barton, would be thirteen by the time the class started and asked if that was okay.

More importantly, all the registrations were ready to pay in full.

"That's pretty cool. Too bad you have to wait until the shop opens," Ada said.

Gracie gaped at her. Did she have to wait? "Once the registrations are paid, why can't I have the class?"

Ada shrugged. "I thought you were waiting until you research the house's history."

"But I don't have to. I can have the classes now, just like I did when I was living in Richmond," Gracie said, still staring at the screen. "I used to host a knitting class at the local art center. All I need is a space to sit and supplies, and I have both. I don't have to wait for the rezoning either, since I'm not opening the retail portion of the shop."

Ada patted Gracie on the back. "Then it looks like you can do it."

Gracie glanced at the space that would be the dining room. Amazingly, she had found an old worktable in the local school system's excess sale. It was the perfect height for instruction. "I would need to finish setting up the classroom space."

"I can help you. It shouldn't take long," Ada said.

"We need some chairs."

"Other than that, I can't think of any reason you can't hold the classes even though the shop isn't officially open." Ada nodded. "I think you should do it."

I need to do this. Gracie returned to the laptop, her mind racing. "First I have to find out if the parents would be willing to start the class early."

"Let me put my stuff upstairs, and I'll get the space set up and look for some chairs," Ada said.

It took only ten minutes to email the parents. Then Gracie helped Ada move the table around and they searched for chairs together. All the while, Gracie had to fight off the feeling of surrealness. She was doing what she never dreamed she would do, and that lightened her heart. But fear tempered her excitement. What if this failed? What if this was just a waste of time?

Chairs ordered, for less than she anticipated, Gracie went back and checked her email. Three of the five parents had agreed to the date change.

"That was quick," Ada said, looking over her shoulder.

Gracie nodded. "I guess I'm going to have to put together the kits for the class."

Ada clapped. "Let's do it."

They went to the front of the store, and Gracie opened a box of yarn. "Each kit needs a pair of size seven knitting needles and a ball of cotton yarn."

"What's the pattern?" Ada asked.

"A knitted dishcloth." It was the perfect first project. It wasn't as long as a scarf, and a new student could finish it without losing enthusiasm. It was the first thing she'd knitted all those years ago when she'd fallen in love with the rhythm of the stitches.

"Ah, the old dishcloth-as-a-first-project trick," Ada said, selecting five sets of bamboo needles.

Gracie stared at her. "How do you know that? And that I needed bamboo needles?"

Ada stepped away from the box of needles. "You taught me, remember?"

Once when Gracie had come to visit, Gran had asked her to teach Ada how to knit as a way to help her lower her stress about school. "I totally forgot."

"I still knit occasionally, but when school is in, I don't do much."

They were halfway through packaging the kits when the doorbell sounded. Ada went to the door and peeked out the window. She looked over her shoulder with a grin on her face. "It's Clarence."

Gracie straightened. She hurriedly smoothed her clothes. Did she forget that he was coming over?

"You look great," Ada said with a laugh, and she opened the door.

Gracie didn't have time to respond before Clarence stepped in, a small bag in his hand. "Hi." He looked around. "I probably should have called first."

Ada waved a hand. "It's okay."

Gracie pressed a hand to her stomach. "What brings you by?"

He held up the bag. It was Ms. Lila's knitting project bag. "I told Grandma Lila I was going to be at a meeting nearby, and she asked me to bring her scarf for you to fix."

Gracie laughed. "Let me see." She took the bag from Clarence, walked to the sofa, and sat. Studying the knitting, she smiled. Ms. Lila knitted beautifully, but she would often get distracted while talking and forget what she was doing. "Oh, this is an easy fix. Shouldn't take more than ten minutes. Would you like to sit? Unless you have to go." Her tone came out more disappointed than she meant.

"No. I already went to the meeting." He sat next to her on the sofa.

The knitting slipped out of her hand and she fumbled as she picked it back up. "I just need to fix one row."

"Grandma tried to explain to me what to tell you was wrong with it." Clarence looked sheepish. "Honestly, it was like she was speaking another language. Finally, I just asked her if you would know what to do."

Gracie laughed. "Knitters have their own secret language. Crocheters too."

"Like a secret club." Clarence leaned over, watching her work.

"Yes, but it's easy to get in the club. All you have to do is learn how to knit." She tinked back the whole row and smiled at the thought of teaching her children's class that the word *tink* was just *knit* backward. Tinking was undoing the stitches.

"I've always found it fascinating." His voice was very close to her ear.

"I can teach you." Gracie lifted her head to look at him, but he was still leaning over. Their noses were inches from each other. Her face flamed, and she turned her attention back to the knitting.

"I think I might like that."

※

Gracie had lived in the house for one month. Hard to believe. Especially since living here nearly drowned her daily. The grief was heavy. However, she somehow kept the sadness at bay. She couldn't be sad.

She had a promise to fulfill, and that promise had kept her moving.

The fact that the house didn't look like it did when Gran lived there helped too. Then there was the brick wall and the door. Although it had been there for decades, discovering it brought a newness to living in the space. More than once, like she was doing now, Gracie caught herself staring at the wall in wonder. If the house was used for a station on the Underground Railroad, was the brick exposed at the time? Did people come to this house and wonder what was behind the door?

Most of all, how did the owners of the house keep their work hidden? That would have been a deadly secret to keep.

She looked away from the wall and continued to put yarn in the cube shelving. The shop wasn't complete, but she did want it to resemble a shop when the kids' knitting class began.

As she organized the cubes by colorway, the doorbell rang. With a skein of yarn still in her hand, she went to the door. Ms. Lila. Gracie peered behind her, looking for Clarence, and sighed with disappointment when she didn't see him. *Cut it out,* she chided herself. Clarence didn't have to accompany Ms. Lila every time.

She opened the door, her smile bright. "Hi, Ms. Lila."

"Look at that." Ms. Lila looked past her. "It looks like you're almost ready to open." She took slow steps to the middle of room, eyeing the yarn in Gracie's hand. "These are some great colorways. I may need to knit Clarence another hat."

Gracie fought the urge to snap to attention at Clarence's name. Instead, she closed the door and calmly said, "Oh, does he like hats?"

"He likes to stay warm. You know he spent all them years in Atlanta. Ain't used to the cold anymore." She sat on the sofa. "He would appreciate anything handmade and warm."

Noted. "To what do I owe this visit?"

Ms. Lila sat up taller. "I—I thought I would stop by."

Then Gracie remembered. Mother Bethel's prayer shawl ministry met every first Friday of the month. Gran and Ms. Lila often spent the majority of the day together, starting with lunch and ending with a trip to the church. Gracie's heart ached. Gran was loved by so many people, and so many people bore the pain of grief from losing her. "It's the perfect time. How about some lunch?"

Ms. Lila gave her a wistful smile. "I would like that."

"I don't have much food, but we can order something to be delivered."

Ms. Lila waved her hand. "As long as you do it. I can't figure out these food delivery services for nothing."

Laughing, Gracie picked up her phone and ordered two chicken and quinoa bowls from a local eatery and sat down next to Ms. Lila.

"While we're talking 'bout food, I want to invite you and Ada to Thanksgiving dinner."

Gracie sucked in a breath. Thanksgiving was two weeks away. "I totally forgot. Gran normally. . ." The rest of the sentence withered on her lips.

"I know. That's why I'm asking. I'm pretty certain your uncle isn't going to invite you to his house."

Gracie chuckled. "Probably not."

"It would be my pleasure to have you." Ms. Lila squeezed her hand. "I told Clarence, and he thought it would be nice for you to come too."

Gracie looked down to hide her blush. "Well, if it's no trouble, I'll talk to Ada. Do you need us to bring anything?"

"Just yourselves."

Determined not to cry, Gracie smiled. "Thank you."

"Now tell me how this shop is going." Ms. Lila opened the bag she carried with her and pulled out a hat knit almost to the crown.

Gracie stared at it. "What happened to the scarf you were knitting? The one Clarence brought over for me to fix?"

Ms. Lila waved her hand like she was clearing the air. "I made a mistake I couldn't figure out and put it in time-out."

"You know I could have helped you." Gracie laughed. That was one thing she loved about Ms. Lila. She lived life on her own terms, like Gran. It was clear why they were such great friends. Would she be as fearless when she reached their season of life?

"Yes, but you're doing the house thing and getting the shop ready to open. How is that going, by the way?"

She told Ms. Lila about her trip to Clarence's office and about the taxes.

"Do you need help with that?" Ms. Lila asked while knitting round and round.

Gracie gaped. "No. It's my responsibility. I can handle it." *Just barely.*

Ms. Lila looked at her over her glasses. "Don't let me find out that you lost the house because you couldn't pay the taxes."

"I—I can handle it, Ms. Lila. I can." Even if she couldn't, she would find another way than to ask Ms. Lila. How would Clarence feel about her taking money from his grandmother? If something was starting between them, it would be over.

Stop it. There is nothing starting between you and him.

Ms. Lila shook her head and let out a huff. "You are as stubborn as your grandmother."

Gracie shifted in her seat. "Gran *was* stubborn."

"So are you." She leaned over and touched Gracie's hand. "And I know you will fight for this house as hard as Marian did."

Gracie frowned. "I thought Gran already owned the house from her mother? Why would she have to fight?"

Ms. Lila leaned back and laughed. "Let me tell you about your Gran. Years back, this man came round, wanting to buy all the properties on this block, including the school."

Gracie leaned forward. "Even this house?"

Ms. Lila nodded. "He wanted to turn everything into high-rise condos. He put a lot of pressure on some of the older residents on the street. Threw a lot of money at them. But your Gran wouldn't budge."

"What happened?"

"The developer bought some of the properties on the block but a few others wouldn't sell either. The property company owns half the block, and they never built the condos. Your Gran stood toe to toe with them. Even threatened to sue them if they didn't leave her alone."

Gracie went to the counter where she had left the socks she was knitting. Knitting them two at a time, a technique where both socks were on the same needles, allowed her to finish them quickly. She would have to cast on something else soon. "That sounds like Gran."

The food arrived, and they had a pleasant lunch together. She peppered Ms. Lila with as many questions as she could about Gran.

"I've been wanting to say this for a while," Ms. Lila said, picking up her knitting again. "Marian would have been very proud of you. So would your mother."

Would they? She was past knowing with both of them, especially her mother. Rochelle McNeil was only a memory. And from what Gracie knew about her, her mother was a fighter like Gran. Gran had told her how she had argued with the doctors who didn't believe how much pain she was in after she gave birth to Gracie. The pain would kill her. Rather, the blood clots that had formed in her legs and lungs would. No matter how hard she argued, no one believed her, and thrombosis had ended Rochelle McNeil's life.

Gracie opened her mouth to reply, but nothing came out. Gran wouldn't be proud of this mess. Couldn't be. Gran managed her affairs with clarity and speed. Not forgetting to pick up the mail for months and paying the taxes late. Gran's gift should have given her a new life. Instead, her life looked very much like her old one.

"I don't think she would be proud." Gracie took a shaky breath, tears brimming in her eyes.

"Oh, sweet girl, why wouldn't she?" Ms. Lila put her knitting aside.

"Because—" was all Gracie could say before the tears started falling.

"Because you're facing some challenges? That's why she would be proud."

Gracie tried to accept Ms. Lila's words, to make them true and apply them to herself. But she failed. Like everything else. And now Gran wasn't there to save her. Regardless of whatever life she had—dead-end jobs, no relationships to speak of, moving from one cheap apartment to the next and nearly being homeless—her life was better with Gran in it. Now Gran, like her mother, had gone to the sweet by-and-by and left Gracie in the grim here and now.

CHAPTER TWELVE

Olivia

*A*lmost a week had passed since Beulah and Hope had arrived. Although their conditions improved some, they were still very weak. Olivia had done all she could to keep them warm and fed.

Even though she knew they were recovering, her anxiety remained high. Particularly now that Walker had disappeared. Not to mention how Saunders' visit had rattled her badly enough that she jumped every time the front door opened. Even when it was Douglas. The first few times, he had studied her with concern. Now he announced himself when he came home.

She vowed to stop jumping. A man should be able to come home from work and not frighten his wife every night. But he had, as usual, not asked why she was so skittish. If he knew she was growing more afraid by the day, he would forbid her to put her life in danger. She shook her head. It was too late for that now.

Olivia was hunched over her sewing table when the door opened. She jumped and then scolded herself. But surprise brought her to her feet when she saw Franklin standing in the doorway in the fading sunlight.

"Franklin. Oh my. I quite forgot myself. Did I ask you to deliver something? Because I have nothing for you." She pushed the pin in her hand into the pincushion.

"No." Franklin took off the brown cap he was wearing and reached in his pocket. "I got a letter for you."

She crossed the room and took the letter. "Thank you. Do you need to wait for a reply?"

"No, ma'am." Franklin shuffled. "Just trying to get warm. Mighty cold out there."

Olivia smiled at the boy. "You can go and make yourself a cup of cocoa. I believe there are a few biscuits left over too."

Franklin grinned. "Yes, ma'am."

She returned to her seat and opened the letter, taking one last peek at the door. Douglas would be arriving soon from work. If she expected him, he would not frighten her. The flap gave easily under her finger. She unfolded the note and began to read.

> *Mrs. Kingston,*
> *I will be arriving at your house tomorrow to collect the passengers that you have been so kind to accommodate these past weeks. Mr. and Mrs. Tomas are ready to receive them and assist them with food and shelter until they can be escorted to our northernmost conductors.*
> *I will come after sunset if that is acceptable to you. There have been strange doings about, and I feel it is best to use the aid of darkness.*
>
> *Yours in service,*
> *Mr. T. Gull*

Olivia refolded the letter, her mind working on all she would need to do before Mr. Gull arrived tomorrow. First and most importantly, she would have to go over the process with Beulah. Extra steps would need to be taken to accommodate baby Hope. Olivia would also have to prepare Beulah that Mr. Gull was white. Some fugitives were unnerved by receiving assistance from a white man because they had trouble forgetting their past. Olivia would make sure Beulah understood she was among friends.

Franklin returned from the kitchen. "Thank you, Ms. 'Livia. That was what I needed."

Olivia laughed. Franklin spoke in a manner that was well above his years. "Glad you enjoyed it." She let the boy out, closed the drapes, and locked the door. Maybe she could get to talk to Beulah a bit before Douglas arrived home.

Olivia removed the panel, but when she opened the door, she was met with a sight she never expected to see.

Baby Hope was sitting on the second-from-the-top stair. Olivia took a step back. "What are you doing here?"

Hope looked up at her, her brown eyes wide, and whimpered.

The next thought slammed into her like a thunderclap. *Where is Beulah?*

After scooping up Hope, she rushed down the stairs as fast as she safely could. The room was dimly lit, and as Olivia's eyes adjusted, she noticed two things.

First, there was a dim light source. Too much light to be coming from upstairs.

Second, Beulah was gone.

She gasped, holding Hope tighter. The panel between the root cellar and the secret room leaned against the adjoining wall. From where she stood, she could see that the outside door was slightly ajar, like someone had tried to close it. Cold air flooded the room. Her mind whirred. Beulah would not have left. Where would she go? And would she have left Hope?

Olivia looked down at Hope. The baby's face was a mask of confusion. *Maybe she would have left Hope.*

One skill all stationmasters needed was the ability to think on their feet. But standing there in the dim room with Hope staring at her with worried eyes, Olivia's mind was as frozen as the air.

She did think of what she could not do: leave Hope in this room alone.

The root cellar door still stood a little ajar. She gently placed Hope on the bed so she could close it. But she had not taken two steps before the child let out a hoarse wail. Olivia rushed back, picked up the girl, and rocked her. "All is well. Don't cry, little one."

Hope pressed her face into Olivia's neck and grabbed a fistful of

Olivia's blouse, making it very clear that Olivia was not going to be able to put her down again.

She caressed the girl's head. "It is nearly suppertime, and I was going to bring food down to you and your mama. How about something to eat?"

Hope watched Olivia's face as if she understood.

The door would have to wait. Besides, if she closed it, Beulah would be locked outside. She shifted Hope in her arms as she climbed the stairs. Maybe once Olivia fed the child, Hope would drift to sleep and Olivia could close the door. Then she could work on solving her next problem, which was getting word to Mr. Still. Beulah had passed through Mr. Still's house first, so it was a possibility she had returned there. Olivia tried to accept that explanation, but her mind pushed back. *But why leave Hope?*

She reached the top of the stairs. Hope buried her face in Olivia's neck and let out a whimper. Poor babe. She had been in the dark so long the light hurt her eyes. "I'm so sorry."

Olivia shielded Hope's face, turned, and plowed right into Douglas.

He was standing next to the door, a puzzled look in his eyes, and when she ran into him, he wrapped his arms around her and Hope to steady them. "Olivia?" His voice came close to her ear.

It was something about the tenderness in his tone that uncorked her emotions. Tears rushed to her eyes. "Douglas. . .I. . ."

Douglas relaxed his hold and looked down at Hope. "And who do we have here?"

Olivia blinked back tears, exhaustion weighing her down. Most of her reserve in telling Douglas about her work slipped. "Hope."

Douglas smiled. "Is this your little patient?"

She swallowed, struggling against the tears forming. "Yes, she—I am not supposed—"

Douglas held up a hand. "Let's not worry about that now. You look like you could use some help."

Her shoulders sagged. "Hope and her mama came here together, but her mama left without her."

Douglas' eyes grew wide. "Why?"

"I do not know." But as soon as she spoke the words, a memory came to mind. Mrs. Wilson having to exit through the root cellar door because Saunders was here. Besides that, how much more had Beulah heard from downstairs? Did she leave to protect Hope and Olivia?

"Let me help you," Douglas said. His voice was firm. A tone she knew. He was going to help her no matter what she said.

Olivia sniffled. Her legs felt like she had run up and down the stairs all day. "The root cellar door is open. I need to close it."

Douglas looked down at Hope. "You tend to the child, and I will close the door."

"Douglas," she started, her words pleading.

"Everything will be all right. We will tend to the immediate needs and then talk."

She nodded. "It may be a little dark. Take a lamp."

He released her, breaking the bubble of warmth his embrace created. He crossed the room and picked up an oil lamp Olivia kept sitting on a table for that very reason.

He lit the lamp and descended the stairs. She watched him until he disappeared, then carried Hope into the kitchen. Hope's eyes had adjusted to the light, and she was studying everything with wonder. "How about some bread to start?" Olivia picked up one of the biscuits she had baked earlier and handed it to the child.

Hope nearly snatched it from her and set to eating it with vigor.

She heard Douglas coming up the stairs, and in a minute he was standing in the doorway, watching Hope. "She is undernourished."

"She and her mama had a long trip."

"And she was sick." Douglas moved around her and began preparing plates of food.

"Douglas, you do not have to do this."

"I think I do." He smiled at her. "Go sit in the dining room. I'll have more food for you before Hope finishes that biscuit."

Olivia obeyed, her emotions in a jumble. When Douglas set the plate of chicken and potatoes in front of her, Hope leapt forward to grab for it. Olivia had to react quickly to catch her tiny hands.

Douglas laughed. "Looks like she's ready for more." He placed his own plate in front of the chair next to Olivia and sat down. After saying a quick blessing, Olivia used her fork to mash one of the pieces of potato and shred some chicken for Hope.

"Go slowly. Her stomach may be too weak for heavy foods."

Olivia smiled at him. His doctor training tended to leak out of him at times.

"What do you do now? By the way you looked coming out of the basement, I assume this was not supposed to happen."

Olivia looked down at Hope, who was chewing on a strip of chicken and reaching for another. "I need to get word to Mr.—" She stopped herself. Douglas was already too far into this than she was comfortable with.

"Word to Mr. Still?"

She let out a sigh. "Yes."

"I will go over to his house as soon as I finish eating."

Olivia sat up straight. "I do not wish to involve you."

He tipped his head and gave her a curious look. "I've always been involved, dear."

CHAPTER THIRTEEN

GRACIE

*S*omething thumped in the room next to Gracie's, and she came awake in alarm. Did Gran need her? She swung her legs out of bed and was almost to the door before reality caught up with her.

Gran didn't need her any longer. She, however, needed Gran.

She shuffled back to her bed and flopped down, the beginnings of a headache building at the back of her neck. After her lunch with Ms. Lila, Gran had been stuffed into her thoughts like she'd filled the cubes with yarn. Memories stacked on top of each other, each one a different color and hue.

Gran telling her the family tree. Gran frying fish and hush puppies. Gran praising the few school accomplishments she'd had. Gran growing weaker and weaker. Gran taking her last breath. Gracie had been there for that. It had been a suspended moment of painlessness. A brief flash before the sharp anguish hit. A second of seeing Gran without pain and Gracie not feeling the pain yet.

She groaned. If her thoughts continued like this, she would spend the day crying.

She showered and then went into the small kitchen. The noise she'd heard was Ada getting breakfast.

Ada gave her a crooked smile. "Good morning?"

Gracie chuckled. "Do I look that bad?"

Ada looked her up and down. "Yes."

Gracie, laughing, pushed Ada aside to get to the coffee. Gracie hadn't expected it, but Ada brought with her a measure of comfort. Gracie had been on her own for so long that she forgot how nice it was to share a space with someone. She had lived with Gran until the end, but that was different. She was Gran's caregiver. She was Ada's cousin and, maybe, friend.

"You're up early," Gracie said, then second-guessed herself. Ada had slept until well after ten the previous week. "I mean, you aren't normally up this early."

"When I'm not in class, I sleep as late as I can. My first class is at nine," she said, looking over at Gracie. "Did I wake you?"

Gracie took a deep breath. "I thought you were Gran."

Ada set her cup on the table. "I'm sorry."

"Don't be," Gracie said with a wave of her hand. "It's like she's all around. I can't help but think of her."

"I know."

Gracie gave Ada a watery smile and moved to toast a bagel. "It's good that I'm up. I need to prepare the last of the materials for the kids' knitting class."

Ada popped the lid on her travel coffee cup. "I don't have class tomorrow, so I can help you with whatever's left."

"You don't have to."

"I know. I want to. This is exciting."

Gracie laughed. "I'm not going to refuse help. I also need to finish filling out the nomination application. And figure out how to pay the taxes."

Ada turned. "I thought you said you could handle the taxes."

"I can," Gracie tried to say confidently, but her voice squeaked. "It's just that I'll have to use the money I had set aside to finish setting up the shop. I still have to pay the contractors."

"You should talk to the family about using the estate money to pay off the taxes."

Gracie was shaking her head before Ada finished speaking. "The house is my responsibility now."

Ada moved closer. "Yes, now. But Gran was still alive when the first tax bill was issued. That makes it her estate bill."

Gracie looked down at her coffee cup. That made sense. "I can see how that could be true."

Ada put her hand on Gracie's shoulder. "It is true. Talk to the family. You already have my vote, and I'm sure my brother and Natalia will agree. I'll talk to Bernard for you."

Gracie didn't point out that Ada had omitted her father. "I guess I could call Natalia and Uncle Rand. . ."

The words hung in the air, and Gracie appreciated that Ada didn't try and sugarcoat Uncle Rand's reaction. She only patted her on the shoulder and said another one of Gran's favorite sayings. "Go with God."

Gracie exhaled. God was going to have to help her.

She waited until Ada left and called Natalia. As expected, Natalia agreed with Ada and gave her consent for the taxes to be paid from the estate account. Then Gracie immediately called Uncle Rand. No sense wasting the boost of courage Natalia's approval had given her. She pushed her shoulders back and listened to the phone ring.

On the third ring, Uncle Rand answered. "Hello, Gracie."

"Hi, Uncle Rand," she said in an airy tone that belied the tension between them. "How are you?"

"I'm fine," he said, his tone sharp, like he was offended that she asked. "Have you called to tell me what you told Ada about the house?"

Gracie grimaced. "Not exactly, but I do need to ask you something."

"Oh, really?"

"Yes, I—"

"I'll be home all day."

Gracie opened her mouth to speak, but all she managed was "Uh. . ."

"What time will you be here? Later is better."

She gritted her teeth. This didn't warrant her driving all the way to Uncle Rand's house. Why did he have to needle her like this? But he probably knew she needed him. "How about two o'clock?"

"Okay," he said and ended the call.

While completing a few tasks, she tried not to dwell on her annoyance, but she wasn't able to rid herself of her irritation before she arrived at Uncle Rand's house. Just as she climbed out of the car, she got a text from Ada saying Bernard was okay with paying the taxes from the estate funds. She stretched out the walk to the front door in slow steps. She rang the bell and waited.

After a minute, he opened the door, not smiling. "I can't talk to you long. I have a meeting."

Then why did you agree to this time? Gracie tramped down a groan. "I'll be quick."

"Hopefully quicker than it took you to walk from your car," he said, closing the door.

She rolled her eyes while his back was turned and bypassed the closet. She didn't want to stay any longer than Uncle Rand wanted her to.

As she walked to the sofa, Gracie noted how quiet the house was. It had always been that way, even when she was a kid. Her aunt and uncle never explicitly said that she couldn't be loud, but the command hung in the air, wordless, sucking the sound out of the house.

"What do you need to talk to me about?" Uncle Rand sat in the armchair, and Gracie sat on the sofa.

She fiddled with the buttons on her coat but got straight to the point. "I need to ask you if you would be okay with using Gran's estate money to pay the taxes on the house."

"Taxes?" he repeated. The word cut through the air, and she resisted the urge to flinch.

"Yes."

Uncle Rand leaned back. His expression changed from a hard stare to amusement. "You didn't pay the taxes?"

"They were due last December." She let out a shaky breath. "I will take care of the current taxes, but I think last year's taxes should be paid by the estate."

His expression changed in a blink from amusement to anger. "I told you the house is your responsibility. That hasn't changed. I know my mother left you money. Use that to pay the taxes."

Gracie moved to shift on the sofa but realized she was perched on the edge with nowhere to go. "All the other heirs of the estate have agreed to pay the taxes from the estate money."

"You went behind my back to manipulate everyone else like you did my mother?" He was near yelling now, his voice booming in the small room.

"I haven't manipulated anyone!" Anger forced the words out of her mouth louder than she wanted.

Uncle Rand studied her for a second, shock in his features.

She broke eye contact and stared at her fisted hands in her lap. "I would have liked to get your agreement on this, but you are in the minority. I don't actually need your approval now."

"My mother used to tell us how special that house was. That it had been owned outright by the family for several generations. That it was special and always needed to stay in the family. And now we're in danger of losing it because of your carelessness."

She flinched but then pushed the sting of his words from her mind. She remembered Ms. Lila saying that her mother and Gran were fighters. She could pretend to be like them. "Uncle Rand, I'm going to pay the taxes this week. We are not losing the house."

"The current taxes are your problem. You will have to pay them yourself. I don't have any more money to throw away on you."

I'm not asking for help on the current taxes. One would think she hadn't repaid the loan he'd given her all those years ago. "I know, Uncle Rand."

She let herself out the front door, her emotions raw.

The tax statements were still spread on Gracie's wobbly coffee table. Right where she had left them. She had meant to take care of them yesterday, but after her meeting with Uncle Rand, she had gone straight to her room and closed the door.

She sighed and rubbed her eyes, grumbling at the morning sunlight that brightened the room. Her mind kept replaying her conversation with Uncle Rand. Particularly the part about her carelessness. She was careless not to think of the mail and the taxes. Something so basic. Something that could cause her to lose the house.

Gran had kept meticulous records and handled her business with decisiveness and urgency. Over the months since she died, it was clear that Gran had done all she could to make Gracie's possession of the house go smoothly, including putting the house in a living trust. That made sure the rest of the family couldn't contest it going to Gracie. It also meant Gracie could move in before Gran's estate was settled.

Gracie shuffled over to the sofa and sat in front of the table. She set the tax notices aside and grabbed the folder with all of the other paperwork from Gran's estate. She lifted the top sheet. It was a receipt and warranty for a refrigerator. Not only had Gran written down the date that she purchased the refrigerator but she wrote down the date and time it was delivered and the first names of the delivery people.

Gracie couldn't help but chuckle. Gran's notes. She had kept them for everything. When Gracie was younger, Gran had sent detailed notes to Gracie's father after Gracie stayed over for the weekend. Whenever Gracie went shopping for Gran, she would leave the house with a very detailed grocery list. One of the phrases Gracie heard often from Gran was, "Let me jot that down." When Gracie would go to Gran's doctor's appointment, all the doctor's comments went into a little journal that Gran kept. Gracie had had to learn Gran's note-taking system once Gran got too sick to take the notes herself.

When she paid the taxes, she would do what Gran did. Add notes.

Gracie wrote two checks, one from the estate account to cover the previous year's taxes, the other from her personal account. Not wanting to leave anything to chance, Gracie decided she would drive the checks for the taxes down to the Office of Property Assessment.

Ada came to the door with her phone pressed to her ear and a frown on her face. She looked in at Gracie and mouthed, *My father.* Gracie slumped back on the couch. Uncle Rand's timing was synonymous with a headache.

"Okay, I'm coming," Ada said, her voice tight. She ended the call.

"My father is outside, and he wants to talk to me."

"Did he say what about?"

Ada huffed and started down the stairs. "I don't know. But he's mad about something."

Gracie stayed where she was for another minute, not knowing whether to pray, scream, or hide. She decided on praying for Ada.

She put the checks into a plain envelope. The Office of Property Assessment had a way to pay the bill online, but she thought it was best to create a paper trail. Maybe for the next person who would own the house. It would be a part of the house's history. Who knew how much more stressed she would be if she didn't have Gran's paperwork.

Raised voices caught her attention. Ada and Uncle Rand.

Gracie rose and went to the top of the stairs. She couldn't completely make out what they were arguing about, but she did hear her name a couple of times. It was probably wiser to stay out of this and let Ada handle her father. But Ada had to be really upset to raise her voice. She might need the support.

When Gracie reached the bottom of the stairs, she heard Ada say, "Dad—" But that was all she could manage before he hurtled inside.

He spotted Gracie and crossed the space between them with more speed than she thought he could. "I don't know what you're doing to my daughter, but I won't allow it," he nearly snarled.

Ada let out an exasperated huff. "My father thinks you're brainwashing me."

"For the last time, I'm not brainwashing anyone. Not Ada and not Gran." Gracie kept her voice as calm as she could.

His hot glare bore down on her. "You convinced her to let you use the estate money for the taxes you should pay. What else are you saying to her?"

"Really, Dad. I'm a grown woman," Ada said.

Uncle Rand whipped around to face Ada. "Did she ask you for money? If she did, don't give it to her." His fists were clenched at his side. He turned back to Gracie. "Then again, if you don't give her money, she'll probably sell the house and waste the proceeds from the sale."

Ada sighed. "Look around, Dad. Does it look like she's selling the house?"

He did look around, starting with all the yarn and ending with the wall that held the secret door, still without drywall or a countertop.

"What on earth?" He took tentative steps toward the wall. "What did you do?"

Gracie tried to feel brave, but her words came out with a warble. "I removed the drywall."

She waited for his angry retort, but he didn't say a word. He only walked to the door and touched it. In a voice that Gracie had to strain to hear, he said, "I never knew this was here."

Gracie glanced at Ada, who was wearing a look of real sympathy. The same feeling settled in Gracie's chest. She remembered Ada telling her that Uncle Rand was grieving Gracie's mother. Now he was grieving his own. "I didn't either. I just found out when I tried to secure the countertop to the wall."

Uncle Rand looked at her, then to the kitchen. "Two doors to the root cellar. That doesn't make sense."

Is this the right thing to do? "It doesn't go to the root cellar," Gracie said. Ada gawked at her.

His gaze snapped to her. "Where else could it go?"

Gracie picked up the flashlight that had come to live right by the wall, and she opened the door. She flicked the flashlight on. "Let me show you."

She went down the stairs first. Uncle Rand and Ada followed. At the bottom of the steps, Gracie shone the beam so that the majority of the little room could be seen.

"I—" Uncle Rand looked back up the stairs. "What is this?"

Gracie peered at him through the dim light. Maybe this was a chance to repair their relationship. Something that could bring them closer. "Maybe a room used on the Underground Railroad."

Uncle Rand gasped as if she had struck him. "What?"

Gracie explained about William Still's house being across the street and how she was working with someone at the Philadelphia

Historical Commission to find out if Gran's house had also been used for the same purpose. Then she waited in silence.

She could hear Uncle Rand's breathing, almost panting. Looking around the room, she tried to imagine what it must have been like for runaways if they stayed here. Only a few at a time could have fit in the room. It seemed crowded with just her, Ada, and Uncle Rand in it. But the relief they must have felt. To have traveled hundreds if not thousands of miles to get here. To know that after this, freedom would begin. Their difficult path wouldn't have been over yet. They would have to avoid getting caught or continue to move north. But this room could have been the first step in the journey.

How precious that must have been.

Still imagining, she didn't notice that Uncle Rand had wheeled around to her. When she did, his anger snapped her back to the present. "And my mother left this house to you?"

"She—"

"You don't deserve this." His voice was a tight string. Controlled but seething.

"Dad," Ada said. Her tone had a note of warning.

He turned to Ada. "She doesn't. She has never done anything to deserve this. She wasted the life her mother died to give her."

His words seared and sliced through what little peace Gracie had. She staggered back a step. She opened her mouth to say something, anything, but only a sob came out. What was she supposed to do? *Say it isn't true.* But it was. She didn't deserve this. She didn't deserve to own Gran's house, and she certainly didn't deserve to own a station house of the Underground Railroad.

She rushed past him and Ada, handing Ada the flashlight as she went.

"Gracie!" Ada called out from behind her.

Gracie bolted up the stairs to her room, where she fell on her bed and sobbed.

CHAPTER FOURTEEN

OLIVIA

*T*he clock chimed noon, and Olivia nearly groaned. Her eyes stung from being so tired. And from crying. She and Douglas had spent a fretful night with baby Hope. Not that the babe was any trouble. She was tired from all the excitement and promptly fell asleep after she'd had a bath and Douglas had examined her. He noted that she was severely undernourished and had lost weight from her sickness.

Olivia's tiredness came from the fact that she had sat and watched the child sleep in the basket they had lined with blankets. If Hope had awakened and not known where she was, it may have startled her. But she didn't wake. Olivia had gone to sleep for a few hours before dawn. It seemed more like a few minutes.

When she began her morning routine, however, she realized she had another complication. What was she to do with Hope during the day? She wasn't as clingy as the night before, but Hope would still cry if Olivia stayed out of her sight for too long. She had thought about putting her in the basket and carrying it downstairs to her work area, but that wouldn't work today. Earlier that morning she had received a note from a Mrs. Pansy Johnson requesting a fitting. Her name was not familiar to Olivia, but the note said that Mrs. Johnson had been referred by Mrs. Mason. With the money Mrs. Mason spent on dresses, having another customer like her would be wonderful.

Olivia rubbed her eyes, and a soft thump sounded from upstairs.

Without any other options, she had raced around to the Wilsons' house before Hope woke and Douglas left for work. Both Mr. and Mrs. Wilson needed to be in the store today, but they could spare one of their older daughters, Milly, to come around for a few hours and sit with Hope.

Olivia had run through the possibilities of what to do with the child. Not sleeping gave her plenty of time to think. They could put Hope in one of the girls' homes. There was one nearby run by Mrs. Brasewell, a member of the Vigilance Committee. But what if Beulah returned, looking for Hope? It was probably for the best that Hope stay. However, if Beulah did have a conductor take her farther north, it may be months before she could make contact. Most fugitives waited until they got themselves established before they sent for their loved ones. It made sense that Beulah would wait, especially if she believed Hope was in good hands with Olivia.

Except Beulah never asked Olivia to care for Hope. Instead, Beulah had asked if she had to leave.

The front door opened. The soft bumps upstairs promptly ceased. Olivia stood from her table to see a very tall, very solid woman coming through the door. She wore an immaculately tailored dress. Her dark curls framed her face.

Olivia smoothed her skirts. "Good afternoon."

"Good afternoon," the woman said. Her words held a southern twang, and she wore a wide smile. "My name is Mrs. Johnson."

"Nice to meet you."

"Ain't you a pretty little thing. The pleasure is mine. I have seen Catherine Mason's dresses. Absolutely delightful."

Olivia dipped her head. "Thank you. I assume you need some new dresses. What is the occasion?" Mrs. Mason normally showed up at the shop when she had an event to attend.

"No occasion. Pretty dresses make me happy."

Olivia smiled. This woman would be an even better customer than Mrs. Mason. "Let us look at some fabric samples." Olivia led her over to the table where she had the samples laid out. "What is your favorite color?"

Mrs. Johnson laughed, high and tinkling. "All of them."

Olivia studied her face and then lifted several selections from the pile. One of the reasons her customers valued her so much was that she could match the perfect color to their skin. "What do you think of these?"

"I love them all." She touched a deep green silk. "Especially this one. Reminds me of my home in Virginia."

Olivia snapped her mouth shut. If Mrs. Johnson had a home in Virginia, the less Olivia knew about it the better. Her home was probably a plantation.

"Are you married, Miss Olivia?" Mrs. Johnson asked, fingering a piece of printed cotton with a delicate yellow flower pattern.

"I am."

"What does your husband do?"

In the normal course of conversation, spouses and family regularly came up, but not before the customer had decided what they wanted made. "He is a doctor," Olivia said slowly.

"A doctor? A real doctor?"

Olivia studied Mrs. Johnson, not sure if she was genuinely as surprised as her tone sounded. "Yes, ma'am."

Mrs. Johnson touched her on the arm. "You're skilled at making lovely dresses, and your husband is a real doctor. I am always amazed at how smart your people can be."

Olivia gritted her teeth. *You would also be amazed at how many fugitives I will help with the money you pay me for your frilly dresses.* "Thank you."

With a little nudging, Olivia steered Mrs. Johnson to make her selections. She chose five squares of fabric and five dress styles. "I want these."

Olivia raised an eyebrow, "You want all five?"

"Ye–es." Mrs. Johnson dragged out the word. "Unless there is a problem."

"Not at all," Olivia sputtered. The woman had picked the most complicated patterns and the most expensive fabrics. "Shall we do a fitting?" She ushered Mrs. Johnson behind the screen. "Just call out when you're down to your corset and petticoats."

While Mrs. Johnson undressed, Olivia grabbed a sheet of paper and tallied up the bill. It was three times what Mrs. Mason spent at once. What a boon it would be to have her as a regular customer.

"All ready," Mrs. Johnson called.

When Olivia stepped behind the screen, Mrs. Johnson had done what she was told. Usually, Olivia would imagine that she was measuring a mannequin, but she couldn't help but notice Mrs. Johnson's strong arms and shoulders. Arms that had seen hard labor.

Olivia stepped to the woman and took her measurements as fast as she could. As she did, another bump sounded from upstairs followed by a giggle. Hope and Milly.

"You have children. Boy or girl? You probably have a whole brood." Mrs. Johnson's voice sounded above Olivia's head as she measured her waist.

"Actually, I do not have children. I have guests staying with me at the moment." That was the best she could come up with.

"Children are so darling. Mine are all grown," Mrs. Johnson said with pride.

Olivia stood. "All done." She rushed out from behind the screen.

Once Mrs. Johnson emerged, Olivia handed her the bill. "I will need a deposit."

"How about I just pay you all of it right now?" Mrs. Johnson reached into her satchel, pulled out a banknote, and handed it to Olivia. "I will return in a month."

Olivia stared at the note and gaped at the ease with which the woman handed it over. And it did not escape her notice how many banknotes Mrs. Johnson had. "Yes, ma'am. If they are done sooner, I will send word to you. Where are you staying?"

"I said I will be back in a month." Mrs. Johnson gave her a pointed stare. Olivia held it until the woman looked away.

Once Mrs. Johnson left and Olivia closed the door behind her, Olivia stared at the note. Another thump upstairs. *This is plenty to help us take care of Hope.*

Olivia decided it was best to go out the back door to get to Mr. Still's house. It sat across the street, the back of her house facing the side of his. The trip needed to be brief since it would be dark soon. She pulled her coat closed and walked with quick steps to the front door of Mr. Still's house. She knocked on the door, and Mrs. Still opened it.

"Mrs. Kingston, how are you?" Mrs. Still leaned forward, studying her face. "You look like you need rest."

Olivia sighed. She needed rest, but she had no time for it. "These past days have been trying."

Mrs. Still led Olivia into her living room. "The weather is changing. All the women are in need of heavier garments." Mrs. Still was a more skilled seamstress than Olivia. Between word of mouth and her advertisement in the paper, Mrs. Still never lacked for customers.

"No, not the dressmaking, although I did get a new customer with expensive tastes."

"Nice to have wealthy customers." She led Olivia to the stairs. "Then you must be here to see William. He is up in his office."

Olivia nodded her thanks and climbed the stairs. She braced herself. Beulah's disappearance would be unpleasant news, especially so soon after Walker went missing. She knocked on Mr. Still's office door, and he called out, "Come in."

She stepped into the small office. Mr. Still sat behind a desk covered in papers. Beside the desk were shelves of bookcases. In front of the desk was an armchair. Olivia wondered how many fugitives had sat in that seat and told Mr. Still all about themselves.

Mr. Still looked up and smiled. "Mrs. Kingston. Please sit. How can I help you?"

She sat and folded her hands in her lap. "I need to consult with you on a matter."

He put his pen down. "Of course."

As she told him about Beulah, his eyes grew wider. "Did Miss Beulah leave a note? Talk to you about leaving?"

"No. She cannot read or write."

"When did she leave?"

"I do not know. I assume yesterday. I only discovered it because I went down to prepare her for Mr. Gull to take her farther north."

Mr. Still rubbed his face. "I will speak with Mrs. Brasewell and see if she has space for Hope."

Olivia sat forward. "But that is nearly a day's travel. What if Beulah comes back for the child?"

Mr. Still sighed. "Very true. You will have to keep her for a little longer."

Olivia sat straighter. "My husband and I came to that conclusion."

Mr. Still's eyebrows shot up. "Your husband?"

"I have hidden many things in that room, but a baby with no mama isn't something I could manage alone," Olivia said. "Or keep hidden from Douglas."

Mr. Still chuckled. "I suppose not. Then if you and Dr. Kingston are settled with keeping the child, I will alert the conductors and stationmasters to be on the lookout for Miss Beulah."

She started to stand and then remembered something. "Did Mr. Wilson tell you about their unexpected passenger?"

"He did. It was very perplexing."

"I wonder if this is connected. He disappeared like Beulah did," Olivia said.

Mr. Still frowned. "That he did. And, now that I think about it, a fugitive disappeared from another station house in the area. The Breer family."

"Could this be a coincidence?"

Mr. Still shook his head. "I would like to believe it is. I will send Franklin around with a note if I hear anything. And I will find other accommodations for any incoming fugitives until we settle this matter with the baby."

Olivia sighed in relief but immediately felt guilty. The idea of no fugitives for a while should not make her feel better. Finding shelter for them was already challenging enough. The Bella Vista network would have one less house. But then, she and Douglas were providing aid to baby Hope. "Thank you," she said.

Footsteps pounded up the steps. Mrs. Still appeared at the door, nearly breathless. "Mr. Williamson has been released!" she cried with tears in her eyes.

Mr. Passmore Williamson had been imprisoned since the summer for participating in a dramatic rescue. A woman and her two sons were to sail north with their owner, but Mr. Williamson, Mr. Still, and five other members of the Vigilance Committee had rushed to the docks, boarded the ship, and informed her that she was free if she so chose. All she had to do was walk off the boat into their care. She did.

All those involved in the rescue were arrested, but only Mr. Williamson remained in jail. The members of the antislavery community had been petitioning the courts for his release for months.

Mr. Still hopped to his feet. "Truly?"

"Yes. Franklin just brought a note from Mr. Williamson himself."

Mr. Still rushed to the door, pausing to face Olivia. "I am sorry, but I must go."

Olivia grinned at them both. "Please do not worry. This is the best news."

And with that, Olivia left. She couldn't stop smiling as she covered the distance between the two houses. Her heart felt a little lighter. There was so much bad happening all around. She must remember to take the time to celebrate the good.

All was quiet when she stepped into the kitchen. She removed her coat and went upstairs, her worry growing. Why was it so quiet?

When she reached their sitting room door, she saw why. Douglas and Hope had made themselves comfortable on the sofa and had fallen asleep together. A book sat on Douglas' knee, and Olivia suspected they had fallen asleep while he was reading to her.

She stood in the doorway, studying them. A pang and longing threaded through her heart. The Underground Railroad was rewarding work, and she was glad for it. But she dreamed of having a family too. To tell her children the story of their history. That their grandparents and parents were conductors and stationmasters and took up this sacred work to help others. But for some reason, God had not blessed them yet.

Or maybe He had, even if just for a little while.

CHAPTER FIFTEEN

GRACIE

S he has never done anything to deserve this."

Days later, remembering Uncle Rand's words still stung. They had sliced into Gracie's already battered heart and left her bleeding. They had played on a loop in her mind since she'd stormed out of the secret room.

Ada had come into her room and tried to console her after Uncle Rand had gone. She kept reminding Gracie that Gran thought Gracie deserved the house. Did Gran really think that? What if the gifting of the house was out of pity? Not deserving the house nor the history it might hold would make things so much worse.

Gran might have just been grateful that Gracie came to take care of her. How many times when she was too weak to leave her bed did Gran tell Gracie how much she appreciated her coming to Philly. Or the day Gran weakly grasped Gracie's hand and said, "No one wants to die alone." Gracie had tried to quiet her, but Gran's eyes had sharpened. "I'm glad you're here."

But that wasn't a reason to reward Gracie with the house. She did what family was supposed to do. She couldn't have let Gran die alone. Most of Gracie's life had been spent alone. She'd spent years wishing there was someone, anyone, to share life with. And then Gran filled the void and made sure Gracie knew she wasn't alone. Made sure Gracie knew that she was a strong Black woman in a long line of strong Black women. Gracie counted it an honor to do for Gran what

Gran did for her. There was no need for a reward.

No matter how she thought about it, inheriting this house was pain on top of pain. She owned it because Gran had died. Gran, the only mother she really knew, died and left her this house. Would she ever feel anything other than the pain of loss when she thought about the house? Even if the house had been a station on the Underground Railroad, there would still be pain. The pain of inheriting it when it should have gone to Uncle Rand and his family.

Today was supposed to be an exciting day. Good exciting. Today was the first session for the kids' knitting class. Yet all she wanted to do was stay in her bedroom with the door closed.

The heaviness of her heart seemed to drag her steps, tears threatening. She went straight to the classroom table and busied herself with checking each of the student kits. It wasn't necessary, but she had to do something so she wouldn't surrender to the temptation to cancel the class. Ada had gone out for snacks, something Gracie had overlooked.

Seeing that there was nothing left to do, Gracie sat down with the hat she had just begun knitting. She worked a row, regulating her breathing as she did.

Down the middle of the table lay the samples she'd knitted. She had selected mostly cowls and mittens, since those projects appealed to younger and new knitters alike. They would act as encouragement for the students. Most would tell her they could never knit something so complex, to which she would reply, they were all made one stitch at a time.

If there was one thing she could be proud of, it was that she was a good knitter. Her childhood knitting teacher had told her that she took to knitting like she was born with needles and yarn in her hands. The compliment stung. She had not been born with yarn and needles. She had been born with trouble.

The back door opened and Ada stumbled inside with a case of bottled water and a few more bags. "I forgot how hard it is to get up those steps."

Gracie raced to her and took the case of water. "You should have come through the front door. It would have been easier."

"I wasn't sure if any of your students were here yet, and I didn't want you to have to leave them to open the door." Ada glanced around. "Besides, it was interesting walking past the root cellar doors and knowing what's really down there."

Gracie didn't look up from arranging the bottles of water. Her thoughts drifted again to the secret room. But instead of thinking of those who fled slavery under horrific conditions, she thought of the people who owned the house. The stationmasters. During one of their increasingly frequent phone calls, Clarence had explained to her what a risk it was to be a stationmaster. Especially for a free Black. If they were caught assisting those seeking freedom, they could have been sold into slavery themselves. They, however, thought that their illegal activities were worth the risk.

Gracie should feel honor for owning such a place. But she could identify more with the newly freed slave. Only knowing hardship all her life. Then to reach freedom and have it be so fragile and fraught with danger. To be free but not, living for days in a dark room. Free but not completely.

The doorbell sounded just as Ada finished arranging the individual-sized bags of chips and pretzels at the other end of the table. When Gracie opened the door, a tall girl and a man stood on her doorstep. The girl's hair was braided with pink tips. She wore a scowl on her dark brown face, her arms folded.

Gracie smiled. "Hello, I'm Gracie McNeil. I'm the owner and your instructor."

The man smiled. "I'm Stanley Russell. This is my daughter, Mia."

Mia gave Gracie a wave that was no more than a wiggling of her fingers.

Gracie bit back a laugh. "Come in."

For all her attempts to look unimpressed, Mia's face transformed when she stepped inside. The three cubes Gracie had assembled were full of yarn. The countertop was lined with notions and project bags. Mia scanned the room, her eyes growing wider.

"I'm so glad you're doing this," Stanley said. "We need something like this in our community."

For a moment, Gracie felt a glimmer of hope. "I'm glad too. It gives me the ability to introduce the fiber arts to a new generation."

"I already know how to crochet," Mia said. Her words dripped with sass.

"Mi–a," Stanley said, drawing out the two syllables of her name.

Mia let out an exasperated sigh. "But I do. I crocheted in my braids." She ran the long strands through her fingers.

Gracie gave her a smile, the first real one on her face in days. "They look amazing. You did them all yourself?"

Mia grinned, her posture relaxing even more. "Yup."

"Very nice," Gracie said. "Let me show you the classroom."

Stanley followed them. "Do you mind if I sit out front and read? The shop is a bit of a distance from home, and I would just be coming right back."

"Of course."

Gracie just had time to introduce Mia to Ada before the doorbell rang. Three more of her students were standing outside. Bella, Trinity, and Rylee. Unlike Mia, the girls rushed inside like chattering birds. Clearly, they knew each other. Trinity's mother asked if she could stay as well, and Gracie agreed. Dani was the last of her students to arrive. Gracie greeted Dani's mother and led Dani back to the classroom.

Bella and Trinity were studying the samples. "Did you knit all this?" Trinity asked.

"Yes," Gracie said. A ripple of pride skimmed over her tender emotions. Seeing the girls' reactions to her work, seeing it through their eyes, made her stand a little taller. She had come a long way from the first lopsided dishcloth she'd knitted back in middle school.

"This is so a-maz-ing," Bella said. "I want to knit myself one of those big cowls that cover your entire neck."

"And you will. Everyone have a seat," Gracie said.

Bella, Trinity, and Rylee sat on one side of the table, and Dani and Mia sat on the other with a seat between them. *So this is how the class dynamics are going to be.* The spot Mia picked didn't have a kit, but there was one in front of the next seat. Mia slid the kit over.

"Look at Mia. Already breaking the rules," Bella said. Rylee and Trinity giggled. Mia's head dropped.

"She is not breaking the rules. She can sit wherever she likes," Gracie said, her tone light.

Mia kept her gaze on her kit. Gracie's heart ached for her, but she knew better than to try to encourage her anymore. She remembered what it was like being the outcast in a class. Besides, Mia had an ace up her sleeve. She already knew how to crochet. Sometimes it was easier for people who crocheted to learn knitting than a person with no experience with yarn.

Gracie smiled. "Shall we get started?"

All the girls nodded excitedly.

A feeling of rightness settled on Gracie's shoulders. All her other problems faded as she began to explain the fundamentals of knitting to five eager girls. She had begun knitting on the student side of the table. Having come so far as to be sitting on the teacher side now felt surreal.

⚜

Four days had passed, and Gracie was still riding on the high of the knitting class's success. Of course, she would have to keep the friction between Mia and the other girls under close observation, but it had gone better than she expected. The girls had left with smiles, and that's all that mattered. When was the last time something good had happened for her so smoothly and gone so well? A long, long time ago. Which meant there was probably disaster ahead.

But now it was time to go back to dealing with the other big stressor in her life: the house. Rather, the nomination for it to be registered as a historical site. Other than the secret room, neither she nor Clarence had found anything that would confirm or deny that the room in the basement was used for hiding formerly enslaved people. At least not officially. Clarence was certain that the date on the house's construction was wrong.

And that was the purpose of today's field trip. Since Clarence had been on the team that discovered William Still's house, he knew how to find the real date the house was built. She'd felt a little better when he'd told her that the records for William Still's house listed the construction date as 1930. He was sure the same was true of her house.

She drove down to Clarence's office. He was standing outside again, bundled up with a red knitted scarf.

Gracie smiled up at him when she reached his side. "Did Ms. Lila knit you that scarf?"

"She did, and I'm so grateful for it." He shivered dramatically, and she laughed. "Let's go inside."

When they reached the elevator, instead of pressing the number thirteen for his office, he pressed GL for ground level. Gracie frowned. "We're not going upstairs?"

Playfulness sparkled in his eyes. "We're going down to my other office."

When the elevator door opened, she saw a hallway much like the one on the thirteenth floor except there were fewer offices. Clarence pulled keys from his pocket and walked to the third door from the end. "We keep the archives down here."

He unlocked the door to reveal that the office was twice as long as the ones upstairs. It was also packed with shelves of boxes and books. The thought of all the history that was in the room, crammed onto the shelves, brought on a feeling of timelessness. It also piqued her curiosity. These boxes contained stories of individuals, families, and communities.

Clarence grinned. "It's a researcher's dream."

He led her past the shelves. Two rows of four large tables sat in the middle of the room. There were cube desks with desktop computers on them at the end of each row. He motioned to the tables. "Tables for pulling boxes. Computers for researching the directories and searching the internet."

She nodded in approval. "Very nice."

"It can get chilly down here, so let me know if it gets too cold for you."

She looked at the boxes. "I'm sure I'll be warm moving the boxes."

He led her to a computer. "I'll move the boxes. You search the digital records. First, we need to access some pictures and plot maps."

"Why those?"

"Because they'll tell us if there was a house on that lot in the 1800s. So will the pictures. I think we'll find one or the other. Bella Vista was one of the larger free Black communities here in Philly." He powered up the computer and entered his password. "Search your street in the system. That might yield us some results."

"What if there's nothing there?"

"There'll be something. It's just a matter of what. Sometimes when you're researching, you don't find the exact thing you're looking for, but you find a clue to lead you to the next place." He smiled down at her. "You know how we found William Still's house?"

"How?"

Clarence broke into a grin. "A newspaper advertisement. Mrs. Still was a seamstress, and she advertised her services in the local papers. The ad listed her address. It was a two-by-two-inch square with fewer than thirty words in it, and it unlocked one of the greatest mysteries in Black history."

"That's pretty cool. Something so small. . ."

Clarence held up his index finger with confidence in his eyes. "It only takes one little clue."

Buoyed by his hopefulness, Gracie turned to the computer and typed in her address. The computer listed only five images. "This doesn't look promising."

"Have hope," Clarence said as he pulled the chair up next to her.

She clicked on the first image and zoomed in. Once again, she found Clarence leaning close to her. "What am I looking for?"

"Everything for now. Anything memorable."

She leaned forward and squinted. "Hmm. Maybe someone with better eyesight should look. I'm afraid I'll need glasses soon."

He squinted too. "You would look even cuter in glasses." His voice had a faraway tone to it. Like he was thinking of something else and not aware of what he had said.

Heat bloomed at the nape of her neck and seared up to her ears. Clarence kept studying the image, seemingly unaware of the effect his words had on her. "If you say so," she said quietly.

He leaned back. "Let's look at the next one."

They looked at all five pictures, and although it was fascinating to see how some of the places she recognized had changed completely or hardly at all, none of them held any clues.

Clarence leaned back. "Let's try a different tack. There are some old land maps in the boxes. I'll pull them. Since the Institute for Colored Youth was a block away from your house, search for images of the school."

A memory flashed in her mind. When she was in elementary school, on one of her weekend visits to Philadelphia, she and Gran were walking to the grocery store and passed an apartment building. It sat one block from the house. Gracie had thought it looked like a school and said so to Gran. Gran told her that the building used to be the Institute for Colored Youth. By Gracie's next visit, Gran had put together a folder of information about the school and its importance. "My gran told me about this school. That it was started by a man born on a plantation in the British Virgin Islands who wanted to help give Black children an education so they could earn a living as adults." Gran had stressed that his help had changed the children's lives. Gran had done the same, changing Gracie's life.

He gave her an approving smile. "That's it. You're going to be a proper historian in no time."

She laughed. "Gran tried to make me one." But then a wave of sadness washed over her. Gran had tried to make her a historian. Wouldn't it be ironic that researching Gran's house would make her one?

Thankfully, Clarence had disappeared in the rows of boxes. She took a deep breath and typed the school's name into the search bar. By the time he returned, she had studied two pages of ten images. Some of the pictures didn't include the school at all. Some were pictures of the early students.

Clarence opened a box and coughed from the little cloud of dust that rose. "Did you find anything?"

"Not yet."

He spread a map out on the table then shook his head. "Too new." He took another out and placed it on top of the first one.

Gracie clicked on the next image. It was a picture of the institute taken from the park across the street and at a side angle. She leaned closer, studying the houses around the school. It took her a moment to orient the picture in her mind, but when she did, she gasped.

Clarence looked up. "You found something."

"I think," she said, coming up out of the chair and touching the screen. "I think this is the back corner of my house."

Clarence studied the angle and then grinned wide. "I think you're right." He reached across her and slid the mouse down to the image's description. "Now, when was the picture taken?"

He scrolled, and Gracie nearly whooped when she saw the date. 1830.

"We found it," she said, bouncing excitedly on her toes.

"You found it." Clarence beamed. "I'm willing to bet that someone accidentally typed 1930 on the city's records site instead of 1830. It won't be hard to find your house on the ward maps now that we found this picture."

All the worry about the taxes and Uncle Rand fell away. She was one step closer to getting Gran's house registered as a historic site.

"Oh, Clarence. Thank you." Before she thought about it, she threw her arms around his neck.

He stiffened at first, then wrapped his arms around her. As soon as she closed the embrace, she realized how improper it was. But she didn't move. He was so warm, his shoulders solid under her arms.

"You're welcome," he murmured.

This is a nice prize.

CHAPTER SIXTEEN

OLIVIA

*I*n a week's time, Olivia and Douglas had gotten a little better rhythm of caring for Hope. A pleasant rhythm.

Milly continued to come over to sit with Hope when Olivia had customers. Otherwise, Hope spent her days playing on the floor or sleeping in her basket. No matter how tired he was after work, Douglas always dropped to the floor to play with Hope for a few minutes when he came through the door. The little girl had fallen into the rhythm too. She began watching the door each day around the time Douglas would come home. Every now and then, Hope would wake in the night and begin to wail. On those nights, Olivia and Douglas moved with speed to comfort her.

The only challenge now was that Hope being in their lives was another topic they could not talk about.

Olivia had awakened this morning, Douglas still sleeping beside her and Hope sleeping in her little basket bed. She had come down and started breakfast. When she returned, she found that Hope had climbed into the bed with Douglas. Or he had gotten up and placed her there. Either way, her heart warmed.

When Douglas came down for breakfast, he brought Hope and her basket with him. She was fully dressed, and Olivia laughed at Douglas' attempt to arrange the baby's hair. "Good morning," she said.

She took Hope from him and sat her at the table where Olivia already had prepared eggs for her. Hope dug right in. Douglas sat

Hope's basket bed by Olivia's sewing table. "Good morning." He looked at Hope. "Her appetite is recovering."

"That it is." Hope had significantly improved. Her skin had almost lost its sickly pallor. She was more active but still not making the noises that normal children would make. But then, she hadn't had any kind of normal life. Douglas said that he thought the girl may be eighteen months or so based on how many teeth she had, but she was much smaller than she should be for that age. With time and continued care, Douglas was sure she might grow to a more normal size.

What neither of them was saying, however, was who would be caring for her.

Olivia sat down, and Douglas took the chair across from her. "Any word from Mr. Still?"

Olivia shook her head. "I had planned to send him a note today. But if he had any news, he would have let me know."

Douglas looked at the little girl. "I hope they find Beulah."

They gave thanks for their meal and for Hope, who was almost done with hers, and ate in silence. Finally, Douglas spoke. "When will you have to work again?" he asked, his eyes drifting to the door to the secret room.

She studied him for a minute. "Mr. Still thinks it may be best not to send more passengers until we have the matter with Hope settled."

"Hmm," Douglas said. "I think—"

A loud pounding on the door cut him off. Olivia jumped. So did Hope, but she didn't cry. Olivia lifted her from the chair.

"I'll get it." Douglas exited the room in long strides, and she heard him open the front door.

She wondered what he was going to say. In a moment, she heard Milly's excited voice. She rushed from behind the staircase to see Milly removing her coat. "Let me take her," Milly said.

Olivia handed the child over, frowning. "Milly, I was not expecting you to come today."

"My ma sent me round to take care of Hope. Mr. Still found her mama. She's in jail." Milly bounced Hope in her arms. "You have to go now. Mama said she's in a bad way."

Olivia stood stunned for a second, then went into motion. "Hope has had her breakfast."

Douglas rushed to the coatrack and snatched up their coats. "I'm coming too."

Olivia opened her mouth to protest, but Douglas held up a hand. "If Beulah is bad, someone may have fetched me anyways. Not many white doctors will tend to a fugitive."

Olivia, her words as scrambled as her thoughts, only nodded. Douglas grabbed his medical bag and ushered her out the door.

The jail sat a block from the port. Walking at a quick pace, she and Douglas reached the small squat building in fifteen minutes. Mr. Still and Mr. Wilson stood outside the building. They looked up in surprise when they saw Douglas accompanying Olivia.

"We tried to go in and see her, but the jailer believes we are going to whisk her away," Mr. Wilson said, turning to Douglas. "But you two may be able to get in since you are a doctor. We were told that she is very sick."

"I will do what I can," Douglas said, moving to the door. Olivia followed behind him.

The jail was rank and dark. The only person not in a cell was the jailer, a thin sneering man. "I already told them two outside I ain't lettin' no one in to see the girl."

"I am a doctor," Douglas said.

"A colored doctor? Sure you are."

"I assure you I am. And are you sure that the girl's owner will like that you turned away a doctor? He probably will appreciate you taking good care of his property," Douglas said.

Although Olivia flinched at the word *property*, Douglas kept his tone level and matter-of-fact, which was more than she could have managed in the moment. The jailer scratched his face. "Guess it won't hurt, unless you kill her." He led them to Beulah's cell, and Olivia had to bite the inside of her cheek not to cry at the sight that met them.

Beulah lay on a blanket on the floor. Her breathing was heavy. The jailer opened the door, and Olivia rushed in, Douglas only a step behind her. Beulah didn't open her eyes when Douglas began his ministrations. The jailer stood at the door and watched.

Douglas put a thermometer in her mouth. "She has a high fever," he said, leaning over so only Olivia heard.

Speaking just as low, she answered, "She was unwell earlier but not this bad."

Douglas listened to her lungs, gave Olivia a grim look, and shook his head.

Olivia looked down at Beulah's troubled face. It had only been a little more than a week since Beulah disappeared, but she'd grown much worse in that short time. Where had she been? She must have been under horrible conditions, because she appeared to be on the mend when she left Olivia. Which was why, Olivia suspected, that Beulah had left her child behind. If she was this bad, how much worse would Hope have fared?

Douglas turned to the jailer. "Can my wife fetch some water to bathe her face?"

The jailer laughed. "You shoulda brought everything you needed in with ya. And hurry it along."

Douglas gave Olivia a sad look. "She will not survive long like this." He glanced around the jail. It was cold and drafty and there was no light. Not to mention the filthy, threadbare blanket Beulah was lying on.

Olivia's heart sank. She wanted to lift Beulah into her arms and comfort her but knew she could not. "Mrs. Kingston?" Beulah's voice creaked.

She and Douglas shot a quick glance at the door. The jailer had stepped to another cell and was loudly berating the prisoner there.

Olivia looked down and saw that her eyes were open but only to a slit. "Yes, Beulah?"

"Hope." The way she said the word, Olivia was unsure if she was asking about her daughter or giving Olivia a command to expect this to turn out better.

Douglas leaned closer to Beulah. "She is well," he whispered soothingly. "We will do whatever we can to get you back to her."

Beulah's expression seemed to brighten for a moment, but then she frowned deeply. "Was tricked."

Olivia leaned in, her mind trying to make sense of what Beulah had said.

"Who was tricked?" Olivia asked.

"Me." She breathed heavily. "Logan."

"Is Logan the person who tricked you?" Douglas asked.

Beulah looked at him. "He said—" She groaned. "He said he came to help. That he was a friend."

Alarm raced through Olivia. "Did he come into the house?"

"No. I went out." She blinked. "He told me to come out when I was with the other man."

Olivia frowned, trying to make sense of what she was saying. "What other man?"

"Mr. Lloyd."

Olivia's scalp tingled. Mr. Wilson had said that something strange had happened with Beulah and Mr. Lloyd. Douglas looked to Olivia for an explanation, and Olivia mouthed, *Later.*

Olivia made her voice even lower. "What did Logan look like?"

"White. Blue eyes. Tall." Her head rolled to the side, her eyes closing. "Tricked more than just me. Took us to another house and locked us in a room. When I got sick, they brought me here." Her eyes closed, and Olivia held her breath until Beulah took another one.

They. With that word, Olivia's worry turned to terror. *They* meant that the Friends had a bigger problem than they realized. That they needed to be on guard for several people.

"Can you tell me anything else?"

Beulah blinked, worked her mouth, and then closed her eyes. Olivia asked her again, but it was clear that Beulah had run out of strength to talk.

Douglas checked her for a heartbeat and then rose. "She is still breathing, but I suspect not for much longer. Not much more we can do." He offered Olivia a hand. It took all her strength to stand and leave Beulah alone in what were probably her last hours.

As they turned to leave, Beulah said from behind them, her voice a hoarse whisper, "If. . .if I don't live, be Hope's mama and daddy."

They both turned. Beulah lay there, eyes closed, like she had not spoken.

The jailer rushed over to them. "Out. You been here long enough," he barked.

Douglas took Olivia's hand and led her out of the cell, tears in his eyes as well as hers.

CHAPTER SEVENTEEN

GRACIE

*J*ust as Gracie suspected, Mia mastered the knit stitch much faster than the other girls. That changed the polarization in the group. In the two meetings they'd had, Bella, Trinity, and Rylee had continued to make snarky comments about Mia that they didn't think Gracie could hear. Once they had outright insulted Mia's hair, and Gracie had to remind them of the rules of the classroom, the first of which was kindness.

But once Mia started sailing through her stitches, the comments stopped. They were too busy concentrating on knitting correctly and trying to catch up with her. Mia, on the other hand, was acting like she'd always been a part of a yarn group, making small talk with Gracie.

"So how old were you when you learned to knit?"

Gracie was nearly at the crown of the hat she was knitting and watching out for anyone needing assistance. "I was younger than you, ten years old."

"Did your mother teach you?" Dani asked.

Gracie grimaced. "No, my mother died when I was born."

"That's messed up," Mia said.

Gracie smiled at the honest assessment. "Yes, it is."

Bella lowered her needles. "You didn't know her at all?"

Maybe I should have just told them how I learned to knit. "No."

"Extremely messed up," Dani said.

"Mia's mother didn't want her," Trinity said.

It was if her words were a poisonous dart, and when they hit, Mia popped up out of her chair. Her knitting clattered to the table. "She does want me!"

Yup. I should have picked a better topic. "Trinity, that was an unkind thing to say." Gracie stood, picked up Mia's knitting, and handed it back to her. It had the intended effect.

Mia took the knitting and flopped down in her seat. Her breaths still came in angry puffs. "You know, a mom can still want her kid even if she doesn't want to stay with her husband."

Divorce then. "If I have to warn you again, Trinity, I will suspend you from the class."

Bella snickered. "How lame. Trinity is going to get suspended from knitting class."

Mia looked up at Gracie. "They aren't going to stop." Then she lowered her voice to a mock whisper. "Mean girls."

Gracie almost laughed. "Still, I will not tolerate this behavior in class." Besides, hadn't she dealt with her share of mean girls?

They worked in silence for a bit before Dani asked, "Did you have a grandma?" Dani was the youngest, so Gracie knew the question came from a place of innocence and curiosity.

Gracie grinned. "I had the best gran in the world."

"You didn't, 'cause *my* grandma is the best in the world," Dani said with animation that Gracie hadn't seen from her yet. A good grandma would do that to a girl.

"I don't know. My gran was pretty great."

"I got it. We should have a grandma battle," Dani said, eyes sparkling.

"Like let their grandmas fight?" Rylee asked.

"No!" Mia said. "Just put them together to see who is the best."

Dani sat up taller. "My grandma is going to win."

"My gran gave me this house, and you are sitting here taking knitting classes, so that means I win," Gracie said, smiling.

"Okay. Your gran wins," Bella said.

"Thank you." Gracie gave Bella a little bow.

"For now." Dani huffed. "But remember, Christmas is coming." She spoke quietly but with conviction.

Gracie laughed and was relieved when the conversation shifted to a popular show they were all watching on a streaming service. She didn't have to tell them that she'd already lost her mother and her grandmother and she wasn't even thirty-two yet.

Ada came down the stairs. "Gonna check email before I start my homework."

Gracie followed her into the office. "I was wondering if you could handle that customer question."

"You mean the question about the skein of green Spinnery Yarn?"

"That's the one."

"I got it."

"Thanks."

When Gracie returned to the table, Mia was gone. "Where did Mia go?"

"I think she went to the bathroom." Dani looked up at Gracie. "I'm stuck again."

Gracie smiled. "Happens to the best of us. Let me help."

Gracie turned her attention to Dani's knitting. She was so absorbed that she didn't notice when Mia had returned. She continued explaining to Dani how she'd made her mistake and how to fix it.

The class ended, and Mia began stuffing her knitting into the plastic grocery bag she carried her yarn in. All the other girls had canvas bags. "Mia, you need a better bag," Gracie said.

"I know, but my dad said he's not buying me something else to lose," Mia said.

Gracie bit back a chuckle. How many bags had she lost before she was fifteen? "Let me see what I have."

Mia looked up at her, eyes bright. "Can I have that red bag over on the counter?"

Gracie laughed. "Sorry. That one is way too expensive to give away."

"Oh," Mia said. She turned her face away, but clearly she was embarrassed. "It's really nice."

"It is. It's real leather. Besides, you don't need something that big yet." Gracie went to the stairs. "But I think I have something nice for you."

She went up to her personal knitting supplies. She had more bags than she would ever need. She selected a red, pouch-shaped cotton one she'd bought many years ago. Even though it wasn't the leather one, Mia's eyes lit up when she presented it to her. "That's nice."

"It's all yours."

Bella sucked her teeth. "How come we don't get one?"

"Because you all have bags already." The doorbell rang, and Gracie headed toward the door. "And because I want to give it to her."

Mia beamed at them, but when Gracie cleared her throat, she pulled her smile down a little.

Dani's mother was standing at the door.

"Come in."

"Oh no. I'm double-parked."

Gracie laughed. "Dani, your mother is here," she called back to the classroom.

The girl raced by her. "Here I am." She slowed when she reached Gracie. "And sorry about your mom."

"Thank you," Gracie said.

She ended up standing at the door for a bit because the parents started trickling in to pick up the girls. Mia proudly showed her father her new bag.

He looked alarmed. "Where did you get that?"

Mia huffed. "Miss Gracie gave it to me."

"Did you ask her for it?"

Mia scowled, staring down at her shoes. "No, Dad."

"I gave it to her from my personal stash. I have more than enough."

"We'll bring it back when the class is over," he said.

"You don't have to. It was my gift to her. Please allow me to be kind to your daughter. Besides, she'll be distraught if she loses something out of that plastic bag. All serious knitters have a real bag."

Mia smiled up at her.

Stanley shuffled. "I guess it's okay then, since she's clearly serious about this knitting thing."

"Great," Gracie said. "See you next time."

As Mia walked down to their car, she turned around and mouthed, *Thank you.*

Once Bella, Trinity, and Rylee left, Gracie realized that their mothers were taking turns picking them up. Gracie closed the door and sighed. As much as she loved knitting, teaching could be taxing. She went back to the office where Ada still sat at the desk. "I've got that order all sorted." She stood. "Another one came in. I'll pull it tomorrow. Let's get some dinner. I'm starved."

"How about pizza?"

"Right now, I'll eat anything."

Gracie sat in the chair and pulled up a local pizza restaurant's website. She was halfway through ordering when Ada called to her. "Yeah?"

"Where is the red Cojo bag?"

"Sitting on the counter where it always is."

"It's not here."

It took a second for Gracie to process what Ada was telling her, but when she did, her stomach sank. She rushed to the counter.

The Cojo bag was gone. "But it was here earlier." She peeped behind the counter. "Maybe it fell on the floor."

"I already checked."

Gracie turned in a circle, studying the room. *Oh, please don't let it be true.*

She didn't want to believe Mia had stolen the bag she had just asked about not thirty minutes ago.

Gracie rolled her shoulders, but the tension remained. After a day of searching, she and Ada hadn't found the Cojo bag. She was reluctant to tell Ada what she suspected, but she did. Ada seemed as distressed as Gracie. "Let's hope for the best."

Gracie was near running out of hope.

"Where do you want me to put this box?" Ada's voice broke through Gracie's thoughts.

"Uh, bring it back to the classroom so I can unpack and inventory it."

The box was filled with a new brand she wanted to test, mostly bulky weight yarn. It would be midwinter when she finally got the shop open. Thicker yarns would be popular for people making hats to keep their heads warm. Clarence flashed in her mind. She could knit him a hat in the new yarn to get a feel for its properties. That was a good reason to knit him a hat, right?

She rose from her computer where she had been sitting staring at the screen most of the day. Staring and willing the Cojo bag to reappear.

Ada came up beside her and began taking yarn from the box and arranging it on the table. "I was thinking." She lifted up a rich blue skein of yarn. She held it out to Gracie. "This would make a great hat."

Gracie's thoughts immediately went to Clarence again, and she blushed. "You were thinking. . ."

"Right. I was thinking. If the rezoning application isn't going to take long, we should order a sign."

Gracie rubbed her thumb against the skein of yarn she held. "It's been a week since I filed all the paperwork. I guess I do need to start thinking about that."

Ada put her hand on her hip. "And did you ever go on your lunch date with Clarence?"

"No. I think that was a onetime offer." She turned her attention back to the box.

"I don't think it was," Ada said. "If he asks again, you should go."

Gracie didn't say anything. Clarence was a very nice man, but he was clearly more interested in the house than in her. Everything he'd done was in reference to the house, except. . . "He said he wanted to learn how to knit. Not sure why he didn't ask his grandmother."

Ada threw up her hands. "Call him and set up a private class. Get all up in his personal space. And then go have lunch."

Gracie laughed. "I can teach him without invading his personal space."

"But he smells so good."

"He does."

They both laughed.

Gracie's cell phone trilled behind them in the office.

"If that's him, you'd better set up his class," Ada called after her.

It wasn't Clarence. It was Preston. "Hi, Preston."

"Hi, Ms. Gracie," he said. "I just wanted to check in and see if you've made any progress."

"Some. We dated the house. It was built in the 1830s."

"That's cool." He paused. "That's kinda why I'm calling."

She sat down in the office chair. "What's up?"

"There's a rumor among the contractors that there's another house in the area besides William Still's that's connected to the Underground Railroad. I think they're talking about your house."

Gracie gripped the phone. "Have you told—"

"Oh no. I wouldn't do that to you, Ms. Gracie. Besides, I'm too afraid of Ms. Lila to do that to one of her friends. And you wouldn't believe how ugly things can get when a historical site is located in this city."

"Oh." She exhaled. "Then how did people find out?"

"Not from anyone on my crew." He spoke with conviction. "But I wanted to warn you. If it gets out that it's true, you might be overrun with calls and visits."

Exactly what she didn't want. "Thank you for warning me."

"I saw grown men, brothers, get into a fistfight over a site a couple of years ago. Nasty business."

She remembered Clarence's telling her to keep this to herself. Unfortunately, she hadn't heeded his warning. She'd told Uncle Rand. She pushed that thought away and grabbed at another thread that had presented itself. She'd been putting off opening the shop because she was afraid of doing something bad to the house. But Clarence said she could do small things, not major renovations.

"I did have a question for you. I spoke to someone at the Historical Commission, and they said it would be okay if I go ahead with the things I want to do for the shop. Do you have any ideas about my counter? I realize it can't be mounted to the wall, but can we do something else? I really need to get my shop ready to open."

"Hmm," Preston said. "I can check to be sure, but we may be able to secure it to the floor instead."

"One more thing. Can you remove the rest of the drywall and build me a panel to cover the door? Something I can easily remove if I need to go down to the room?"

"That I can do. I can swing by tomorrow. We'll have to look at the drywall and see how far up the wall the brick goes, but I think that would work."

Gracie grinned. "Thank you so much."

"You got it. See you tomorrow."

She returned to the box and told Ada about her conversation. Ada beamed. "Yay! One step closer."

Gracie took a shuddering breath and looked around the room. She was so close. Could it really be just a matter of days before she could announce that she was opening? Tears pricked her eyes. Gran's dream would come true.

Ada saw the tears and pulled her into a hug. "Almost there. Gran would be so proud."

And that opened the floodgates. She sobbed into Ada's shoulder. "I miss her so much."

The doorbell rang, and they broke the embrace. Ada smiled at her. "I'll get it."

Gracie tried to compose herself, swiping tears from her cheeks, when she heard Ada say loudly, "Hi, Clarence."

Gracie stood up straight, feverishly wiping her face. She took a deep breath and stepped out from behind the staircase and walked confidently to Clarence. She nearly chuckled when she saw him holding Ms. Lila's project bag. "She made another mistake?"

"She says she did. You know I can't tell." He paused, studying her. "Have you been crying?"

"I'll go and finish unpacking the box," Ada said, and scooted out of the room at lightning speed.

"I—uh—got some good news today."

Clarence brightened. "Hooray for good news."

"I have you to thank for it." She took the bag from him and sat on the sofa. He sat next to her. She tried not to focus on him being so close and told him about her conversation with Preston.

"That would work. Actually, if this was a station house, the home-owner probably had a removable panel too."

She pulled out Ms. Lila's knitting. "She did make another mistake."

"Okay. Because I was beginning to think that she was sending me over here—" He snapped his mouth closed.

She fought to keep her fingers from trembling as she fixed the mistake. They sat in silence for a moment, then spoke at the same time.

"About your knitting lesson—"

"I was wondering about our lunch—"

She looked up into his eyes and laughed. "How about tomorrow?"

"For the lunch or the knitting?" His voice lowered.

"Either."

"That works."

He smiled, and she turned her attention back to the scarf. But from the corner of her eyes, at an angle Clarence couldn't see, she spotted Ada jumping up and down, pumping her fist in the air. Gracie rolled her eyes at her.

A soft metal clank sounded. Gracie looked up to see two pieces of mail float down from the mail slot.

She hopped up, startling Clarence. "Oh my goodness." She practically ran to the door.

"What happened?" Clarence followed closely behind her.

She turned to him, knowing she had the most ridiculous smile on her face. "I got mail!"

Clarence, mouth slightly ajar, looked down at the mail in her hands and back up at her. "You did." She could tell he was trying to sound as excited as she was, but he sounded mostly confused.

She laughed. "This is my first mail delivery. Gran had put her mail on hold, so I hadn't gotten any mail since I moved in."

Clarence grinned and offered her a handshake. "Then, congratulations."

She giggled and gave him a hearty handshake, joy she hadn't felt in a while washing over her. She flipped through the two pieces of mail. One piece was the weekly circular from the grocery store on the other end of the block. The other was a letter from some investment company. Junk mail but mail nonetheless.

With all that was going wrong with the house, it was nice for something to go right. It would only be a matter of time before her rezoning permit would fall through that slot.

CHAPTER EIGHTEEN

Olivia

*M*r. Still and Mr. Wilson were waiting outside when Douglas and Olivia exited the building. She tried to keep her posture upright and hopeful, but soon both men were wearing expressions as grim as she felt. *Oh, Beulah.*

"She will not survive two days in conditions like that," Douglas said, looking back at the door.

"Any progress on getting her released?" There was no need to ask if Mr. Still was trying to get her released. Olivia was certain he had already set that in motion.

"We sent word to some of our lawyer friends to try and get her released to our care, but it will take time," Mr. Still said. "The courts are still open, so there may be a chance that something may be decided today."

Olivia glanced back at the door. Helplessness weighted her shoulders. "She said something. She said she was tricked."

Mr. Still's eyebrows rose. "Tricked?"

"She said someone named Logan told her that he was a friend and had come to help. She also said there were other fugitives who were tricked," Olivia said.

Mr. Wilson's eyes widened. "Walker. He said he met with someone named Logan at the docks."

"I think it is safe to assume that whoever this Logan person is, he is not working for us." Olivia fought off a tremble. She relayed Beulah's information about there being more than one person.

"How did they get to her without coming in the house?" Mr. Still asked, his gaze passing from Olivia to Douglas.

Olivia looked at Douglas, who was now wearing an expression of worry. Was he thinking the same thing she was? Thinking of how thin the line between danger and safety was for them, and now Hope?

"I think it was prearranged," Olivia said. She turned to Mr. Wilson. "Remember you said she left Mr. Lloyd and that you found her in the woods. I think this Logan person is luring fugitives away from their conductors."

"Only to let them go back?" Mr. Wilson asked.

Olivia shook her head. "It is strange, but it is the scenario that makes the most sense."

"This could be a problem." Mr. Wilson eyed Douglas. "I know your wife wished to keep you out of her work, but I am relieved you are here. We have no idea how close this Logan person came to your house or where Beulah met him once she left."

Cold dread blasted Olivia colder than the breeze coming off the Delaware River. She pulled her coat tighter. "I already have Saunders becoming more interested in my house." She relayed to Mr. Still what Mr. Wilson already knew, about Saunders pursuing Thea to her house. "We all know about Saunders, but this is the first time he has come inside."

Douglas frowned. "A slave catcher confronted you in our home?"

Olivia froze. *He did not know that.* She sighed. "A patrolman. I am certain you have seen him around. Yes," she said, heart aching.

Douglas's jaw twitched. She could well read his anger.

"It looks as if nothing can be done right now. We should not linger any longer," Mr. Wilson said.

"I will notify you if I hear anything," Mr. Still said.

It took all of Olivia's remaining strength to turn away from the jail and start the walk home.

Douglas wrapped his arm around her. "This reminds me of something."

She looked up at him. He was talking to her. "What?"

He let out a long exhale. "Sometimes there are patients who you've done all you can for and there is nothing more to do but wait. You want to do more. You want to ease the pain and suffering, and you spend your time fretting about it. It is a part of the work, but it is never easy."

Olivia gripped Douglas' arm and allowed herself to cry. His description fit her feelings perfectly. He reached inside his coat and gave her his handkerchief. She dried her tears and prayed for relief and release for Beulah. As she pocketed the handkerchief, she turned her head slightly to see a man in a suit following a few paces away.

Her heart hammered. When they turned a corner, and then the man did too, she leaned into Douglas and whispered, "There is a man following us."

Douglas stiffened but kept his gaze forward. "Are you certain?"

"No, but we can see if he is." She tightened her grip around his arm. "Turn at the corner."

Douglas nodded, realization in his eyes. The turn would take them away from the house. They turned, and when they reached halfway up the block, they saw the man round the corner too. They walked another block before Douglas asked, "Is he still there?"

Olivia, using Douglas' shoulder as a shield, peeked behind her. "Yes."

"Now what?" He leaned his head closer to hers. "It is too cold to continue walking."

The cold had numbed her nose and her toes through her boots. She ran scenarios through her mind. "We will go to Mr. Still's house."

Douglas steered her, and they walked past the Institute for Colored Youth. The play yard was full of screaming boys, their delight filling the air despite the temperature. Douglas looked over at them. "So happy. It never ceases to amaze me how they can find joy in such difficult situations. They could teach us all."

"I am worried about what will become of Hope," she said, almost too quiet to be heard.

He looked down at her, his eyes warm. "I am also, but we cannot worry now. Our thoughts must be on freeing Beulah and finding out who Logan is. I am sure that whatever God has planned for our little Hope, it will be good."

Our little Hope.

But she was not theirs, and her mother was on the point of death. Her future was so uncertain. But Olivia vowed that she would make sure Hope was as happy as she could be.

⁂

Hope reached up, grabbed a tin of stick pins, and snatched them off the table. She moved so fast that the pins were clattering across the floor before Olivia realized what had happened.

"No, no, Hope," she said gently but firmly.

Not that it did any good. Hope grinned, delighted at the noise the pins made.

And that smile warmed Olivia. She carried Hope to her basket bed. Thankfully, Hope had yet to figure out how to get out of it. "Having a bit of fun with my pins, are we?"

Hope sat in the bed, smile still on her face and intent in her eyes. She would knock the tin over again as soon as she had the chance. Once she retrieved them all, Olivia set the pins to the back of her sewing table and then lifted Hope into her lap again.

She had kept Hope close, expecting the news of Beulah's death at any moment. Or expecting word that the slave catchers had transported her back to Virginia. But no word came, no hurried Milly showed up at her door, so she believed the best. Not that she could go and check. Hope had kept her at home, away from the work that had been her only thought for many years. Before Hope, Olivia had loathed the thought of not spending every free moment planning and organizing for the Friends or the school or Mr. Still. Before Hope, she believed she would despise a slower pace.

Now that Hope was here, she found it not as unpleasant as she thought. Besides, it was temporary. She would be back housing fugitives soon.

In all the years Olivia had worked for the Underground Railroad, being able to sit still was an infrequent occurrence. There was always more to do. Now there was very little she could do but care for Hope. She did whatever work she could do with Hope in her lap but not as much as she used to. Olivia found herself twitching to be in motion. To be at work. Instead, she had to force herself to be still and available for Hope.

The bigger challenge was not getting too attached to the child's sweet smile. This was not her child. Hope was Beulah's blessing, not theirs.

But in a way, she was their blessing too.

She worked as much as she could on Mrs. Johnson's dresses. That was made easier by the fact that the dresses the woman picked were mostly decorated with small appliqué-like pieces and lots of lace. She handed Hope a scrap of pink fabric that seemed to delight her as much as the pins. Olivia hummed quietly to the girl and was so engrossed in her work that when a loud rap sounded on the door, she jolted hard enough that Hope slid forward on her lap. Olivia grabbed the girl around her middle to steady her. Then she stood and walked halfway to the door, dread making her tighten her grip on Hope. Was this it? Would the person on the other side of the door have news about Beulah?

But then she spied who was at the door. Mrs. Johnson. A great sense of uneasiness stopped her in her tracks. It had not been a month since her visit, so the woman could not expect her dresses to be done. No matter Mrs. Johnson's reasons for being at her door, the feeling that Mrs. Johnson should not see Hope rang like a shrill bell in Olivia's mind.

Sidestepping out of the view of the window, Olivia pivoted and picked up Hope's basket bed. She carried it to the other side of the staircase where it would be hidden. "Stay here, little one." She went into the kitchen, grabbed a piece of bread, and handed it to the girl as she passed to go to the front door.

She plastered a smile on her face and opened the door. "Good morning, Mrs. Johnson."

Mrs. Johnson stepped forward, but when Olivia remained blocking the door, she frowned. "Good morning. I told you I would stop back in."

Olivia gripped the doorjamb. "Yes, you said you would be back in a month. I am afraid you are a little early for the dresses."

Mrs. Johnson smiled. "Oh, I understand. I only wanted a look at your progress."

"I am not yet finished with the piecework. I am afraid everything is just a jumble of fabric and pins." She fought to keep her smile in place. "Maybe come back in a week or so and I will have more to show you."

"Oh, let me take a peek."

"I—" Olivia started, but a soft thud sounded behind her. As if Hope had. . .

Before she could finish the thought, she heard a small whimper. She turned, praying Mrs. Johnson did not hear Hope, but the woman was peering past her into the house. "Is someone in there? What are you hiding, Mrs. Kingston?"

Olivia stood taller, her stomach knotting. "Remember, I mentioned I had guests staying with me."

"Oh yes. But you never said what kind of guests. Is it family? Mrs. Mason told me your family lives farther north."

Olivia pushed the door closed a little more. "Please come back tomorrow. I should have something more than fabric squares to show you by then."

Before Mrs. Johnson could make another protest, Olivia shut the door. She raced back to the dining room. Hope's little basket bed was empty. She nearly panicked until she saw that the child had crawled under the table and was happily eating her bread. Olivia sighed. "I guess you can get out of the basket." She bent down to pull the girl out. "You are learning fast."

Hope smiled, settling Olivia's nerves a bit. Why was Mrs. Johnson so curious about her guests? And to ask Olivia what kind of guests she had in her house. Odd.

It was time for Olivia to find out more about her mysterious new customer.

CHAPTER NINETEEN

Gracie

*P*reston arrived promptly at ten. Gracie had plenty of other things to do, but she stood mesmerized, watching more and more of the brick wall get revealed. Preston and Jo had to use a ladder to reach the sections of drywall higher up. Fine powder fell like snow. Thankfully, the fixtures holding yarn were covered with a tarp.

Ada came down, eyeing the wall then Gracie. "Shouldn't you be getting ready?"

Gracie gaped. Her lunch with Clarence. He had said he would call this morning. "Oh boy." She rushed to her phone and groaned. Three missed calls and two text messages, all from Clarence. All were differently worded requests for her to call him.

She pressed the call button, and Clarence answered on the first ring. "I'm so sorry. I can't make lunch," he said before she could say hello.

"It's okay. The contractors are here."

"I'm in an emergency meeting." He sighed. "I thought it might be over before lunch, but it's still going."

Gracie stood taller, taking a deep breath. "How about dinner?"

His voice grew softer. "That'll work. Pick you up at six?"

"Great."

His voice grew muffled, and he said something to someone else. "I gotta go. See you tonight."

"Okay." Gracie ended the call and looked at Ada, who had come into the office.

"No lunch?"

"No, he had an unexpected meeting." Gracie tried to sound serious, but a grin escaped. "We're having dinner."

"Then let's go try on that dress."

Ada didn't just let Gracie try on the dress. She gave Gracie a full makeover. When Ada was done, a curious happiness slipped over Gracie. "It's been a long time since I got dressed up. Last time was—" She took in a sharp inhale.

"Gran's funeral. And you looked fierce."

Gracie shook her head. "I needed to do Gran justice. She always looked incredible."

"You succeeded. The black leather jacket was—" She made the chef's kiss motion.

"I got that thing from the thrift store," Gracie said, laughing.

"Doesn't matter. You rocked it. Just like you're rocking this dress."

Gracie put her hand on her hip. "There's an unspoken rule that if you wear a person's clothes better than they did, then you get to keep them."

"If you and Clarence have a magical night, you can keep it as a memento," Ada said with a laugh.

Gracie wore the dress for the rest of the day paired with some high-heeled boots. Every time she walked past them, Preston and Jo gave her approving smiles. Once, Preston said, "You're glowing, Ms. Gracie."

Hopefully Clarence will think so. The thought was so foreign that she paused. Of all the things she thought would happen in her life, this wasn't one of them. A relationship was so far beyond her. Her life in Richmond had been all about the hustle. She had to work several jobs to make enough money to cover her bills. She never had time to date. But Clarence was in her life now, and she found herself thinking about him more and more. Caring, smart, handsome, and totally devoted to his grandmother. He ticked all the boxes and then some.

When Preston and Jo had left and the orange rays of sunshine lit the front room, she touched up her makeup and tried to calm her nerves. When the doorbell rang, she jumped. She went down, trying to measure her breathing and convince herself that it was ridiculous to be feeling this way. How many days had she spent with Clarence? Or talked to him on the phone? Why was this any different?

When she opened the door, she saw the answer to her question.

Clarence stood there, looking like he'd gone through a Clark Kent/Superman transformation, except he still wore his glasses. He normally dressed like a graduate-level professor. Sweater vest, casual loafers, khakis, maybe a blazer added for warmth. He dressed smart. Tonight he dressed. . . She swallowed. Tonight he dressed. . .wow. He wore a black wool peacoat, the red scarf draped over his shoulders instead of around his neck, dress shoes, and slacks. And he had a fresh haircut.

He stood there gaping at her the same way she was sure she was gaping at him. "Hi," he said.

"Hi."

He blinked. "Uh, am I early?"

His question cleared the fog in her thoughts. "No. I—let me get my coat."

He stepped inside, and Gracie had to fight the urge to stare at him. The peacoat was properly fitted across his shoulders. "I'll be right back."

She went up the stairs as fast as she could. Ada met her at the top. "Go down and look at him," Gracie said in an urgent whisper.

Ada grinned. "Yes, ma'am."

When she returned, Clarence looked up at her and smiled. He stepped over and helped her put on her coat. The back of her neck tingled.

"You kids have a good time," Ada said, opening the door for them. She wiggled her eyebrows at Gracie when Clarence wasn't looking.

The November air was crisp and helped cool her face. Clarence led her to his car. "I hope you don't mind my picking the restaurant."

"Not at all." With her stomach knotted in nerves, she probably couldn't get a bite down.

He drove to The Rochester Restaurant, a brightly lit brick building.

They parked a few doors down and walked the distance. Clarence edged closer to her, like he wanted to hold her hand, but suddenly they were at the door, and the moment passed.

They were taken up to the second-floor seating area. Clarence helped her out of her coat and pulled out her chair. Then he removed his coat, and Gracie had to remember to breathe. He was wearing a suit, and it was as well tailored as the coat.

Before he sat, he caught her staring and looked down at himself. "Too much?"

"Oh no. It's nice."

He sat and unbuttoned the suit's jacket. "It was a bit of a splurge. A good suit is essential for all the commission employees. Especially with the number of presentations we do. I really like this suit and wish I had more places to wear it."

"It's not too much."

Clarence smiled, and the tips of his ears darkened a shade.

They chatted comfortably through dinner, and she learned quite a bit about him. She listened as he told her that he'd gone to school for architecture but changed majors. "I realized I'd rather study the history of buildings than design them. Switched to a history degree. What about you?"

She squirmed. "I—um—started a degree in business administration."

"Really?" He leaned forward, interested.

"I didn't get to finish." She looked down at her plate.

"I thought you would have majored in art." His tone wasn't judgmental.

She shrugged. "I needed a degree that could get me a job quick."

"Will you go back now?" Again, curious not critical.

"I don't know. I'm not really rolling in cash from my unopened yarn store."

He nodded. "School isn't cheap. Took me years to pay off my student loans." He shook his head. "A lot of nights eating ramen."

She laughed. "Been there." But not for the reasons Clarence had.

She'd been there because she didn't have money to buy anything else, not because she was paying for an education, like Clarence.

She was relieved when the conversation drifted to the upcoming Thanksgiving dinner. Clarence's family sounded much tamer than hers, and she was honestly looking forward to seeing their dynamics. Plus, being around strangers might keep her from crying all day. Her first Thanksgiving without Gran.

When the bill came, she reached for it. Clarence put his hand on top of hers. "If it's okay, I'd like to pay for dinner. You can pay next time if you'd like."

So there would be a next time. "Okay."

With all the talking they'd done at the restaurant, they still found more to talk about on the ride back to her house. But when they arrived, Gracie struggled to find words. Did this night have to end? He helped her out of the car, and this time he did take her hand as they walked to her front door.

"Tonight was wonderful," she said when they reached her stairs. She stepped up the first step.

"It was." He stood on the sidewalk, which put him below eye level.

She stood there, waiting for something to happen. "So. . ."

He cleared his throat. "Gracie, I would like—" He straightened his shoulders and looked up at her. When those beautiful brown eyes shifted to her lips and back to her eyes, she knew what he would like. And what she would like too. Her whole life felt like a dream. Some parts good, some bad. This moment was a good part. One where she could be happy.

She leaned down, cupped Clarence's face, and kissed him. She felt him jolt, but his surprise only lasted a second. He reached up, grasping her waist and pulling her forward, and returned her kiss with enough warmth to make her forget the cold night air.

When they separated, he rested his forehead on hers. "I've been wanting to do that for a while."

She laughed. "Me too."

He gave her one more quick peck. "Good night."

She grinned. "Good night."

He was in his car before her heart stopped racing. She unlocked the door and stood in the doorway as he drove off. When she turned, Ada was standing at one of the cubes, trying to look like she was casually browsing for yarn. "Oh, you're back. How was it?"

Gracie gave her a big grin. "I'm keeping this dress."

Gracie felt like she could take over the world.

Thanksgiving at Ms. Lila's house ended up being just what she needed. Ada had gone to her father's house first and then stopped by. The dinner was full of laughter and good food. And Clarence was the most attentive boyfriend. *Boyfriend.* Gracie smiled at that.

After her previous date with Clarence, and that kiss, he had called to tell her that he had arrived home safely. They had talked for a while longer, and during the whole conversation she kept thinking about how soft his lips were.

At the end of the call, he asked, "So are we a couple now?"

She had sat stunned for a second. "Do you want us to be?"

"Yes."

"I'm—" She searched for a word. "Complicated."

"And?" He laughed. "I'm not bothered by complicated. I'm complicated too. And I picked the most complicated profession in the world."

She smiled. "Okay, then. We are a couple."

They were a couple, and he wasn't afraid to make that known at the Thanksgiving dinner. He introduced her to his parents, aunts, uncles, cousins, and family friends. Gracie thought more than once that Ms. Lila was going to burst with happiness every time Clarence held Gracie's hand.

She had eaten too much. Clarence's mother, Sonya, was an incredible cook. And Gracie had laughed until her sides ached. Clarence pulled her into a kiss as she and Ada were leaving.

"Young man, slow down!" His father, Zachary, who had been teasing Clarence all night about their new relationship, yelled out, and the room erupted into laughter. Gracie didn't know who blushed more, she or Clarence. Clarence had also set up the date of their next research trip. Gracie could have floated home. She fell asleep that night with more joy than she knew was possible.

This morning she'd gotten up feeling like something was righted in her life. She went downstairs to the office, humming a nameless tune. Ada was already at the laptop. "You look like you're in love," she said after giving her a once-over.

Gracie stopped. "In love?"

Ada chuckled and went back to the laptop. "Yes."

Gracie was frozen to the spot. Was she in love? What did that even feel like? She liked Clarence, but love? It was possible, but how would she know?

The click of the mail slot brought a welcome distraction, and she bolted to the door.

"You gotta stop getting so excited about the mail," Ada called from behind her.

When she lifted the mail from the floor, she saw that her excitement was not in vain. There were two letters. One was from the Permit and License Center. The second was from the Office of Property Assessment. She ripped into the latter and, after skimming it, let out a whoop. Ada came rushing to her.

Gracie held up the letter, stating that her rezoning had been approved. Even though she knew this letter was coming, it didn't stop the rush of emotions. Tears blurred the room, and she let them fall. It was such a relief, she couldn't have stopped the tears if she wanted to. "We can open the shop now."

"I'm so happy." Ada, tears in her eyes, threw her arms around Gracie. "You did it."

"I couldn't have done it without you."

When they broke the embrace and their tears lessened, she opened the letter from the Office of Property Assessment. It was a receipt for last year's and this year's tax payments. The tears began afresh.

"I think we should order your sign as a celebration. And call Clarence." Ada rushed back to the office.

"Let me put these documents away," Gracie said with a laugh. She went upstairs and retrieved the folder with Gran's documents and put the tax receipt in it. She put the rezoning letter in the folder with her shop plans.

As she did, the doorbell rang. She ran her hand over her wooden box before she left the room.

But when she came downstairs, there was no one there but Ada holding another letter. She looked up at Gracie, all of the joy of a moment ago changed into concern. "This came certified."

Gracie took the letter. It was from the same investment company whose correspondence she'd received a week ago. The letter was addressed to Gran. Gracie opened it and read, her heart sinking with every word.

Ada stepped closer, peering down at the letter. "What is it?"

"It says that Gran has an outstanding account with them," Gracie said slowly.

"What kind of account?"

Gracie skimmed the letter again. There was very little in the letter. "It really doesn't say. It just says that I need to contact them immediately." She looked up at the name. First Trust Loans and Investments. "I've never seen their name in any of Gran's paperwork."

"Maybe they're a creditor who saw your Letters Testamentary in the papers." Ada put her hand on Gracie's shoulder. "Don't worry. It's probably something simple like the taxes."

"What if it isn't?" But she already knew the answer to that question. If it was something concerning the house, it wouldn't be simple. And if it was some large bill, how would she pay it?

Ada grabbed her arm. "Let's find out before you worry yourself into an ulcer." They went back to the office, and Ada lifted Gracie's phone from the desk. "Call them right now."

Gracie swallowed. Ada was right. The sooner she knew what this was about the sooner she could resolve it. A few quick breaths and she dialed the number.

The company had several directories to drill down. New customers.

Returning customers. By the time Gracie reached "Press 1 to speak to a customer service rep," her anxiety had been replaced with annoyance.

"Thank you for calling First Trust Loans and Investments. This is Cara. How may I help you?"

Gracie sighed. *Finally.* "I have a question about an account."

"Great. I can help you with that. What is the account number?"

Gracie frowned. "I don't have one."

"What's the address?"

Gracie recited it twice.

"Let me just pull this up. . . ." Gracie could hear the tap of a keyboard. "Um, can I place you on a brief hold?"

Gracie's stomach dropped. She knew what that meant. How many times had her landlord, bosses, or utility companies put her on a "brief hold" before they delivered devastating news? "Yes."

She heard a click, and then very terrible instrumental music began to play. Gracie gripped the phone. Ada rubbed small circles on her shoulder. Gracie's stomach roiled as she tried to imagine what was on the account. It had to be bad. Her thoughts nudged her toward hope, but she ignored them. Hope hadn't always been reliable.

Cara returned. "Ma'am, I'm sorry, can you confirm your address again?"

Gracie repeated it a third time. "I am the homeowner and would like to get some information about this account."

"Am I speaking to Mrs. Leander?"

"No." Gracie fought to keep her tone level. "My name is Gracie McNeil. As I said before."

"We'll need to speak to Mrs. Leander in order to release information on the account."

"Well, that's not going to happen. Mrs. Leander is dead." Her voice came out at nearly a yell. Ada flinched, and Gracie regretted the outburst.

Cara sputtered on the line. "Oh, I'm so sorry."

"I am her granddaughter, and I inherited the house," Gracie said in a calmer tone.

"I see," Cara said, her voice the most human it had been since the call began. "Unfortunately, we have to verify that you are now the homeowner." Cara recited a list of paperwork that Gracie could use to confirm that she was the homeowner. One of them was a copy of the deed. She wasn't going to send them that. They would have to take the paperwork stating she was the executor of Gran's estate.

She rubbed her temple. "What's the best way to get the documentation to you?"

"You can email it." Cara rattled off an email account, and Gracie scribbled it down.

"I'll get that information to you as soon as I can."

"Thank you. I'll add a notation on the account."

Gracie's heart dropped. "And you can't tell me anything about it?"

"No. I'm sorry. Is there anything else I can help you with?"

This is going to be bad. "No, not right now. Have a good day."

Gracie ended the call, her head starting to throb.

"Hey," Ada said quietly, stooping beside her. "Don't get yourself all worked up. If the account, or whatever this is, is in Gran's name, it's probably a part of the estate."

"But what if it isn't?" If it wasn't, Gracie was going to have to come up with more money she didn't have.

"Then you'll figure it out. You always figure something out," Ada said confidently. "And you have people who will help you."

Gracie heard her, but the words competed with her growing dread. She would have to delay the shop. She could always get a job. But the shame and disappointment that overwhelmed her booted that idea from her mind. She'd promised Gran she would open the yarn shop. She would have to keep at it until it was absolutely clear that she couldn't.

"You're right. I'll think of something."

CHAPTER TWENTY

OLIVIA

Olivia rolled her shoulders and continued sewing. She had stayed up late working on Mrs. Johnson's dress so she would have something to show her when she arrived. And to put her plan in motion.

She had explained Mrs. Johnson's unexpected visit to Douglas as they sat down for dinner the night before. All day she had agonized about telling him what she was going to do, but in the end, she needed help. Besides, she didn't believe that Mrs. Johnson was dangerous. Just too curious.

Douglas had a different reaction to her retelling of Mrs. Johnson's visit. He grew more and more concerned as she talked. "What do you think is happening?"

"It is hard for me to guess. Her behavior is too odd and unlike any of my other customers," Olivia said. "It would be unfortunate if she is not who she says she is and the banknote she gave me is not good. I will have done all that work for nothing."

Olivia could tell by the way Douglas shifted in his seat that he disliked the plan, but he had agreed it was the most harmless way to find out information. She promised to be careful and not follow Ms. Johnson out of the Bella Vista community. Only then did Douglas relax a little.

"I will stay home from work tomorrow."

Olivia protested. "Your work is far more important than me following a customer."

"You will need someone to sit with Hope. And I can position myself in our bedroom window. That way I can watch which way Mrs. Johnson goes."

Olivia considered the plan. With Douglas watching, she wouldn't have to leave right after Mrs. Johnson, making it less obvious that she was following her. "All right," she agreed.

As expected, Mrs. Johnson was at her door as early as acceptable. Probably trying to catch Olivia off guard again.

Douglas rose, picking up Hope. He slowed as he passed Olivia to go up the stairs. He leaned in like he was going to kiss her, then seemed to reconsider. "Be safe."

Olivia nodded. "I will."

She took a deep breath before she opened the door to Mrs. Johnson. The woman's expression was a notch less cordial than yesterday, but she still smiled at Olivia. "Hope I am not too early."

"Not at all." She opened the door wider and let Mrs. Johnson inside. From her position, she could see Mrs. Johnson glancing round the room. Olivia moved to the table.

Even though it was a part of the ploy to follow Mrs. Johnson, Olivia was very proud of the work she'd done last night. Most of the outer layer of the dress was done; she only had to finish the lining. And she'd done it all with Hope sleeping in her lap.

Mrs. Johnson ran her hand over the fabric. "Very nice. You do such good work. Quick too."

"The other four are still in the pinning stage, but I expect to have them done on time."

"Very good."

Olivia decided to try one more attempt at getting information from the woman. "I still don't have your address," she said, holding Mrs. Johnson's eye contact.

The woman scowled. "I told you I'll come back." Her tone grew a little sharper.

Olivia smiled graciously. "I was merely trying to avoid repeating what happened yesterday. I could send your dresses as soon as they are done instead of your coming back and possibly finding that they are not ready."

"As I said, I am in no hurry to get the dresses."

Olivia broke eye contact. "Very well."

"Are your guests gone?"

She looked up at the woman. "No, probably resting. It is still quite early in the morning."

"I suppose it is. Will they be staying with you much longer?"

"That is uncertain right now," Olivia said, her nerves starting to jitter.

"It is such an inconvenience for guests to stay longer than they should."

"But not guests you enjoy." Not a lie. She enjoyed having Hope here.

"True." Mrs. Johnson gave the room one more glance. "This is a lovely home. So are the other homes in the area. When I pick up the dresses, I would love to see more of it."

Olivia eyed her. "Are you considering living around here?"

Mrs. Johnson shrugged. "Maybe, yes. I am very interested in this neighborhood. So quiet, and everyone seems to know everyone. Very different than my home in Delaware."

"I thought you lived in Virginia."

Mrs. Johnson blinked. "Uh, you must have misunderstood me. I think I said my son lives in Virginia."

"Oh," was all Olivia said. Mrs. Johnson had said her home was in Virginia.

"Until next week." Olivia showed her out and, as soon as she closed the door, grabbed her coat and hurriedly put it on. She would have to move quickly.

As soon as she'd fastened her coat's top button, Douglas called down the stairs. "She went right, toward Bond Street."

And with that, Olivia was out the door. She walked briskly up the street, angling herself to stay out of Mrs. Johnson's view. Thankfully, even though it was early, there were many people on their way to carry out their business for the day. Olivia blended in. Mrs. Johnson turned and continued her progress up Bond Street.

Olivia followed, nodding to several Black shop owners opening for the day. Shop owners who were conductors or stationmasters. If this was a normal route for Mrs. Johnson, maybe one of them had seen her pass by before. Or had interactions with her. It would not hurt to ask them when she passed them again to go home.

Mrs. Johnson kept walking, and soon they were only a few blocks from the wharf.

To Olivia's surprise, Mrs. Johnson began to slow as she approached Shipper's Inn. Olivia slowed her steps and watched Mrs. Johnson go inside and shut the door.

It was possible that Mrs. Johnson questioned her about guests because she was herself hosting guests and, growing tired of them, had put them up in an inn. But Olivia could find out for sure. She slipped around the side of Shipper's, cut through the alley, and arrived at the back door. She smiled at Mr. Abrams when he answered her knock. His face was red from the kitchen heat.

He smiled when he saw her. "Good morning, Mrs. Kingston."

"Morning. Sorry to trouble you, but I need your help."

His face turned serious. "Come in."

"That would not be wise. I followed one of your guests here. Mrs. Johnson."

He let out a huff. "Strange, that one."

"How so?"

"Her story keeps changing." He rubbed his hands absentmindedly on his apron. "First, she's visiting family. Then she is here on a trip and forgot all about the family."

"When we first met, she told me she lived in Virginia," Olivia said. "Today she said she lived in Delaware."

Mr. Abrams shook his head. "Odder than that, she gets a lot of gentlemen callers."

Olivia felt her shock showing on her face. "She is a—"

"No, no. Not those kind of visitors. That is not allowed," Mr.

Abrams said. "But lots of men come to meet with her here. Some of them respectable. Some not so much. She meets with them down in the sitting room, and they talk very quietly."

"She could be doing anything," Olivia murmured.

"Whatever it is, something's not right about it."

"She's having a few dresses made, and I thought she was too curious about my doings. Will you keep me aware if anything changes?"

"Sure will."

Olivia left Shipper's, her mind a whir. It was possible that Mrs. Johnson was simply an odd woman who liked dresses. Still, Olivia's uneasiness was too strong to accept that explanation. As she rounded the building and walked up the alley, she spotted a familiar form. It was Henry. She opened her mouth to call out a greeting to him but saw that he was deep in conversation with another man. The tall white man seemed familiar, but she struggled to place where she knew him from. He and Henry were having a very animated conversation. Olivia hurried away before he spotted her, not wanting to interrupt them.

Her feet carried her home, even though her thoughts were still at the inn. She opened the front door and found Douglas sitting in one of her chairs, holding Hope close to his chest. His expression was one of pain and shock. He stood and crossed the room to her.

Olivia studied him, then Hope. They appeared to be well. "What is the matter?"

"Mr. Wilson came by while you were gone." He draped his arm around her. "Beulah is dead."

The words hit her chest hard, winding her. Her eyes filled with tears as they went to Hope. *Her mama is dead.* Douglas pulled her into his chest. Olivia wrapped her arms around him and Hope and cried.

CHAPTER TWENTY-ONE

GRACIE

*G*racie couldn't wait any longer to ask Mia about the bag. It was clear that she and Ada had not misplaced it, and there were no other customers in and out of the store. That didn't leave many other explanations. It was not something she wanted to do, but she had to find out. She knew that talking to Mia was going to take some delicacy. Gracie needed to ask about the bag but not accuse her of stealing it. Before the girls started to arrive, Ada helped her rehearse what she wanted to say.

Mia came in, actually smiling. "Hi, Ms. Gracie." She swung the bag Gracie had given her on her wrist. "Wait till you see how far I got."

"Hi, Mia." Gracie nodded at her father. "Head on back."

Mia grinned and bounded back, but when she reached the place where the bag had been, she slowed and stared.

A warning note sounded in Gracie's heart. The other girls' arrivals didn't give her much time to process the feeling.

When Gracie rounded the corner to start class, which now was no more than instructions on fixing mistakes, Mia had already taken out her knitting. She wasn't acting like she'd stolen the bag. It could be a performance, but how many thirteen-year-olds could act that well? She decided to talk to Mia's father. If the girl hadn't taken the bag, she would promptly go back into her shell if Gracie accused her.

Bella looked up at Gracie and let out a whine. "I messed up again. And mine doesn't look like Mia's."

"I can help you," Mia said.

"No." Bella's tone was sharp. But when she saw the stern look Gracie shot in her direction, she sputtered, "I think the teacher should teach."

Mia shrugged. "Whatever."

Gracie moved to Bella's side and looked at the stitches. They were mounted on the needles backward. "Did your knitting come off the needles?"

Bella gave her a pleading look. "Yes, and I tried to put them back. I need a better bag. A bag like Mia's."

Trinity looked up from concentrating on her knitting. "You told me your cat pulled it off."

"If that's true," Gracie said, studying the girl, "then a better bag wouldn't help you."

"Just ask your mother to buy you one," Rylee said. "Didn't she just buy you that—"

Bella spoke over her. "I did ask my mother."

Rylee gave her a skeptical look. "Your mother told you no. That's new, I guess."

"Well, this is a perfect opportunity to teach you how to put your stitches back on your needles correctly." Gracie moved to the head of the table to a sample she was using to demonstrate stitches. She picked it up, pulled the stitches off the needles, and undid a couple of stitches in the middle of the piece.

Dani let out a gasp.

Gracie laughed. "Rule number one to fixing your stitches: don't be afraid of mistakes. Come around and see what I'm doing."

All the girls gathered around her, Dani still looking slightly horrified, and listened to her explain how to fix the mistakes.

Mia huffed. "You make it look so easy."

"With a little time and patience, any mistake can be fixed." What a true statement. With all the mistakes she had made in her early life, time and patience had put her in a better place. Much better.

Mia looked down at the sample. "Not all of them."

"Yeah, you can't keep failing at math and bring your mistakes in for Ms. Gracie to fix."

Mia jumped like she had been pinched. She scowled at Bella. "Mind your own business."

"Girls," Gracie said, "if you don't follow the community kindness rules, I will have to ban you from the class."

Mia sulked back to her seat. "Go ahead and ban her. She's going to say something else anyway."

Gracie schooled her face. Mia had all the sass Gracie had when she was her age. "Last warning."

The rest of the class went well. Bella and Mia didn't take any more swipes at each other. Dani practiced putting the stitches back on the needles of Gracie's sample. When they started packing up to leave, Mia excused herself to use the bathroom.

As soon as she was out of sight, Bella eased up to Gracie's chair. "I wanted to warn you, Ms. Gracie. Mia has been getting into a lot of trouble at school."

Gracie looked at the girl. Did Bella really think she was going to fall for this? "I'm sure it isn't your place to tell me that."

"It is. Because what if she starts being bad here?"

"Then, as the adult, I will handle it." Gracie smiled brightly. "Why don't you tell me how you're doing in school?"

"Huh?"

"How are your grades?"

"She's failing math too," Destiny cried out, and she and Rylee laughed.

Like Mia said. Mean girls.

Bella huffed and returned to her seat, obviously done with the conversation.

To Gracie's relief, all the parents showed up at once. She ushered the other four girls and their mothers out the door but stopped Stanley. "Can I speak to you for a moment?"

"Sure." His expression grew wary.

"After the last class, did Mia come home with something—" She didn't want to put the idea in his head if Mia hadn't taken the bag.

"With something she didn't have before?"

He looked perplexed. "The red bag? I thought you gave it to her."

"I did. But did she have anything else?"

She could see the moment Stanley realized what she was asking him. His face went from confused to angry. "Mia, did you steal something?" he yelled across the room.

Mia whipped around. "Steal—no, no I didn't."

"No, no. Stanley, I'm not saying she stole something." She'd deviated from what she and Ada had practiced but not by much. She should have factored in the family difficulties Stanley and Mia were having. She knew about them, and she knew her own life. How her family's dysfunction had crept into her behavior.

"Yes, you are. Mia?"

"I didn't steal anything, Daddy."

He turned to Gracie and pulled out his wallet. "Whatever she stole, I'll replace it."

Not a two-hundred-dollar leather bag. "Wait one second. I'm not saying she stole it. I'm asking—"

Mia's eyes grew wide. "The red bag."

Stanley huffed. "You do know about it?"

"I asked for it because it was nice." The poor girl looked like she was ready to cry. "But I didn't take it."

"Then why does Ms. Gracie think you did?"

This was not going how she planned. Gracie held up her hand. "Stop. I just need to figure out what happened to it. Mia might have thought it was okay to take it because I'd given her the other one."

Mia folded her arms. "Why would it be okay to take a two-hundred-dollar bag? Which I didn't take, by the way."

Stanley paled. "Two hundred dollars?"

"Daddy, I didn't take the bag." Mia rushed across the room "Ms. Gracie, I didn't take it. I wouldn't do that. I like it a lot, but I didn't take it. I love the bag you gave me."

"She does love it. Showed it to anyone who would look at it," Stanley muttered.

Gracie looked down at the girl. She was probably getting duped, but she didn't believe Mia had taken the bag. "All right. I believe you."

Mia let out a sigh, her shoulders sinking. "I promise I didn't take it."

Stanley harrumphed. "Let's go, Mia."

Mia let her arms drop beside her and shuffled out the door.

"I am so sorry," Stanley said as they reached the door. "I'll check her room. I'll find the bag."

"Please don't. I believe her."

"You don't understand. Mia has been trouble since. . ." He looked out the door at Mia, who was leaning to look at something down the street.

"I was trouble all through school." She touched his arm. "And I still may be trouble. I'm not bothered, and I do believe her."

He gave a sad smile. "I guess I should have hope since you turned out well."

"Not quite. I'm still a work in progress. But I do believe Mia. Please don't be too hard on her. She's dealing with a lot, just like you are."

Stanley looked over at Mia. "Work in progress."

Gracie nodded. "Absolutely."

She watched them go, praying she hadn't just made Mia's life worse.

⁂

Clarence arrived at the house as scheduled on Tuesday morning. Seeing him boosted her mood a little. The fact that she had handled the Mia situation so badly had saddened her. She greeted Clarence at the door with a tight hug.

He held her close, like he knew she needed it. When they separated, he looked down at her. "Are you all right?"

"I had a tough situation to deal with this weekend."

"Is it resolved?"

She shook her head, remembering the hurt on Mia's face. "Not yet. But I hope it will be soon."

"If you need help, I'm here."

She hugged him again to hide her face. She knew he would help her if he could. Having more than Gran to help was a new feeling.

Now she had Ada, Clarence, and Ms. Lila. "I know."

When they broke the embrace, he grinned at her. "Are you ready for this adventure?"

"Yes," she said, letting herself smile. She was allowed some joy in all this.

He laughed. "You're a little too happy for someone about to strain her eyes looking at maps and barely legible records."

"But I'm about to find out about this house. That's exciting."

Once in his car, she asked where they were going. "First stop, the library," he said.

She looked at him quizzically. "Really?"

"Yes. I hope you have a library card." He navigated his car out of the parking space in front of her house and turned left, slowing as they passed William Still's house.

Gracie stared at it with a mix of emotions. Even if her house turned out to be just a house with an extra-large root cellar, it was amazing to think that she was living this close to a real historical location. "I don't. I haven't had the chance to get a library card."

He reached over and squeezed her hand. "Easily fixed. You can get one while you're there."

As they drove, Gracie fell silent, remembering the field trips she and Gran went on around the city. She smiled as they passed Love Park and City Hall.

"I don't know any city in the country that has better architecture than Philadelphia." Clarence stole glances at City Hall with its dome and columns as they passed.

"I always loved the way there was a little bit of everything here. From City Hall to the modern condos to Freedom Park." A shadow of sadness clouded Gracie's heart. She missed Gran and her love for this city. Most of the things Gracie knew about Philadelphia history she knew because Gran had told her.

They arrived at the Parkway Central Branch and parked nearby. As they walked over the large circular area in front of the building, Clarence held her hand, and she grinned at the way his shoulder kept brushing hers.

"Why are we coming here first?"

"Because this branch has been in the Federal Depository Library Program since 1897. Older city records are held here. Ones older than the property taxation site can provide."

They walked into the grand marble foyer, and although people were milling around, the area was hushed. It felt sacred.

"First things first." He led her over to the information desk and informed them that Gracie had just moved to town and needed a library card.

The woman at the desk beamed. "Absolutely." She handed Gracie a form. Gracie filled it out, handed the woman her ID and form back, and within a few minutes she had a library card.

She beamed at Clarence, who gave her a knowing look. "Pretty fantastic."

From there he led her to the government record department. A tall, lean man with skin the color of her gran's heavy brown family Bible looked up and smiled at Clarence. "Mr. Evans. Good to see you again."

Clarence shook his hand. "Same here. Mr. Moore, this is Ms. Gracie McNeil."

Mr. Moore gave her the same warm handshake. "Nice to meet you." He looked at Clarence. "What are we looking for today? You give me the best challenges."

"Actually, Gracie has a challenge for you."

Mr. Moore beamed at her. "She looks like she has a good one."

Gracie laughed. "I don't know. I would think it was hard."

"Those are the good ones," Mr. Moore said with a chuckle.

"All right then. I want to trace the ownership of my grandmother's house." Mr. Moore's enthusiasm made her feel more hopeful.

"Hmm. Sounds promising." Mr. Moore leaned toward her, peering over his glasses. "How far back?"

"Mid-1800s?" Gracie's words came out more as a question than a statement.

Mr. Moore's smile returned. "Yes, she's got a good one." He motioned for them to follow him.

He led them to a large, glass-enclosed room with long study tables. It reminded Gracie of Clarence's archives. "The first thing we need to start with is the address."

When Gracie told him, his eyebrows rose. "That's up the street from William Still's house."

"Yes," she said cautiously.

"That makes it a little easier. I've pulled the Still records for Mr. Evans so many times that I almost have them memorized. How far back do you have information about the house's ownership?"

"When my great-grandparents owned it in the 1930s."

"Then we'll start with property deeds and ward maps."

Clarence nodded. "Good idea." He turned to Gracie as Mr. Moore walked back to the stacks. "Before 1854 the city was divided into townships and boroughs. They consolidated them into ward maps. That information isn't necessarily listed on the deed, unless you happen to have a copy of your great-great-grandparents' deed."

She shook her head. "If Gran had that paperwork, she didn't give it to me."

Mr. Moore returned, giving her a reassuring smile. "That's okay. You have one of the best researchers in the city right beside you. If information is recorded, he will find it. I'll check in on you in a bit."

Clarence proved every bit as helpful as Mr. Moore thought he would be. He understood the ward maps' numbering system. Since her house was so close to William Still's house, he already knew what ward it was in.

Mr. Moore returned after twenty minutes. "Ms. McNeil, I thought you might leave the heavy research to Clarence and do something a little closer to your heart."

She looked up at him. "What's that?"

"Why don't we find the rest of your family in the birth records?"

To her surprise, tears sprang to her eyes. The offer to search for her family made her feel connected despite all that the past year had brought. She sniffled, and Clarence gave her hand a squeeze. "I would like that."

Mr. Moore took her to a bank of desks with a microfiche machine, computers, squares of scrap paper, and pencils on them. "I think the best place to start is with ancestry records." He motioned for her to sit at one of the computers. "We have access to some of the top online ancestry sites, but many of them are user managed and only go so far. Once we go as far as we can, we'll switch to microfiche."

He logged her on to one of the sites. "You will have to trace your family members backward to get the names you don't have."

Gracie looked up. "I actually already have a couple of generations." She lifted one of the slips of scrap paper and listed the names Gran had drilled into her.

Mr. Moore's eyebrows rose with surprise. "This goes significantly faster when you have names. Good luck."

When he was gone, Gracie clicked on the first ancestry site listed and typed in her own name to test how much information she would be getting. She held her breath as the returns flashed onto the screen. There was her name and the long list of residencies she'd held in Richmond. Next, she typed in Uncle Rand's name. It returned with more info than the search on her name did. Aunt Elle, Bernard, and Ada were listed along with Uncle Rand's military service.

Uncle Rand was a mystery to her. Whenever she saw him on his visits to Gran's house, he didn't talk to her more than necessary to be polite. But she had watched him with his children and Gran. He was very different with them. Laughing, talking. Someone Gracie didn't know, with a personality that dried up whenever he addressed her. After Gran died, Gracie had prayed that their shared grief would bring them closer, but it didn't. Uncle Rand only became more distant.

She closed that search with a sigh and typed in her mother's name. The sting of seeing that the first listing was her obituary nearly took her breath away. She swiped tears from her cheeks and read it once again.

Her mother gone. Gran gone. The longer she stared at the screen, the more the pain of loss increased. If only she could have them both back. Have them back and not have their deaths searing her heart.

She noticed movement from the corner of her eye. She looked

up and saw Clarence standing a few steps away. When she made eye contact, he came to the desk. "I didn't want to interrupt."

"I don't think I can do this."

He leaned over and looked at the screen. "Oh."

She stood. "No, I can't do this."

He took her hand. "Then let's look at some ward maps."

She followed Clarence back to the table with the maps, but now that the tears had started, she couldn't get them to stop. By the time they reached the table, she was sobbing. Clarence navigated them into an empty row, put his arms around her, and held her close enough that she could feel his heart beating. Shame crept up her neck. *Why did I think I could do this?*

Clarence nuzzled his face into her hair. "Do you want to go?"

She sagged, more tears. She should be strong. She should stay. "Yes."

"Okay," he whispered.

He left her standing in the row while he went and spoke to Mr. Moore. As he talked, Mr. Moore looked up at her with pity, at least that's what it looked like, on his face.

Clarence returned. "You ready?"

She nodded and took his hand, humiliation tingeing every step. Clarence didn't release her hand until they got to the car. Gracie turned her head to the window and didn't speak the whole ride back to the house. Clarence didn't try to talk to her. He just walked her to her door, gave her a kiss on the cheek, and left.

Before she went inside, she looked up at the house. And just like the day she moved in, she didn't want to go inside and face the memories.

CHAPTER TWENTY-TWO

OLIVIA

*M*r. Still, Mr. Wilson, and Thea arrived at Olivia's house just before sunset. Olivia took a seat on the sofa, and Douglas sat very close to her. Hope had fallen asleep, and every time Olivia looked down at her in her arms, tears returned afresh. Beulah was dead, and Hope was an orphan. Beulah had suffered great hardship to get herself and her daughter to freedom. Both had found it. One in Olivia's home. The other in the great by-and-by.

Olivia knew that they had gathered to come up with a plan, but she was unable to contribute. Thankfully, Douglas kept some of his wits, but his eyes were still red from the tears they had cried together.

None of her passengers had affected her like this. It was hard not to have strong feelings doing work for the Underground Railroad, but she had managed to keep an emotional distance from her passengers. It was almost a requirement. Care with the understanding that the passengers would move on, *must* move on. To send them from her heart in order to accept others.

But not with Beulah and Hope. That distance had closed the minute she saw Hope in Beulah's arms and the desperate look on Beulah's face. Olivia's heart broke anew. Beulah traveled all the way to freedom only to die alone.

"We will find a place for the child," Mr. Still said. "I was planning to ask Mrs. Brasewell but delayed until we knew something of the child's mother. I can check tomorrow."

"That means Hope will have to say here another night?" Douglas asked.

"Maybe longer." Mr. Still sat across from them. "Mrs. Brasewell runs one of the few orphanages in this area and is usually caring for as many children as she can."

Olivia shuddered at the thought of Hope in a home with strangers. "You know she can stay here as long as she needs. It is not as if we have children of our own to care for."

She felt Douglas shift beside her. She looked at him. His eyes were filled with pain.

Mrs. Wilson gave her a sympathetic look. "Of course, Milly can continue to come around and help when you need it."

"What will happen to Beulah's body?" Douglas asked.

Mr. Wilson looked at Olivia when he answered. "Common grave."

Olivia stifled a sob. "I wish—" .

Mr. Still leaned forward. "We did everything we could for Beulah, and that is nothing to be ashamed of. She got herself and her child to freedom. Our job is ensuring that Hope has the life that Beulah suffered and sacrificed for."

Olivia looked down at Hope, her heart breaking. This sweet child could not go into an orphanage. She needed a family. Someone to teach her to read. "Yes, of course."

"If you are willing to care for Hope until we can find another solution, I will agree that is the best option," Mr. Still said. "The child is still too frail and small to travel farther north to another orphanage."

She does not know what she has lost. Olivia nodded.

"The next order of business, I think, would be finding out who this Logan fellow is," Mr. Wilson said.

"I have put everyone I can on alert, but no one seems to know who he is." Mr. Still steepled his hands. "I tried to find out at the jail who brought Beulah in."

"The slave catcher?" Douglas asked.

"If it was him, why didn't he just take her back to the South?" Thea asked.

"Maybe he was waiting to find out where Hope was," Olivia said quietly. "Once Hope grew up, she would fetch a good price at auction."

They all sat in silence for a few moments. "If the owner knew Hope existed. Beulah could have hidden her from her owner. It has happened many times before," Thea finally said.

"That still does not change the fact that someone is luring fugitives away from the station houses," Douglas said. "How could they do this without watching your movements?"

"Maybe they're not," Olivia said. "Remember, Beulah said she met Logan before she reached here. Maybe it is all prearranged."

"But it doesn't make sense," Mr. Wilson said. "If that is so, why not take them then? Why arrange a later meeting?"

"We need to find out," Mr. Still said.

"Maybe we can have the stationmasters speak to all the fugitives we have hidden right now," Douglas suggested. "Maybe they know something but don't realize it."

Olivia glanced at him, her heart swelling at his use of the word *we*. He, unaware of the love and pride swelling in her heart for him, squeezed her hand.

"An excellent idea." Mr. Still rubbed his hands together. "We will send word around to ask. I will start asking the fugitives coming in about Logan. Maybe the connection to all this is him."

"There is something else I was planning to relay before. . ." Olivia shook her head and forced herself to continue. "I have a strange new customer." She told them about Mrs. Johnson and her trip to the Shipper's Inn and Mr. Abrams's information about her.

Mr. Wilson let out a huff. "We will have to be extra careful."

Mr. Still stood. "I will ask Mr. Abrams if he recognizes any of the men visiting Mrs. Johnson. I find it interesting that all these unknown people have shown up in the area now."

"Me too," Olivia said. They had seen something like this before. Slave catchers flooding the city. It normally happened in late October and November because that was the most favorable conditions for a fugitive to run. And where the fugitives went, the slave catchers followed.

Mr. Still walked over to Olivia and placed his hand on Hope's head. "She is so peaceful. It is a hard thing for a child to be in the world without a mother."

Olivia sniffled. "Yes, but she will be well cared for here."

Mr. Still smiled at her. "I am sure."

They left quietly, and Olivia carried Hope upstairs to their bedroom while Douglas extinguished the lamps. She sat on the edge of the bed, holding the sleeping child to her chest. Another flood of tears coursed down her cheeks. How could her heart break for someone she barely knew? How could it hurt this bad? She had never tried to fool herself that she should avoid all feeling for the fugitives. Their pain and their stories became a part of her story the minute they came into her house.

Hope was different. She was a child alone in the world. No known family. Beulah told Mr. Still that she did not have any more family than Hope. If she did, Olivia would move heaven and earth to reunite them. But this baby had no one but her and Douglas.

Douglas came into the room and paused at the door, staring at her. Then he came to sit next to her. "This is heartbreaking."

"I wish I could have done more." The tears were falling freely now. "Protected her better."

"You could not do anything about what you were unaware of."

"Hope now has no family."

"No," Douglas said quietly. "But she has us."

⁂

If Olivia didn't know the baby was too young, she would have sworn that Hope knew about what was happening in the wider world. She seemed to know her mother was gone. In the days following Beulah's death, Hope clung to Olivia and Douglas, crying for the first time when she awakened in her basket bed but didn't see either of them. Olivia soothed the girl, singing a soft lullaby, until she stopped crying. But she ended up having to hold her for the rest of the day.

Since she was running out of time to finish Mrs. Johnson's dresses, Olivia employed Milly to come and sit with Hope more often. Milly happily agreed. The two of them had grown attached to each other. Olivia would watch them together, her heart breaking in advance for the day when all of them would have to say goodbye to Hope. She had had no word from Mr. Still that one of the orphanages had a bed for Hope. Olivia began to count every day as a stolen blessing.

Sitting at her table, Olivia trained her attention on the dress in front of her. The fifth one Mrs. Johnson had ordered. It was almost done. She also turned her attention to the woman herself. Mr. Abrams had continued to watch her, but nothing had changed. Mrs. Johnson still came and went at the Shipper's Inn as before. She also still continued to meet with different men in the inn's parlor. Solving that mystery would have to wait.

The front door opened and Franklin came in. "Hi, Miss 'Livia." He went over to the babe, took a piece of sweet bread from a napkin in his pocket, and gave it to her.

Olivia fought back a laugh and tried to sound stern. "You have to stop bringing her treats."

Franklin grinned. "But she likes them."

"She is going to expect sweet bread every time she sees you."

"That's okay. I always keep a piece in my pocket." He patted his pocket and then seemed to remember why he had come. "I have a note for you."

He pulled it from his pocket, and Olivia took it. She immediately recognized Mr. Still's handwriting.

> *I know what we agreed, but we have a party of friends just arriving in the area.*
>
> *They will only need one night's accommodations. We will be dividing the party between several houses. There will only be two, brothers, coming to your house. If this is acceptable, they shall arrive at your door after sundown with Mr. Wilson.*
>
> *Please send word back by our young messenger.*
>
> *W. Still*

She folded the letter and put it in her pocket. "Tell him this is acceptable." They had agreed that Olivia would resume taking fugitives after something was decided with Hope, but with Douglas involved, she could do it sooner. Her heart warmed. He would help. At least with this part. After Hope was settled, she would have to find a way to return to her previous level of secrecy.

But she did not want to.

"Bye-bye, baby," Franklin cooed at Hope. Olivia laughed.

But when Franklin started toward the door, he pulled up short.

Milly shot him a quizzical glance. "What's wrong with you?" she asked in a tone that only a big sister could.

"That man's been followin' me." Franklin took a step back away from the window.

Olivia crossed the room and looked out the window. "What man?"

Franklin pointed. "That one."

Olivia looked out the window and saw Saunders standing across the street. It was not unusual to have patrols around, but seeing Saunders so often sent alarm bells ringing in her mind.

"Stay here for a minute. If he continues to watch the house, you can go out the back door," Olivia said. "But you need to let Mr. Still know that he followed you."

The boy nodded. "He followed me straight from Shipper's."

Olivia glanced down at him. "You were at Shipper's this morning?"

"Delivering the bread like always," Franklin said. "That man was standing outside, watching everyone walking up and down the street. Like he was guarding the place."

Olivia gave Franklin a smile, not wanting to alarm him. "Do you have any other pressing deliveries?"

"No," he said. "Just going back to Mr. Still with your answer to his message."

They waited a quarter of an hour, and when they checked again, Saunders was gone. Olivia hustled Franklin out the door and told him to get to Mr. Still's house as fast as he could. She and Milly spent the rest of the day jittery, jumping every time the door opened.

When Douglas came in, Olivia sighed with relief and gave him a hug. "I am so glad you are home."

He froze. "Is all well?" She released him quickly. Surely he thought her affection would be strange after her being reserved for so long. He studied her for a moment then looked past her to where Hope and Milly were sitting on the floor.

"I am not certain, but I was wondering if you could escort Milly home. Saunders followed her brother here," Olivia said. "We will have dinner when you get back."

Douglas nodded and helped Milly with her coat, and then Olivia locked the door behind them. A sense of dread continued to grow in her mind, and she was nearly shaking by the time Douglas got back.

He came in wearing a frown. "She made it home safely. Mr. Wilson told me Saunders was in his grocery this afternoon."

Olivia sat down next to Hope, her emotions sinking. "Saunders must have figured something out."

"Mr. Wilson thinks that as well. But how?"

"He watches Mr. Still's house all the time. Maybe he put the pieces together by seeing how often Franklin and I go in and out of Mr. Still's house."

Douglas sat down in the seat next to Olivia and placed his hand on hers. "Obviously, he does not know too much, or he would have arrested you by now."

"If he keeps watching, he will figure something out." She glanced over at Hope who was feeding herself fistfuls of potatoes. She moved to divide the food into smaller bites. "Mr. Still sent me a note today. He wants to know if I can. . ." She paused. "If I can work tonight."

Douglas nodded. "Olivia—"

"I promise I will be careful."

"I know you will."

"It will be well after Hope falls asleep, so you can go to bed as usual." She turned her attention to her plate.

"Nothing is as usual now." He said the words with so much conviction, Olivia looked up.

"No, it is not."

They finished their dinner, and Douglas played a bit with Hope. But Hope, who must have been tuckered out from all the excitement of the day, was soon nodding off. Douglas carried her upstairs, and Olivia got her little bed ready.

As he lowered her to the bed, Douglas asked, "Do you think we should get a crib?"

Olivia watched Hope adjust in the little basket and drift back to sleep. "Is that wise, since we do not know how long Hope will be with us? Mr. Still is checking with Mrs. Brasewell for a spot at her children's home." The thought of sending Hope away soured her stomach. Maybe she would tell Mr. Still that Hope could stay longer—maybe forever. She shook the thought away. Hope was not theirs.

"She will soon be too big for the basket. Besides, we will eventually need a crib for our own children."

The words seared Olivia's heart. "If we ever have children."

Douglas stopped and pulled her into his arms. "God will bless us somehow."

She fought back tears. Douglas was right. God had already blessed them with Hope. Why not more?

After one more check on Hope to make sure she was sound asleep, Olivia returned downstairs.

As she was removing the panel, Douglas came down. He had changed into the clothes he used to work in their summer garden. "What do we need to do?"

Olivia gaped at him. "I—uh—"

"Olivia," he said. "I am going to help you. What do we need to do?"

"There is no need. I can handle it myself."

"I know you do not need me, but I want to help." Douglas took a step forward.

"But if you know what I am doing, how will I keep you safe?" Her words came out as a strangled plea.

"A slave catcher has been in my house without my knowledge. How safe am I?"

She looked down at her shoes, unable to argue against his point. Danger had come close to him, and if Saunders was watching the house, what would stop him from following Douglas to his work? Olivia fought to keep Douglas from knowing what she was doing, but Saunders was unaware of that.

"Very well," she said. She listed all the items they would need.

Douglas gave her a smile and went to work. He carried the basket, and Olivia went before him with a lamp. They sat on the little cot, waiting for Mr. Wilson to knock on the door.

Douglas exhaled. "I have never been down here this long. It must get dark with no lamp."

Olivia shifted to face him. "It does, but I try and make it as comfortable as possible."

"I am certain you do, but it is hard to imagine what the fugitives go through to get here. And then to come to this dark room."

Olivia swallowed. She knew. Miles and miles of walking. Pain. Hunger. Cold and heat. "But when they get here, they are free for the first time in their lives."

Douglas nodded. "Tomorrow, we need to talk."

"About?" She rubbed her arms to hide the tension in her shoulders.

"Us. And this."

She looked at him. The faint lamplight cast flickering shadows over his face and made it difficult to read his expression.

The clock upstairs chimed ten, its tones floating down the stairs like mist. Olivia froze. "Something is not right. They should have been here by now."

Douglas stood. "Maybe we should go look for them."

Olivia shook her head. "That is not how it works. They come to me. I wouldn't even know where to begin looking."

Just then, they heard a noise. Not a knock on the door, but something clattering against it. Neither of them spoke, taking quiet breaths. After a moment, the sound came again. Olivia's eyes widened and her blood chilled as she recognized the sound.

Mr. Wilson—or someone—was throwing pebbles at the door.

She turned to Douglas. "That is the signal Mr. Wilson is to use when it is not safe for them to come in. We need to go up and extinguish the lights as if we are going to bed. To show we know they are not coming tonight."

Douglas grabbed the basket, and as fast as they could, they extinguished the lamps in the house. When they got to their bedroom, Olivia turned off the lamp and the room went dark. As her eyes were adjusting, she heard Douglas say, "Olivia, come look at this."

She navigated the dark room to the window and peered out.

Saunders stood across the street, watching the house.

CHAPTER TWENTY-THREE

GRACIE

Ada had to remind Gracie that the girls would arrive for class soon. Her thoughts were still tangled on her shameful behavior at the library. How she could break down like that? Her mother had been dead for more than thirty years, and Gracie had never met her. Such an extreme reaction. But then, was it? Gran had told her about her mother. Occasionally, Gran would say, "You sound so much like your mother." Gran made sure Gracie felt connected to her mother. Now that Gran was gone, the connection was gone.

Clarence had called or texted every day since. One text in particular stuck in her mind.

GRACIE, I CARE A LOT FOR YOU, AND I HOPE YOU KNOW I WOULD DO ANYTHING TO EASE YOUR PAIN.

His words had made her cry more, and then she scolded herself for crying so much. Just like the situation with Mia, she should have known that researching her family was going to be hard. Why hadn't she factored in the pain of seeing the names in black lettering on the screen? Instead, she thought she would just breeze through it. Now her heart was hurting, and she couldn't stop it.

Four of the girls arrived almost at the same time and went straight back to the table and started working. When Mia arrived, she was much more subdued than usual. She greeted Gracie readily enough but didn't really talk during the class, even when Gracie tried to draw her out. She would give the shortest answer possible and turn her attention back to her knitting.

The other students noticed too. Dani, who had kept to herself since the class began, tried to strike up a conversation with her. Mia responded, but again, with none of her normal enthusiasm. Mia even stood at the back of the group when Gracie called them around her to demonstrate the next technique they were learning—how to join a new ball of yarn when the old one ran out.

Gracie helped Trinity get back on track. She had forgotten to bring the yarn to the front of her knitting in order to work the purl stitch. When Gracie looked up, Mia wasn't knitting. She was just staring at the wall. Gracie moved around the table and touched her work. "Looks like you'll be ready to cast off next week."

"That's if my dad lets me come," Mia said in a low voice.

"Why wouldn't he let you come?"

"'Cause he still thinks—" She stared across the table. When Gracie turned to see what Mia was looking at, she saw Bella staring back at them, hanging on every word.

Gracie straightened. "Do you need help, Bella?"

Bella looked down at her knitting. "I'm cool."

Gracie turned back to Mia. "What's up between you and her?"

"Not much to tell. She's mad that I got picked for a special leadership program at school and she didn't."

"Congratulations." Gracie gave Mia a sympathetic look. "But sometimes people don't know how to deal with their hurt and embarrassment."

"Yeah, they do," Dani said, not looking up from her knitting. "They take it out on other people."

Gracie looked over at Bella, who was making sure she wasn't going to get caught eavesdropping again and was having a very loud conversation with Trinity and Rylee.

How many times had she been bullied by girls like Bella? Girls who needed very little to start a campaign against her. Back then, she wasn't strong enough to do anything. But now she had the power to prevent Bella from bullying Mia and Dani, at least while they were here.

And Bella tried. She made a comment about Dani knitting too slow. Gracie gently rebuked her, but not five minutes later she took a swipe at Mia about getting in trouble at school again.

"She had her locker searched yesterday. You should watch her, Ms. Gracie," Bella said, her tone soft and full of fake concern.

Gracie sat up. "Bella, you have been repeatedly warned about violating the class kindness policy. I will be calling your mother later today."

Bella's eyes grew wide. "I was just telling you what happened."

"After I've repeatedly told you that it's not your place to do so," Gracie said. "I will speak to your mother and decide if you can come back."

"But you let Mia stay after she stole the bag!" Bella said.

The room grew quiet, and Gracie fought to keep her expression neutral. This girl needed a job as an investigator. How did she even know about that? But Gracie decided to turn the tables on Bella. "What bag?" she asked in an extra sweet tone.

"The red one," Bella said. "The one she asked you for. She stole it."

"I did not!" Mia screamed.

Gracie held up a hand. "And how do you know she stole it?"

Bella's mouth snapped shut. Not a question she probably anticipated.

"Yeah, Bella. Tell us how you know." Mia egged her on but piped down when Gracie shot her a *let me handle it* look.

"Because she asked for it but you told her no. So she stole it. She's probably using the little bag inside for all her stolen earrings. That's if she could figure out how to open it," Bella said, triumphantly.

"I'm still going to speak to your mother, and I'm also going to tell her that you are making serious accusations against Mia," Gracie said as the doorbell rang. "That's probably her now."

Bella tried to protest, but Gracie ignored her pleas. It wasn't, however, Bella's mom but Mia's dad. "How did Mia behave today?" he asked.

"Not like herself."

"Then I'll pull her out of the class."

"That's not necessary. When I say she wasn't herself, I mean she was withdrawn and quiet."

"I told her she'd better behave or she couldn't come back."

"But Mia hasn't misbehaved at all. She is energetic, yes, but not bad." Gracie sighed. "I don't want to tell you how to raise your daughter, but I started this class because I was always in trouble as a kid and someone started a knitting class at my school. I was struggling with learning to live without a mother."

He looked down at his shoes. "Mia told me about that."

"Maybe Mia's troubles are just her trying to figure out to live without hers," Gracie said. "She mentioned your divorce."

Stanley took a deep breath. "It's been very difficult."

"Then maybe give Mia some grace. She's struggling just like you are." Gracie gave him an encouraging smile and wondered if anyone had given her father that talk. Then she realized that someone had. Gran.

Gracie called for Mia, and she crossed the front room with her shoulders slumped. "Thank you for taking up for me today. People usually don't," she said to Gracie as she walked out the door.

"You're welcome."

Dani's mother arrived next, and a few minutes later Trinity's mother picked up the other three girls. As they were walking out the door, Bella stopped and looked up at Gracie, something like remorse in her eyes. "Are you still going to call my mom?"

"Yes, I am. Unfortunately."

Bella huffed and stomped out the door.

Gracie closed the door and leaned against it. Ada came downstairs. "Class that bad, huh?"

"Bella is a handful and, apparently, a bully."

Ada shook her head. "I'm always amazed how mean children can be to one another."

"You know she accused Mia of stealing the Cojo bag. Said she was probably using the little bag inside for—" Gracie covered her mouth.

"What?" Ada said.

"Bella said that Mia was probably using the little bag inside for her stolen earrings," Gracie said. "But how did Bella know there was a little bag inside? It was just that. Inside."

Ada's eyes widened. "Bella took the bag?"

"She also said something about figuring out how to open the bag."

"I'm a grown woman, and those Cojo bags are still hard for me sometimes. Took three times to figure out how the snaps were supposed to close," Ada said. "We both saw that bag day in and day out. It never moved or looked like it had been tampered with."

Gracie rubbed her face. "But how do I find out for sure?"

An idea came to her mind. It was clever, but Gracie couldn't be happy about it. It hurt her as much to know that Bella could have stolen the bag as it did when she thought Mia had.

The day dawned cold and gray. Much like Gracie's mood. It had been gray for days, looking like it would snow at any minute. The sun had withdrawn, and it fit her feelings perfectly.

Gracie hated to admit it, but she was dreading Clarence's phone calls.

Not because she didn't want to talk to him. She did, if to do nothing more than explain her behavior at the library. But she was also afraid that he would ask her when she would be ready to go back to the library. Could she ever be ready to face that pain? To see her family members' names listed when they were no longer here for her to know and love?

With a sigh, she dragged herself out of bed, the cold floor a jolt. Probably needed to turn up the thermostat. After having some breakfast, she padded downstairs. As she did, her thoughts went to her mother. How many times had her mother walked these steps? Or Gran and Paw-Paw? Or her great-grandparents? Did they think of the people who would walk these steps after them? Family like her and Ada?

Or did they think of who had already walked these stairs, back to the people who first owned the house? Did those first owners, possibly stationmasters, think about who would follow in their footsteps?

Ada came out of the office as Gracie reached the bottom of the stairs. "Good morning," she said quietly.

Gracie hadn't told Ada what had happened at the library. Thankfully, Ada was out when Clarence had brought her back home.

"Gracie, did something happen?"

Gracie looked around at the shop. All looked in place. "Why?"

"You haven't been yourself the past couple of days. Did you and Clarence break up?" Ada touched Gracie's arm.

"No, we didn't."

"It's just that I noticed you've been having really short conversations with him and, if I'm not mistaken, avoiding his calls."

Gracie dropped her head. "I got a little overwhelmed on our last research trip. Just thinking some things through."

"Okay," Ada said with a sigh of relief.

There was a loud knock on the door.

"I'll get it," Gracie said, glad to get out of the conversation.

Ada groaned behind her. "I hope that's not my father. He called me this morning, wanting to talk about what you're doing with the house."

"I'm sorry," was all Gracie had time to say before her phone rang.

Ada went back to the office and lifted the phone from the table. "It's Clarence," she called.

"Answer it and tell him I'm coming."

But when she opened the door, her heart dropped. Two officers stood on the front step. "Are you Gracie McNeil?"

Speechless, she nodded.

"We have an eviction notice. You are to leave the premises immediately," the officer closest to her said.

"What? No." Gracie stepped back.

"Ma'am, please don't make this more difficult than it needs to be. We have a court-issued warrant to remove you and your guest from the house."

She was vaguely aware of Ada's frantic conversation with Clarence. Then she remembered something. "Can I see the warrant? You can't expect me to just leave without some proof."

The officer huffed and pulled it from his pocket. "It's official, I assure you."

She opened the paper, trying to keep her hands steady. It was almost useless to ask for it. The words swam in front of her as she tried to calm herself. What she was seeing looked official. Hot tears filled her eyes. After all this. Fighting with Uncle Rand. Finding the room. The taxes. All the research, and she was about to lose the house.

Before she could reach the bottom of the sheet, she saw Clarence running up the street. He had his phone pressed to his ear.

He rushed up the stairs nearly breathless. "Let me see the warrant," he said between breaths.

It took a second for Gracie to realize he must have been already on his way and that Ada must have told him about it.

He shook his head as he studied the sheet. "Officers, you know you can't do this."

"The warrant is official," the taller officer said.

"It may be," Clarence said, "but there wasn't a court date for Ms. McNeil to hear from the party who filed the claim against her."

The officer folded his arms. "My job is to remove Ms. McNeil from the premises."

"But she has ten days to vacate. And as I said, Ms. McNeil has gotten no notification that she is being evicted. She stays until this is sorted out." Clarence didn't budge.

The shorter officer addressed Gracie. "Is this true, Ms. McNeil?"

"Yes. I don't know who is evicting me. I have paperwork. I can prove that I own this house outright and that it was paid for many years ago."

"Can you show us that paperwork, please, ma'am?"

Gracie let them inside. Clarence stood right beside her, shoulders back and spine straight.

"Let me get it." Gracie's knees felt like mush as she walked up the stairs. She got her ID and grabbed the folder of Gran's paperwork.

The officers went through her paperwork, although she was sure they hardly knew what they were looking at.

The taller officer glanced up at her. "We were sent here to evict you but. . ." He looked at all three of them, and Gracie held her breath. "But we thought there was something weird about it."

"Weird, how?" Ada asked.

The officer took the warrant back from Gracie. "This is incomplete."

Clarence nodded. "I noticed that too. I was going to point it out to you if you tried to remove her from the house."

"We asked our chief if this was valid, and he said the rest of the paperwork was on its way over but we were to come here now."

Gracie tipped her head. "Is that normal procedure?"

The officer frowned. "No. The warrant needs to be complete, or the department could get sued."

"You will get sued," Ada huffed.

The officer looked guilty. "And we should if this isn't valid. I don't think it is. I've been on the force for a long time, and I've never seen an eviction done with an incomplete warrant."

Gracie's heart thumped, but a question came to her mind. "What would you suggest I do?"

"If you truly don't know who filed the court paperwork, get a lawyer and find out," the shorter officer said. "The lawyer should be able to buy you some time."

"But if it is valid?" Gracie asked, forcing out the words.

"Then you have to leave," the officer said grimly.

Gracie closed her eyes, her heart aching. *If it is. . .*

The taller officer gave her a card. "If you need us to testify on your behalf, we can. We've seen all your documents."

Gracie took the card and was only able to mumble, "Thank you."

She stood frozen as Ada and Clarence showed the officers out. She studied the warrant again. After a few seconds, her vision had blurred the words. She was going to lose this house. Uncle Rand was right. She was careless. So careless that she had gotten to the place of eviction not even two months after moving in. She should have been more diligent. She should have. . . She didn't even know what she should have done.

Clarence and Ada returned with compassion and worry on their faces.

Clarence slipped his arm around Gracie. "It's going to be all right."

She looked up at him. "How do you know that?"

"Gracie, you heard what the officers said. The warrant is incomplete," Ada said, her voice soft.

"But that doesn't mean it's invalid," Gracie whimpered. "People can't just go around issuing fake eviction notices."

"I have a lawyer friend you can talk to," Clarence said. He looked down at his watch. "The courts are closed for the day, so we'll go see her tomorrow and check the court records."

"Are you sure you didn't get something in the mail?" Ada asked.

Gracie shook her head. "You saw all the mail we got. It was only the rezoning letter, the tax receipt, and. . ." Her words dropped off.

"And?" Clarence asked, hope in his voice.

"And that weird certified letter from the investment loan company," Gracie said, frowning. "They said I had an account but not what kind or what the balance was."

"Can I see the letter?" Clarence asked.

"It's in my office,"

"I'll get it," Ada said.

Ada returned and handed Clarence the letter. She eyed him. "Why do you know so much about this process?"

Clarence continued reading. "My first job when I came back here was in the property center. I've processed enough evictions to know how this is supposed to go."

Gracie watched him read. "Well?"

He rubbed his chin. "This name looks familiar, but I can't place why. I need to look in my records to see where I've heard this company name before. I'll go back to the office and look now."

"You don't have to do this right now, especially since we're going to see the lawyer tomorrow."

"I know, but I want to." He gave her a kiss on the cheek. "I don't think I can bear seeing you in any more pain."

"Thank you," she said softly.

She walked him to the door and then watched until he was out of sight. As she stood there, the cold air pouring in the door added to the chill forming in her bones. The reality was that she had failed to live up to her promise to Gran.

Ada came to her side and put an arm around her. "It's going to be okay."

Gracie let out a heavy sigh. "I wish I was as hopeful as you."

"You should be. I can't imagine this being legit. There has to be some other explanation."

"We only have ten days to figure it out," Gracie said, closing the door.

"Clarence is going to help, and I'm here. We could even ask my father and Natalia to help."

Gracie grimaced. "Natalia, yes, but I don't think Uncle Rand would help. You saw how reluctant he was about letting me use the estate money for the taxes."

Ada grasped Gracie's shoulders. "He would help. He may not be happy about you owning the house, but he would fight to make sure you didn't lose it just to keep it in the family."

"Again, I wish I was as hopeful as you are."

"He's not all bad. He has his moments, but I think if you're going to have to fight for the house, it would be a good time for him to prove he's on your side."

Gracie moved away from Ada, unable to respond. Uncle Rand wasn't going to help, and this was her problem. "I'm going up to my room."

"It's going to be okay," Ada called up the stairs behind her.

CHAPTER TWENTY-FOUR

OLIVIA

The day dawned cold and dreary, a gray rain tapping on the windows. Olivia sighed, the weight of the night before still heavy on her. Mr. Wilson and the two brothers had never arrived. She had gone to bed with Douglas, but neither of them slept much, both stirring at every little sound. She had told Douglas that it was not so unusual for plans to change because of some unforeseen circumstance. She said it not only to comfort him but also herself as well.

She rose, prepared breakfast, and tried to focus on sewing until Douglas carried Hope downstairs. He gave her a tired smile. "No word?"

She shook her head. "I was considering going to the Wilson house to see if I could learn something."

They ate in silence. Olivia watched Hope, who seemed to sense that something was amiss and was less animated. There was so much uncertainty about her future. And danger.

Douglas rose and was collecting the dishes when there was a knock on the back door. They both jumped.

He set down the dishes. "I'll get it."

Olivia picked up Hope and waited a tense moment while Douglas checked the back door. She sighed with relief when she heard Mr. Wilson's voice. But all her relief drained away when Mr. Wilson stepped out of the kitchen into the dining room. He looked haggard, and there was a large cut on his forehead, an angry red line above his eyebrows.

Douglas led him to a chair. "Sit down. Let me get my kit."

"What happened?" Olivia asked, placing Hope on the floor to play. She went to the kitchen and brought him a cup of tea.

"We got ambushed last night." His voice was hoarse, and he took the cup with both hands. "Slave catchers. We stayed out all night trying to avoid them, but they caught up to us a few blocks away."

"Where are your passengers?"

"One got away, I think. The other was captured."

Douglas returned and began cleaning Mr. Wilson's wound as the man recounted how his night went. "We left the docks after dark. It took a little time because the brothers were so weak and tired that we had to stop by Shipper's to get them some refreshment and warmer clothes." He took another drink of tea. "We waited a bit in the kitchen until they got warm and then headed here."

"Were you followed?" Douglas asked, pausing in his ministrations.

"Not that I saw. We were a block from here when three slave catchers came out of a side street. I told the brothers to run back to Shipper's while I tried to hold off the catchers. That's when one of the men hit me. I saw them take one of the brothers, and the other disappeared into the night."

Olivia sat down. "Did you see where the men took the passenger?"

"No," Mr. Wilson said. "Head was ringing like a bell. After I threw the pebbles at your door, I hid in the trees across the street. Didn't want the catchers to come to your house."

Olivia sighed. This was getting more and more complicated. "Have you been home?"

"No. I know Thea is probably worried to the end of her nerves," he said. "And there was something else unusual. I saw Henry down at the docks."

Douglas shot her a quizzical look. "Who is Henry?"

"He is a member of the Friends of Bella Vista. He works at the docks, but it is unusual that he would still be there late at night."

"I saw him, but it was like he didn't want me to see him."

Olivia glanced over at Hope, who was chewing on the end of her blanket. "Funny, I saw Henry in an odd place too. The other day. I saw him at Shipper's."

"Did he see you?" Mr. Wilson asked.

"Not that I know of." She rubbed her forehead. What did Henry have to do with this? She had no doubt something was amiss. Henry had been acting strange since their last meeting. As much as she hoped for the best, it was too much of a coincidence that he was at the docks last night. The same place Walker said he had met this Logan person.

"The cut is already starting to close, but with a blow to the head, you may be dizzy for a few days," Douglas said.

"You rest, and I will go around to your house," Olivia said, rising.

Douglas frowned. "Are you sure it will be safe?"

"I believe so. There are too many people on the streets for them to accost me. Besides, our slave catchers and Logan seem to like to work at night."

In a matter of minutes, she was out in the dreary weather. She pulled her collar up and rushed in the direction of the Wilson home. As she did, she saw one of the maids at Shipper's, Molly, rushing toward her. When they made eye contact, the girl waved.

Olivia changed directions and went back to her. "Mornin', Molly."

The girl was not wearing her normal cheerful look. "Mornin'. Mista Abrams sent me to your house to give you this."

Olivia took the note but, because of the mist, tucked it inside her coat. "Thank you, Molly. Now get out of this weather."

"Yes, ma'am." She trotted back up the street.

Although Olivia knew the note was important, letting Thea know that her husband was well held a higher priority. Thea's face proved how important it was when she opened the door. The woman's expression went from disappointment to hope to fear when she saw Olivia.

"Come inside." She pulled Olivia through the door. Franklin and Milly stood by the sofa, worried looks on their faces.

"Your husband is at my house," Olivia told her once she was inside.

Thea's shoulders sagged with relief. "Is he well?"

Olivia put her arm around her friend. "He was hit on the head, but

Douglas says it will be all right."

Thea sat on her sofa and rubbed her face. "What happened?"

Olivia relayed what Mr. Wilson had told her. When she mentioned Shipper's, she remembered the note in her pocket. "I have a note from Mr. Abrams." She unfolded the paper and read it.

Miss Olivia,

One of Mr. Wilson's passengers arrived here last night shortly after he left. I will take him to Mr. Still's if you cannot accommodate him. He says that Mr. Wilson was injured and that his brother has been captured. If the brother arrives at your house, let him know that John is safe here.

Also, Saunders visited the inn last night while I was out. Molly told me he was here for a short time and she thought he talked to someone here, but she didn't see who. I believe it was Mrs. Johnson, since Molly says she went out shortly after Saunders left.

Please take care,
M. Abrams

Olivia folded the note with trembling fingers. Saunders talking to Mrs. Johnson. How were they connected? Mr. Abrams did not recognize the men she was meeting with. They could be slave catchers, or they could be friends or relatives. But it was too much of a coincidence for Saunders to be at Shipper's after watching both her house and Mr. Still's house.

And they needed to find John's brother as quickly as possible before he was returned to the South.

❧

Olivia left Douglas with Hope at home and walked down the street to Mr. Still's house. It was a rare night. The Friends of Bella Vista normally did not gather under the same roof outside of their meetings. Tonight was different. Granted, it was under the cover of a Vigilance

Committee meeting, but many of the Friends would be in attendance.

Olivia went inside, and Mrs. Still greeted her. "William is with the Vigilance Committee in the dining room. Everyone else is upstairs in William's office."

Olivia thanked her and went up the stairs. Crowded in the office were the Wilsons, Mr. Abrams, and Mr. Gull. She moved straight to Mr. Wilson. "How are you?"

"On the mend, thanks to your husband." He touched the bandage. "Not so much dizziness now."

Thea linked her arm through his. "You need your head to be as clear as possible."

"We all do." Mr. Gull said.

They made small talk until Mr. Still's daughter, Caroline, came to the door. "Daddy said you can come down now."

They went down. Mr. Still was standing next to his dining room table, looking at a paper. "Friends, please take some refreshment if you like."

No one did. It seemed everyone else was as eager as she was to start the meeting. They needed a plan, quick.

Mr. Still sat. "I have made Mr. Gull aware of what has been happening here. Is there any new news?"

Mr. Abrams spoke up. "Not new, but John is doing well. He is very anxious to find his brother though."

"And I think that is the first order of business," Mr. Wilson said. Olivia couldn't be sure, but it appeared the man's shoulders were weighted with guilt.

"Has anyone checked the jail? Maybe they are holding him there until they take him back south," Olivia suggested, thinking of Beulah.

Mr. Still shook his head. "I have had someone watching the jail. No new prisoners were brought in for the night."

"I'm traveling south in a few days. Maybe I can make inquiries at the plantation they ran from," Mr. Gull said. This was a service he had provided many times for the group since, as a white man, he had the freedom to travel.

"That's a good idea," Olivia said. "I also think someone needs to keep an eye on Mrs. Johnson." She told them how strangely Mrs. Johnson had been acting at her house. Asking strange questions. "The night Mr. Wilson was attacked, Douglas and I saw Saunders outside our house."

Mr. Abrams frowned. "Then he showed up at Shipper's and, according to Molly, spoke with Mrs. Johnson."

The room grew quiet.

"There is one more unpleasant item I need to mention." Olivia took in a deep breath. "Henry has been acting strangely lately. He was at the Wilsons' store when Walker arrived. Then I saw him at Shipper's in the middle of the day when he should have been working."

"And I saw him at the docks the night I was attacked," Mr. Wilson said.

Mr. Still shook his head. "Very strange. He came to see me just yesterday, asking if I'd gotten word about his family. He left a wife and a daughter in Maryland when he ran. He has been looking for a way to get them free."

"I had no idea," Thea said. "Can we help him?"

Mr. Still shook his head. "His old master is asking for two thousand dollars to free his family. Henry has some money saved, but not that much. Unfortunately, the committee cannot provide that amount. He seemed quite desperate."

"How are Saunders, Mrs. Johnson, and Henry all connected?" Mr. Gull asked.

"Mrs. Johnson is having several dresses made by me," Olivia said, and the attention in the room turned to her. "I tried once following her to Shipper's, but maybe we can get someone to watch Shipper's to see who is visiting her."

Mr. Gull rubbed his beard. "When did you tell her the dresses would be ready?"

"In a few days," Olivia said.

"But why follow her if she's just going to go back to Shipper's?"

Mr. Abrams asked.

Olivia's thoughts pulled at all the threads of this story. "If she is involved in these disappearing passengers, she has to be holding them somewhere. Her appointment to pick up her dresses will be the perfect time for us to start following her."

Mr. Still nodded. "Very true. But since Mrs. Kingston has other responsibilities right now, someone else will have to follow Mrs. Johnson. And it has to be someone she has never seen before."

"I will do it," Thea said. "I will stop by Mrs. Kingston's house every morning until Mrs. Johnson comes and help with the baby instead of Milly. Milly can take my place at the store."

Olivia shook her head. "I think I should follow her. I already have a rapport with her, and I have the best chance of coming up with an excuse for following her."

"You already do too much," Thea said, placing a hand on Olivia's arm. "And you have Hope to think about until we get this mess sorted."

"We all have to think of our families," Olivia said with a surprise flash of anger at her friend. Mrs. Johnson had come to her house, and Beulah was gone possibly because of Mrs. Johnson. Beulah, who had been in Olivia's care. "But I believe it would be better if I do it."

"I agree with Mrs. Wilson. It will be difficult for Mrs. Kingston to follow without being seen. Mrs. Wilson has a better reason as the neighborhood grocer," Mr. Still said. "But please be careful. All of you."

They adjourned the meeting. Thea moved to Olivia's side. "I know you are angry with me."

"Mr. Still believes it is best if you go—"

Thea put her hand on Olivia's shoulder. "You are not responsible for everything, Olivia."

Olivia folded her arms across her chest. "I know."

"Do you?" Thea asked, tipping her head. "You head the committee, sew dresses, and house fugitives, all while being a wife and now caring for a child. You can let others help you."

Olivia's mind flashed to Douglas. His insistence in helping her.

Help she nearly refused.

"Well, I guess I will have to let you do it this time."

Thea studied her, then gave her a hug.

When they separated, Olivia was surprised at the tears forming in her friend's eyes. "What was that for?"

"Because you are very stressed and you needed it."

As the Friends began to depart, Mr. Gull offered to walk Olivia back to her house before he returned to his room at Shipper's. He normally lodged there when he was in town for more than one day. They chatted about a dress he was considering having Olivia make for his wife. Olivia only half listened. Her mind was still on the meeting. She could have handled following Mrs. Johnson.

Once at her front door, Mr. Gull turned back toward Shipper's. Olivia took one last look around before putting her key in the lock. As she did, she saw Mr. Gull turn the corner and then a figure slip from the darkness of the woods and follow him. She dropped her key into her pocket and rushed down the street. She should go inside and get Douglas, but he would only tell her to stay inside or go get Mr. Still. Whoever this was would be long gone by then. Besides, she only needed a glimpse of the person following Mr. Gull.

She reached the corner, but realization stopped her cold.

It was Henry. He was slinking along in the shadows. She started to call out to him when a hand closed over her mouth and an arm locked around her waist.

The shock stunned her, but then she began to thrash with all her might, fear fueling her strength. The hand was clamped so hard that she could only make muffled sounds, but she continued to fight. The man holding her grunted, "Hold still, or I'll hurt you."

Despite the threat, she continued to struggle. She had to get away. The man dragged her up the street toward where Mr. Gull had gone. She let all her weight hang on the man and kept struggling. By the time they reached the next street, the man was panting heavily. Another man appeared from around the corner. "I took care of the two up there," he said, motioning in the direction Mr. Gull had gone.

"I think this one will fetch a nice price," the man behind her said.

"Too spirited," the man in front of her said. He reached into his coat and produced a gun.

Olivia froze.

The man grinned. "That's better."

Then he hit her and the world went black.

CHAPTER TWENTY-FIVE

*E*xhausted, Gracie went to her room without dinner. She couldn't eat if she'd wanted to.

Ada had invited Gracie out, promising her that food would make her feel better. Gracie hadn't responded because Ada going out to dinner would give her what she really wanted: to be alone. She was so tired. Tired of crying and worrying. But most of all, tired of fighting. Her life was a wreck, and she needed to accept that. It would always be filled with trouble and pain. Pain she wanted to stop but had no way to do so.

She trudged up the stairs to her room, closed the door, and collapsed into bed, too tired to even cry.

Gran had gone to great lengths to make sure Gracie got the house. She had to know that it would put Gracie at odds with Uncle Rand, but she did it anyway. Gran had put all her hope and expectations in Gracie. She shouldn't have. Why didn't Gran see that Gracie couldn't pull this off? It was so obvious. Gracie's life had been disaster after disaster. She had almost believed that inheriting this house would change the dark trajectory of her life.

It hadn't. It had only accelerated her failure.

She rolled over and groaned. How could she ever live with herself, knowing that Gran's house was gone from the family?

She thought of Ada, Ms. Lila, and Clarence, the people dearest to her now. They were so supportive. So helpful. Had they all wasted their time on her? Their opinion of her would certainly have to change if she lost the house.

The doorbell ringing interrupted her thoughts. Ada must have an armful of food and couldn't get the door open.

Gracie dragged herself back down the stairs to the front door. When she opened it, Uncle Rand, not Ada, stood on the steps.

"Not tonight, Uncle Rand," she said, not caring how sharp her words were. If there was anyone she was not going to have a break-down in front of, it was Uncle Rand. Because in breaking down, she would prove to him what he'd always believed. She didn't deserve the house or Gran's trust.

To her surprise, he didn't light into her immediately like he normally did. He only gave her a sad look.

Gracie let out a huff of exasperation. "Ada isn't here and—"

"Can I come in?"

Gracie paused. He normally didn't ask. He'd just barge in like he owned the place. "Yes, but I'm warning you that I am in no mood for—" She let her words drop off. She wasn't in the mood for anything.

He stepped inside with none of his normal bluster. His demeanor was more like a dog with its tail between its legs.

"What do you want to talk about?" Gracie said, hugging herself.

"I guess I don't want to talk."

Gracie threw up her hands. "Uncle Rand, I can't tonight."

He reached into his pocket and produced a key. A small, ornate one.

Gracie stared at it and then back up at Uncle Rand.

He didn't make eye contact with her. "It's the key to your box."

All her strength evaporated, and she staggered. "My box from Gran?"

He nodded.

"You had it the whole time?"

He didn't speak.

"You had it the whole time!" The words came out loud and with tears.

"It was on a key ring with the spare house key." He spoke slowly.

"Mom accidentally gave it to me. I told her that I was going to bring it back but forgot. At the end, she made me promise that I would give it to you as soon as possible."

Fat, hot tears rolled down her cheeks. "Why would you keep it from me?"

"Because I didn't think you deserved it."

She covered her mouth, crying so hard she couldn't catch her breath.

"I'm sorry." He walked over to the table in the seating area of the yarn shop and put the key on it. Without another word, he left.

Gracie couldn't get her legs to move. Her thoughts swirled, pain heavy in the mix. All those times she asked Uncle Rand about items in Gran's estate and he had never said a word. Her heart ached. Could she ever forgive him?

But now she had the key. She could open the box.

Taking slow steps, she went to the table and picked up the key. It was cold but almost weightless in her hand. She closed her fingers around it and went upstairs to her living room. To the box. She lifted it off the stand, carried it to the couch, and set it next to her.

Tears blurred her vision as she put the key in the lock and turned. She heard a soft click, and the lid popped open.

Taking a deep breath, she sat the key aside and lifted the lid.

The first thing she saw was a letter in a pink envelope with her name written on it in Gran's handwriting.

She tried to regulate her breathing as she lifted it out and carefully opened it. When she unfolded it, she saw it was dated a few months before Gran died. She ran her fingers over the paper and began to read.

> *Gracie Girl,*
>
> *This is not how I wanted this to go, but it's clear that God had other plans. I prayed, as I'm sure you did, that this cancer would be healed. I'm not giving up all hope yet, but I am settled that my healing may be in eternity.*
>
> *I don't want to leave you.*
>
> *You have had so many people leave you and have had to struggle through so many things alone. But in these*

past months, seeing God's love working through you as you have sacrificed your life to come care for me, I know you are not alone. You have God. And trust me, Gracie Girl, He is more than enough.

I realize that your life is going to get more complicated and painful after I'm gone. But I want you to go forward knowing that I love you and your mother loved you. And my love is the love I received from my mother and her mother and all the mothers in our family, past and present. That is why the house had to come to you. To continue the unbroken line of loving mothers.

If your mother had lived, my beloved and only daughter, she would have inherited the house. And she would have given it to you, and you would have given it to your daughter. That's the way the house gets passed down, from mother to daughter. I am not your mother, but I stand in her place with pride.

You are loved with a love that has traveled down through history and arrived at your heart.

Live in that love, my sweet angel.

Gran

Gracie dropped the letter, sobs wracking her body. She would have given anything to hold Gran again, but this was the next best thing. Gran's words and God's love, her mother's love, all wrapping around her like a warm blanket. Securing her and soothing her.

And not just their love. Ms. Lila's and Ada's love. Clarence's love. The love of knitting. The love of watching the girls develop their stitching skills. The love in the history of this house. She was surrounded.

And she now knew that no matter how bad things were, she could always hope in love.

CHAPTER TWENTY-SIX

Olivia

*T*hrobbing pain brought Olivia awake. She groaned and tried to move but found herself restricted. Thoughts in a jumble, she tried to focus. Where was she? The answer didn't immediately come to mind. She instead turned her attention to the sensations around her. Wherever she was, she was lying on her side on the floor. Her wrists were in pain, and when she tried to move her arms, something restrained them. Rope.

Realization cascaded over her like a flood.

Someone had grabbed her outside her house. White men she didn't recognize.

She opened her eyes, and her head spun. She was in what looked like a basement. Like her secret room, on a dirt floor.

Tears sprang to her eyes. Why had she followed Mr. Gull? She had ignored all their safety measures of not traveling alone. And for what reason? Because she thought she could do so without asking for help. How foolish. How absolutely foolish not to recognize her limits. Not to see that her so-called "protection" of Douglas was her own delusion. No matter what she did, he could not be completely safe in a city of slave catchers. Her tears fell at the thought of Douglas. If she did not escape, she would never know what he wanted to talk to her about.

Steadying herself, she tried to roll to sit up. A voice spoke in the darkness. "I wouldn't do that if I was you, Mrs. Kingston."

She strained to see the speaker, although she instantly recognized the voice. "Henry?"

"Yes, ma'am."

Shock added to her dizziness. "What are you doing here?"

"Paying for my sins," he said quietly. "They said they would help me free my family."

"They who?" Olivia asked.

"Saunders, Logan, and Mrs. Johnson." She heard him sigh. "I was a fool to think they would keep their promise. And now, you're here."

Olivia's skull throbbed with pain. "I do not understand, Henry."

"They told me if I helped them find out who was helping the fugitives, they would free my family."

She lay back on the floor and sucked in a breath. "Oh, Henry."

"I knew what all of you were doing. I gave them little bits of information. I didn't think they could figure it out. I am so sorry."

That jolted Olivia to action. "We will sort this all out later, but right now we have to get out of here. Are your hands free?"

"No."

"Can you untie mine?"

He remained where he was and silent.

"Henry, you have to untie me. If we remain here any longer, there will be no way for you to make this right." He was not the only one who needed to do some atoning.

A moment later, she felt Henry's rough fingers working the knots in the rope at her wrists. "How long have they been gone?"

"Not long. Sounds like they all left. Lots of walking upstairs." Henry pulled the rope, and Olivia let out a hiss of pain. "Sorry."

"Just keep going." In a few more seconds, she was free. She pushed off the floor to a sitting position and studied Henry. He looked haggard and thin. She untied his hands. "Let's go."

He nodded. She tried to stand, and the room spun. She braced herself against the wall. *You have to be strong right now.*

"Mrs. Kingston?" Henry asked from behind her.

"Follow me." She took shuffling steps over to the stairs, her muscles stiff from lying on the floor. She slowly crept up the stairs, Henry one step behind her. She stopped at the top, hoping her suspicions were true. That if she and Henry were bound, their captors would not feel the need to lock the door. She turned the doorknob, and it opened easily.

She paused before peeping out into the room in front of her. It was sparsely appointed. Only a few chairs and a single lamp sat on a table. Other than that, the room was empty.

"Guess they all did leave."

"We should do the same," Olivia said, and the room swam again. "Grab that lamp."

He moved across the room to retrieve it and then handed it to her. She motioned toward the back of the house.

"Door's over there," Henry whispered, pointing the opposite direction.

"They probably have someone watching the front door."

Henry nodded, and they came to a short hallway leading to the kitchen. When she heard someone at the front door, she paused, Henry ahead of her and out of view. With steps that made her head pound, she rushed into the hallway just as the door opened.

Voices filled the room, and she instantly recognized two of them—Saunders and Mrs. Johnson.

"Your and your men's incompetence is unacceptable," Mrs. Johnson hissed. "Catch slaves and people look the other way, but you assaulted a white man, and now the law is looking for you."

Mr. Gull.

"He didn't see us." Saunders sounded like a child being chastised.

"Does that matter?" Mrs. Johnson yelled. "They will be looking for someone who did see you. And then you bring the girl here. Why didn't you just kill her and dump her body somewhere?"

"We can get information from her and then sell her."

"The goal was to infiltrate the network here without raising suspicions. That would have provided us with as many slaves as we needed. We would have all gotten paid well. But she knows who I am. I have been to her house, fool."

So that was the plan. Olivia's heart thumped so loud that she was sure they could hear it. If they had succeeded. . . Olivia shuddered to think.

There was a pause, and then Mrs. Johnson said, "Did you leave the door open?"

"No."

We need to move, now. Olivia listened and heard two sets of footsteps rush down the stairs. She leaned into Henry. "Find the back door."

He crept two steps away from her, checked the kitchen, and nodded.

"Go," she whispered.

But when she tried to step away, she staggered, the room tipping.

"Would you look at this?"

She focused on the hall in front of her and saw Mrs. Johnson and Saunders standing at the other end.

Mrs. Johnson glanced back at Saunders. "I told you this one would be trouble."

"All the better that we sell her quick."

Olivia took a step back, assessing her options. As light-headed as she was, she would surely be caught before she made it out the kitchen door. Henry might make it but could be caught before he found help.

Then she remembered the lamp in her hand.

She said a quick prayer, then raised it above her head and threw it down the hallway toward Mrs. Johnson and Saunders with all her might. The lamp sailed through the air, and for a second she wasn't sure she had thrown it hard enough. But when it hit the floor, it shattered, and oil and fire splashed across the floor.

Mrs. Johnson let out a cry, but Olivia did not delay any longer. Henry had already opened the back door. They rushed out and found themselves in an alley between rows of houses. As they ran, they heard Mrs. Johnson and Saunders shouting.

Olivia tried to keep pace with Henry, who was much faster than she was, scanning to see if she recognized anything around her. After running full tilt down two streets, she realized they were near the wharf. Which meant they were near Shipper's.

"Follow me," she called to Henry.

Head throbbing and breath stinging her throat, she ran until they reached Shipper's. She staggered as Henry pounded on the back door.

The door opened and Molly appeared, her expression shocked. She reached out, grabbed Olivia's arm, and pulled her inside. "They've been looking all over for you."

Olivia made it to just inside the door before she collapsed.

CHAPTER TWENTY-SEVEN

GRACIE

As soon as Clarence texted her to meet him at the Historical Commission's office with all her paperwork for the house, Gracie grabbed the hat she was knitting, wrapped a scarf around her neck, tossed her phone in her purse, and was out the door with a quick explanation to Ada. Her nerves had been in a knot since the officers threatened her with eviction. No amount of reassurance could untie it. Clarence was sure they would get to the bottom of things with his lawyer friend's help. But what if the eviction was valid?

But what if it wasn't? She allowed herself to hope a little. Hope in the love Gran had for her.

As usual, Clarence was standing outside the building housing the Historical Commission, his expression brighter than the sun reflecting off the buildings. She realized she hadn't seen him since he'd come to her aid at the house. He leaned in and placed a soft kiss on her lips. "Let's go see Ms. Shaw and get this mystery solved."

He led her two blocks to another office building. They bypassed the front desk and went straight to the elevator. When the doors closed, he leaned over to her. "You have bags under your eyes. Have you slept?"

"Nice thing to say, new boyfriend."

He chuckled, pulling her close. "You know what I mean."

She looked at the sweater vest he was wearing. "I don't know what I'll do if the eviction notice is valid. Not just losing Gran's house—" She closed her mouth.

"You'll have to go back to Richmond?"

She didn't bother to tell him that she didn't have anywhere in Richmond to go back to. Her mind couldn't even imagine what that would be like. She would have to go back to square one with the yarn shop, searching for a location and praying to find something affordable. Once Gran's bills were settled, there might be a little money left, but she would have to divide it with Uncle Rand, since he was Gran's only living child. She still had a little of the annuity money, and if she sold all the fixtures she'd bought, that would provide a little revenue. Like Ada said, she would think of something. Not the bright future Gran tried to give her but one that looked more like her dark past.

A feeling pushed back against all her dread, pushing her to hope.

The elevator doors opened, and they were facing an all-glass wall. The door read SHAW AND ASSOCIATES. He led her through the door to a reception desk. The office was a different kind of quiet from Clarence's office. People talked and phones rang, but it was muffled, like she had cotton in her ears.

The receptionist looked up. "Mr. Evans. How are you? Haven't seen you around much. I haven't had a chance to congratulate you on the William Still discovery."

"Thank you. It was quite exciting." Clarence gave her a gracious smile.

The receptionist's phone rang. "Ms. Shaw is in her office," she said as she picked up the receiver.

Another short walk and they were at the corner office. Behind the desk sat a striking Black woman, hair flowing over her shoulders, makeup expertly applied to her butterscotch skin. Gracie was suddenly self-conscious. Ms. Shaw dripped in confidence. She looked like success. Gracie was sure she looked like a tired, stressed-out failure, even though she'd worn her repurposed cashmere sweater and an A-line skirt with high-heeled boots.

Ms. Shaw rose and shook Clarence's hand. "Clarence, how are you?"

"I'm well." He motioned to Gracie. "This is Ms. Gracie McNeil."

"Nice to meet you." She shook Gracie's hand. "Have a seat. Tell me how I can help you. Clarence, you made your issue sound quite urgent when you called."

"I'll let Gracie explain," he said, giving Gracie's hand a squeeze.

Gracie shifted in her chair and explained most of the story. She left out the secret room, but she had to force herself to keep talking when she talked about Gran passing. Clarence reached over and squeezed her hand.

Ms. Shaw gave her a sympathetic look. "I'm so sorry for your loss. And this must be adding a great deal of stress to your life in addition to grieving."

"Thank you." Gracie said. "Is there anything I can do?"

"There is plenty we can do. Let me start with a few questions. Was there anything in your grandmother's estate about a sale?"

Gracie shook her head. "Not anything I saw."

"Could paperwork be somewhere else? Safety deposit box or such? Maybe with other family members?" Ms. Shaw asked.

"Again, not that I know of." Gracie pulled out her sock and started knitting, needing to soothe her nerves. "And the judge in the probate court ordered all parties involved to turn over all paperwork. I believe everyone in the family did."

"When people are grieving, sometimes important things slip through the cracks. Were any of the bills paid late? Particularly taxes?"

Gracie's jaw dropped. "How did you know?"

"Because nonpayment of taxes is one of the few ways a person can lose a house that's already paid for." Ms. Shaw glanced down at Gracie's knitting, a curious look on her face. "One more question. Did either of you do an auction sale search?"

Clarence shook his head.

"I didn't even know that I should look." Gracie tried to stay calm, but her palms were sweating. She placed the knitting in her lap.

"You wouldn't have known to look." Ms. Shaw smiled and put her hands on her keyboard. "Let's start there." She asked Gracie for the address and for her ID. She typed something, waited a beat, and then leaned forward.

Gracie held her breath.

"Well, that's interesting." She tapped a few more keys. "There is no record of a tax auction sale for your house. I'm looking back to last year."

Gracie let out a long breath.

"Nope, nothing." Ms. Shaw tapped more keys. "Eviction notices are public records, so I'm checking the court records."

"The officers who came to my house said the warrant was incomplete." Gracie reached into the folder. "Here is the copy they gave me." She set it on the desk in front of Ms. Shaw.

Ms. Shaw paused and glanced at it. "It's very incomplete."

"I thought the same thing," Clarence said, frowning.

Ms. Shaw turned her eyes back to the screen. She typed for a few moments, then her eyebrows raised. "Oh, it's them."

"Who?" Gracie leaned forward.

"First Trust Loans and Investments," Ms. Shaw grumbled.

Gracie jumped. "They sent me a letter." She flipped through the folder and gave Ms. Shaw the paper. "I got it a few weeks ago. I called them to get information about the account, but they wouldn't tell me anything because it was in my gran's name."

"Did they ask you to send them a deed as proof?"

Gracie leaned forward. "Yes, they did, but I didn't do it."

Ms. Shaw smiled broadly. "Ms. McNeil, you're about to make history."

"I am?" Gracie squeaked.

"Yes. First Trust Loans and Investments has been defrauding people for years." Her fingers typed furiously now. "As a matter of fact, there have been a few victims in your neighborhood."

Gracie turned to Clarence. "Ms. Lila told me about it." She turned back to Ms. Shaw. "Clarence's grandmother and my gran were friends, and she told me how someone had come around and tried to buy the whole block but that some of the homeowners, like my gran, held out."

"But some of them gave in," Ms. Shaw said sadly. "More like were tricked into thinking that they owed a massive amount of back taxes. It happened the same way with you. Officers show up, stating they have an eviction notice. Strange or incomplete filings at the courts. Threats and, more importantly, requests for a copy of the deed."

"But wouldn't the homeowners research their tax history?" Gracie asked.

"Most of the victims were elderly and didn't have a Clarence to help them."

Gracie smiled, her gratitude to him overflowing. And love. Yup. She loved him. "So now what?"

"Every time someone has tried to take them to court, they haven't succeeded because of lack of evidence. The people at First Trust Loans and Investments are very good at their game and cover their tracks well. I believe they even have someone in the courts or government working with them. But with you, we have proof and can take them to court, even if it's just for falsifying documents," Ms. Shaw said.

Gracie thought for a moment, her heart aching for the families who already lost their homes. Their history. "Let's do it."

Ms. Shaw grinned. "Great. Do I have permission to start working on this on your behalf?"

Gracie fought to stay upright. Retain a lawyer? "I—um—am not exactly in the position—"

Ms. Shaw smiled at her. "Pro bono. Clarence called in a favor."

Gracie looked at him with shock. His ears turned pink. "You needed some answers immediately."

"Thank you both." Gracie fought back tears. "And yes, you have my permission to look into this."

Ms. Shaw's expression transformed into a look that meant trouble. "It will be my pleasure. Stealing people's homes makes me very angry. I will send all this information over to the state revenue department and make some other calls."

Gracie and Clarence thanked her and left the office. Gracie wasn't sure her feet were touching the ground. She wasn't going to be evicted. Not only that, she might save someone in the future from losing their home. She grinned all the way to the elevator, but as she walked and reality set in, tears formed in her eyes.

She was going to have the life Gran wanted for her. The house would stay in the family, and she would keep her promise to Gran and open the yarn store.

She had lots of bad in her life, but this—this was really good.

Saturday dawned, and Gracie lay in bed for a few minutes before moving.

She had slept soundly last night. The first time in a long while. With the house issues resolved, her mind seemed to be able to fully rest. After she showered and had some breakfast, she called Clarence.

He answered, his voice low. "I was just thinking about you."

"You were?"

"Just thanking God that your house issue got resolved."

"Yes, thank God," she said. "I don't know how much more I could have taken."

"Are you busy today?"

"I have my knitting class this afternoon." She told him about the situation with the bag.

"That's pretty serious. Are you okay?"

"Yes. Like you've told me before, it's going to be okay." She leaned back on the sofa. "But I do want to go somewhere with you."

"Dinner?"

"No. The library."

There was silence on the line for a second. "You want to go back to researching? The last time. . ."

"I know. I had a really hard time seeing my mother's and Gran's obituaries. But I'm better now. I can handle it because I now know how much they loved me. How much I meant to them." The letter she'd found in her wooden box had wiped away any doubt she had about their love. "I want to find out if there are more amazing women in my family."

"You're amazing."

"You are too."

"How about Monday?"

"Great."

"And dinner tonight?"

She laughed. "Okay."

"And my knitting class."

She tried to make her voice sound stern. "Okay, now. You're asking for a lot."

"Can I ask for more? If I did, would you still say yes?"

She gaped, unable to formulate words in response. What was he hinting at?

"Gracie?"

"I think. . . ," she said. "I think it would depend on what you're asking. I'm not down for searching dusty boxes."

He laughed. "That's fair. See you tonight."

"I look forward to it."

Gracie had to practice not grinning as she got the classroom ready for the girls. She needed to be serious, but every time she thought of Clarence asking for more, she couldn't hold back her smile. She finally sobered when she thought of what she was about to do. She prayed it would go as she planned.

Gracie had talked to Bella's mother about the girl's behavior. "I will certainly talk to her," the woman had said. "I'm surprised she acts like that since she loves the class so much. It's all she talks about. She even asked me if she could enroll when you offer the next class."

Gracie was cheerful as usual when the girls arrived. Dani, Bella, Trinity, and Rylee went straight back to the table and took their normal seats. Mia lagged behind while Gracie closed the door.

"Is everything all right, Mia?" she asked as they started toward the classroom.

"Yeah. Well, I wanted to say thank you for talking to my dad."

Gracie tried not to look surprised but failed. "You don't have to thank me."

"He canceled my punishment." She beamed up at Gracie.

They had stopped near the foot of the staircase. "He could have decided that on his own."

"He told me that you talked to him. And about my mom." She looked down at her shoes. "Thanks."

"You're welcome."

Mia looked over to where the red Cojo bag had been. "It's still missing?"

Gracie took a few steps away from Mia, motioning her to stay where she was, and peeked around the staircase. The girls were still at the table, engrossed in their conversation. She moved back to Mia. "Tell me what you know about the bag."

Mia's face morphed into a frown. "You still think I took it."

"No, I don't," Gracie said. She had to choose her words carefully. "I think I know what happened to it. But I need to know, did you pick it up or anything? Open it?"

Mia shook her head. "I never even touched it. My dad says, 'Look with your eyes, not with your hands.'"

Gracie smiled. "My gran used to say that to me too."

"Please believe me, Miss Gracie. I didn't even touch it."

She put a hand on the girl's shoulder. "It's okay. Please don't worry. Remember, whatever happens in class today, don't worry."

Mia gave her a quizzical look but nodded.

They went back to the classroom. Gracie let them talk a little more before she gave the lesson for the day—how to tell the right side from the wrong side of their work. "It's really simple," she said.

Dani shook her head. "You always say that. None of this was simple. Learning to purl was hard."

Gracie laughed. "But you mastered it. It only took a little practice."

At the halfway point of the class, Gracie stood up. "Girls, I have something uncomfortable to talk to you about."

They all put down their knitting and stared at her. "What's wrong, Miss Gracie?" Dani asked.

"I haven't been able to locate the missing bag."

"The red bag," Trinity said. "The one Mia stole."

Mia balled her fists. "I didn't steal it."

Gracie held up her hand for quiet. "I don't know who stole it. But it has been stolen. This class is the only group of people who have come into the shop since we aren't officially open." She took a deep breath. "Because of that, I am going to have to cancel the rest of our classes."

All the girls reacted like she suspected they would, with protests and pleas.

"But we already told you that Mia has it," Rylee said.

"I have spoken to Mia's father," Gracie said, keeping her voice calm. She hoped that the girls would deduce from her words that Mia was innocent, like she wanted them to.

"Then who took it?" Rylee looked around the table and then back at Gracie.

"I don't know, but I think it would be best if we end the classes until we figure it out," Gracie said. "Next week will be our last class until the bag is found."

Dani perked up. "So if the bag comes back, we can have class again?"

Gracie studied the girl. "Yes. If the person who took it returns it, classes will resume." She didn't add that the thief wouldn't be allowed to come back.

Trinity folded her arms and let out a frustrated sigh. "So we all get punished because someone"—she looked at Mia—"stole a bag?"

"Until I know who stole it, this is the only option we have," Gracie said, returning to her seat.

The class was significantly duller after her announcement, as she expected it would be. Except for Mia. She had brightened. She chatted and laughed like nothing had happened.

Bella sneered at her. "Why are you so happy?"

"'Cause I didn't steal the bag." She returned her attention back to her knitting. "Someone else is about to ruin the whole class, and it's not me."

The other girls groaned.

Rylee had a hard look on her face. "I like this class."

Trinity huffed. "We all do, but somebody had to go and mess it up."

They ended the class dejected, faces long as they went to the door. Trinity's mom picked up the three carpoolers, and Trinity immediately began explaining what had happened. Trinity's mother looked at Gracie. "Is that true?"

Gracie nodded. "I'll be giving parents a call later."

Except for Mia's dad.

CHAPTER TWENTY-EIGHT

*O*livia awakened with a start. She stared at the room around her, but when she tried to sit up, the room swam.

"Stay still, sweetheart."

Douglas.

The whole evening rushed back to her. She opened her eyes to find him sitting in a chair next to the bed. He looked haggard, eyes puffy and collar slightly askew. "Douglas." She tried to move again and realized there was a heavy lump on her right arm. When she turned, she found Hope sleeping next to her, a handful of Olivia's blouse in her fist.

"She would not stop crying until I let her get in the bed with you."

Tears sprang to Olivia's eyes. "I am so sorry."

Douglas frowned. "For what?"

"Many things. For worrying you so."

"This is not your fault," he said with conviction. "You didn't do anything to deserve this."

She looked around the room. "Where am I?"

"Shipper's. I did not want to move you until you healed a bit."

"How long have I been here?"

"All night," Douglas said. "You collapsed at the door, and Mr. Abrams carried you up here. They waited until daybreak to come for me."

She sighed. He had been up all night, probably worried beyond sleep. Then she remembered the rest of the night. "Mrs. Johnson."

"Henry told us what happened. Several members of the Vigilance

Committee, including some lawyers, went to the house you escaped from. They caught them. They were trying to put out the fire." Douglas gave her a grim smile. "Henry told us what you did."

"I didn't have many options."

"Rest assured that was the right one." Douglas gingerly took her hand. "Mrs. Johnson and Saunders were able to extinguish it before it burned down the entire house. When the ruins were searched for survivors, there were three more fugitives and two free Blacks locked up in other rooms."

Olivia closed her eyes. The seven of them would have been on their way to the South. She shuddered. "Thank God."

"Thank God, indeed, because apparently Mrs. Johnson has been running a very successful gang of slave catchers for years. They suspect she has sold at least fourteen free Blacks to the South. The police are also charging her with your kidnapping."

Olivia remembered the shrewd look in the woman's eyes. "I can believe it. I guess that is how she paid for all those expensive dresses."

"Saunders was a member of the gang as well as Logan. They have gone to jail also." Douglas rose. "You need to rest."

She nearly sat up but immediately thought better of it. "Do you have to leave?"

"Yes. I have not slept, and it would not do your head any good if Hope and I jostled you trying to sleep here with you." He lifted Hope off the bed after prying Olivia's blouse from her fingers. "I'll be back in a couple of hours to check on you."

"I love you."

He lifted her hand and kissed it. "I never thought I could love you more than I already did, but I do."

She spent another two days at Shipper's, Molly waiting on her hand and foot, before she was strong enough to go home. Douglas carefully escorted her even though her head felt much clearer. As they walked through the streets, gratefulness settled over her. The work she did was dangerous, but she was blessed to do it. To help in such a significant way. But she also knew that she did not have to do everything alone. She would accept as much help as she could get.

Which brought her to her next thought. She gripped Douglas' arm.

Over the past two days, she had only had brief conversations with Douglas, although she had many conversations with others. The Wilsons came to visit her, keeping her abreast of what was happening with Mrs. Johnson's and Saunders' court cases. Mr. and Mrs. Still visited and told her that although Mr. Gull was injured, he would recover.

The police had come to talk to her about what had happened. Thankfully, they did not ask about John or any of the other fugitives they found in the building. They recorded that she, a free Black, had been kidnapped, and that was enough for them. There had been such an uproar about the kidnapping of free Blacks since the Fugitive Slave Act passed a few years ago that the city officials were on edge.

Douglas had lingered silently in the background with all these visitors.

Once they arrived home, she would no longer avoid talking about her work with the Underground Railroad and how Douglas felt about it now that she had been injured.

Milly and Hope were playing in the living room when they came through the front door. Hope looked up and, to Olivia's delight and surprise, gave them a big smile. She scrambled toward them, still not quite strong enough to walk. Douglas bent down and scooped her up, swinging her in the air. Hope laughed and then held out her arms for Olivia.

Olivia pulled her close, the child nuzzling her face in Olivia's neck. Tears formed in her eyes.

Another conversation she and Douglas would have to have.

Milly gave them the update of all Hope had done that morning and then went home. Douglas led Olivia, still holding Hope, to the sofa and helped her sit. Olivia smiled at him. "It is good to be home."

"It is good to have you home." He sat down, watching her settle Hope on her lap. "I thought I had lost you."

Olivia lifted her gaze to him. She expected to find anger in his eyes, but it was not there. His eyes were filled with love. She took a deep breath. "I know you were very worried about me, but I cannot stop doing this work, regardless of the danger. I promise not to take any unnecessary risks, but I cannot stop."

Douglas leaned back, surprise on his face. "I could never ask you to stop this work. God willing, I want to help you."

She beamed at him. "I love you."

"I love you too."

CHAPTER TWENTY-NINE

GRACIE

With joy bubbling in her heart, Gracie typed in an official grand opening date of her brick-and-mortar yarn store, Stitch Wishes. With the cloud of doubt lifted, she could get the shop ready for business.

She sat back in her office chair and grinned at the screen. This was really happening.

She could now turn her attention to planning the grand opening event. Ada was more than ready and had been throwing ideas around for days. Gracie didn't know who was more excited. They both had let out a loud whoop when Preston finished installing the pegboard. They started putting the pegs and yarn up before he was done putting away his drill. They had also watched as a tech installed smart technology security cameras and a smart doorbell.

As Gracie watched the tech install the camera system control panel, she thought of all her family members who had lived in their house. Wondered what their lives were like. Wondered how they felt about how they lived. It was a nice daydream to wrap herself in.

When she and Clarence had talked over dinner, he told her he had only managed to trace the house deeds back to the 1920s. He was confident that he could keep going and find more. They had leaned over their notes in the restaurant, heads almost together. It wasn't until later that she realized how right it felt. To be close to him, watching his eyes sparkle with excitement when he talked about the history of her family. How he would hold her hand or wrap his arm around her shoulders when they were walking together.

As if he knew she was thinking of him, he texted, GOOD MORNING.

Clarence was something she hadn't expected in all the activity surrounding the house. She hadn't anticipated how helpful he would be with her research. She also hadn't anticipated how much she would love to be near him. That she would love him and he would love her.

GOOD MORNING, she texted back. HOW IS YOUR DAY GOING?

She turned on her computer and waited for his reply. Her heart beat faster when she read, SPENT THE MORNING THINKING OF YOU.

She grinned and was glad Ada wasn't here to give her that knowing look she gave when Gracie talked about Clarence. BEEN THINKING ABOUT YOU TOO.

I'D BE INTERESTED TO HEAR WHAT YOU WERE THINKING. Then a pause. MR. MOORE CALLED ME. HE FOUND SOMETHING.

Gracie stared at the message. Unable to contain her excitement, she punched the call icon. "What did he find?" she asked as soon as he answered.

He chuckled, and she realized that was another thing she loved about him. "I knew you were going to call. He didn't say, but he wanted to know when we would be at the library again."

She stared at the list of things to do for the shop. It wasn't that long. "Can we go this morning?"

He laughed again. "No, but I can go this afternoon. I've got to go and replace some high light bulbs in my grandmother's house."

"Oh, I can wait." She tried not to sound disappointed.

"You know that you don't have to wait for me."

"I know."

"All right. I'll see you this afternoon. Love you."

She paused.

He cleared his throat, and she could imagine his ears turning red. "Gracie?"

"Yes. I'm still here. Just not used to you telling me that you love me."

"Oh, good. I thought maybe it was too much."

"Uh, no. Just need to adjust to hearing it."

"Okay. See you later. Love you. Might as well practice hearing it."

She laughed. "Love you too."

When it was close to his arrival time, she stood outside in front of the house. She was so ready to know what Mr. Moore had found that she didn't want to wait for Clarence to park. As she stood there, she glanced over at William Still's house. Would she ever stop being amazed at knowing such an incredible person had lived there? Amazed at all that had happened in that house?

She let out a small laugh. If Clarence's suspicions were right, someday someone would stand looking at her house and think the same.

Clarence arrived, putting on his hazard lights long enough for her to climb in.

"Hey," she said.

"Sorry to keep you waiting. It took a lot to convince my grandmother not to come along with us."

"She could have come."

"She may one day."

The conversation died out, and Clarence drummed his fingers on his knee as he drove. It was as if they couldn't talk about anything, the suspense taking their words. Clarence parked as close to the library as he could, and they walked at a quick pace to the door.

They arrived at the government records office desk, and Mr. Moore beamed when he saw them. "There you are. I've got something exciting to tell you."

Instead of leading them to their normal spot at the tables, he picked up a folder and took them to a smaller room with just tables and closed the door behind them. "I did a little more digging on your family."

Gracie sat. "You did?"

"There is so much information stored in this building that I can't research it all, but when someone comes looking for family, it gives a focus to some research."

"You didn't have to do this for me," Gracie said.

"I know, but Mr. Evans is a great asset to the historical community, and it was slow one day last week." He sat next to her with a laugh.

Clarence sat on the other side of Gracie, scooting forward to see. He was close enough that she could lean back against his chest. "What did you find?"

He pulled out a piece of paper with a photo on it. In the photo were two rows of Black people, men and women. They wore stoic and serious expressions. "Last time Ms. McNeil was here, she wrote down her family's names on a piece of paper. She left it on the desk, and I decided to search their names."

The caption on the bottom of the photo read *The Society for the Betterment of Orphans*. "I think I found your great-great-great-grandmother."

Gracie gasped. "You did?"

Mr. Moore nodded. "She served as a member on the society's board." He gave Gracie a look and pointed to the list of names under the picture. The third person in the top row was her great-great-great-grandmother, Elizabeth McDonald.

"But there is someone else of importance here." He pointed to another woman in the picture. "Caroline Still."

Gracie sucked in a breath. "Like William Still?"

Mr. Moore nodded. "His youngest daughter."

Gracie lifted the paper, hand trembling. "This is amazing. I wish my gran—" A lump formed in her throat, and she bit back tears.

"That's amazing. I never heard of this organization before," Clarence said.

Mr. Moore grinned. "Me either. Back in the early 1800s, a lot of organizations popped up run by newly freed Blacks. This was one of them. They set out to battle the issue of orphans. Slavery had left many children without parents or unable to find theirs. The Civil War orphaned even more. It was a significant problem at the time."

Clarence leaned over. "How long was this society in operation?"

"Ten years before it disbanded," Mr. Moore said.

She pressed her hand to her heart. "I can't believe it."

"I wonder how she got involved in the group," Clarence said.

"Me too," Gracie said, searching her great-great-great-grandmother's face for any hints of familiarity.

"There are not many records on the society, since it was one of the smaller ones, but there may be more. I'll see what I can find," Mr. Moore said.

After he left, Clarence whispered, "I think he's on to us and why we're looking for records. He's a very observant man."

"Will he tell anyone about this?"

"No. We can trust him. But I think he's just as excited as we are."

Gracie returned to the microfiche and continued her search. It took a little time to trace all the names she had recorded. She would have to compare the names to the names on any deeds Clarence found.

But after an hour of searching, she found herself at a dead end again. She'd nearly cheered when she found two records for her great-great-great-grandparents. One was for Cornelia Murray. Cornelia's mother was listed as Beulah Murray, but that was where the records ended. No matter how she searched, she couldn't find any information on her.

Mr. Moore returned, and Gracie told him what she had found. "But I can't seem to find any records for Beulah Murray."

Mr. Moore looked thoughtful. "There may be more information for you to find here, but I think with the proximity of your house to the Still house and this connection between your great-great-great-grandmother and Caroline Still, it's time to introduce you to one of my friends—Ms. Darlis Quinn, the curator of the Still collection at Temple University."

Clarence shook his head and smiled. "I suspected you were on to us."

Mr. Moore gave him a sly look. "I figured it out the minute you told me the address."

"Do you really think there could be more information?" Gracie asked.

"If there is anything anyone needs to know about William Still, it is that he kept meticulous records. So there is a good chance that there is more." Mr. Moore jotted down Ms. Quinn's number and handed it to Gracie. "Now, go and see what else we can find out."

CHAPTER THIRTY

GRACIE

*S*aturday arrived, and Gracie's excitement about the family research put her on a high. She had called Ms. Quinn's office at Temple University and scheduled an appointment for Monday. She had hoped they could go sooner. But today she would hopefully resolve the Cojo bag mystery. She would find out if one of the girls she had grown quite connected to was a thief. Whatever happened, it would clear Mia, she was sure. Clearing the innocent was important.

She set up the classroom space, fully expecting that at some point in the class, the Cojo bag would magically return.

Mia and Dani arrived first. Gracie welcomed them warmly but watched as they both stared at the place where the bag was supposed to be, and their shoulders slumped. Trinity, Bella, and Rylee arrived next. Or rather, Trinity and Rylee. Bella wasn't with them when Gracie opened the door. "Where's Bella?" she asked once the girls came inside.

"She went back to the car. She left her phone," Bella's mom told her. "I just parked down the street, so she should be right back."

Gracie smiled. "Tell her the door is open when she gets here."

After Bella's mom left, Gracie closed the door but didn't lock it. As she passed the stairs, she looked up. Ada was sitting at the top of the steps, slightly in the shadows. If the plan went the way Gracie suspected it would, the thief wouldn't see her there.

Gracie went to the table and began asking the girls how their week went.

"Horrible," Trinity grumbled. "Are you still going to cancel the class?"

"If the bag doesn't come back, yes."

Trinity let out a sigh. "But I didn't take it."

A few minutes later, Bella came rushing into the classroom space. "I'm here, and I locked the door."

Gracie nodded and began the class instruction. The girls paid attention to everything she said, hanging on her every word, knowing this may be their last class. After the girls returned to their seats, Ada came down and asked Gracie to step into the next room.

When they were out of earshot, Ada whispered, "She brought it back."

Gracie lifted her phone. The smart home software allowed her to check the footage from the security camera in the system's app. She watched, let out a sigh, and returned to the table. She fought to act normally for the rest of class, but it wasn't easy. Now that the thief was caught, there would have to be consequences. It was hard, but she thought about what she had told Stanley about her overcoming her childhood troubles. If she could, so could anyone else.

Class ended, and the girls rose with long faces and packed up their things. Bella was ready before everyone else so she was leading the group as they walked toward the door. When she passed the place where the Cojo bag had been, she looked surprised and pointed. "The bag. It's back."

The other girls wore expressions of shock.

"Oh, Bella," Gracie said. She turned to the other girls. "Could you all please wait in the classroom? Except you, Bella."

Their shock turned to confusion, but Ada came out and ushered them around the end of the staircase like a flock of ducks.

"The bag is back, Ms. Gracie."

"Please sit out here until your mother arrives."

They didn't have to wait long. Bella's mom arrived with Stanley. Gracie directed Stanley to the classroom where the other girls were waiting but pulled Bella's mom aside. "Mrs. Bland, can I speak to you for a minute?"

"Of course."

Gracie called Bella over to them. "Mrs. Bland, I'm afraid that your daughter stole a bag from my shop. When I threatened to cancel the class, she brought it back."

Mrs. Bland looked from her to Bella and back again. "Bella wouldn't do that."

"I had my assistant watching from upstairs when she came today, and we have security cameras installed. I can show you the footage of Bella putting the bag back. What's worse is Bella accused another girl of stealing it."

"I didn't take it," Bella cried.

"Then explain how you got it and how you knew what was inside it."

"I—I guessed."

Mrs. Bland scowled at the girl. "Bella, did you take the bag?"

Gracie kept her face neutral. She didn't want Bella to think she was angry with her.

Bella's face became redder and redder. "It wasn't fair."

"What wasn't?" Gracie asked.

"You gave Mia a bag but wouldn't give me one," she said, anger flashing in her eyes. "I asked just like she did."

Mrs. Bland gaped. "You took the bag because Ms. Gracie gave Mia a bag but didn't give you one? Didn't I buy you a bag?"

"She should have given me a bag too." Bella folded her arms.

Compassion washed over Gracie. Bella could be facing some hard years if she didn't change.

"I am so sorry," Mrs. Bland said. She still looked a little shocked. "I will reimburse you for the bag."

"No need if it's not damaged." Gracie stooped to look Bella in the eye. "That was a very unkind thing you did by accusing Mia. But I believe you know that now and you'll apologize to her."

For a moment, Gracie thought the girl was going to remain

defiant, but tears began to flow down her cheeks. She didn't speak, only nodded.

Gracie called for Mia, who came out of the classroom with her father. Gracie stepped back and left the rest to Mrs. Bland. "Bella, do you have something to say to Mia?" Mrs. Bland said.

"I'm sorry for saying you stole the bag." Bella spoke so quietly Gracie barely heard her.

"So you took the bag?" Mia said.

Bella nodded.

Pride filled Gracie's heart when Mia said, "I accept your apology."

"Now let's go home. We need to have a talk," Mrs. Bland said to Bella. She collected the rest of the girls.

"Does this mean we can come back next week?" Dani was bouncing on her toes.

"Yes, we'll have class next week."

The three girls, two of them all smiles, and Dani left, but Stanley and Mia lingered. When they had gone, Stanley said, "Thank you. You believed Mia even when I didn't."

"You're welcome. And remember, I was a lot like Mia when I was her age." Gracie smiled. "I just treated her and Bella the way I wish someone had treated me when I was their age."

Mia gave her a tight hug. "You're the best. Can you marry my dad?"

Stanley turned pink then red in quick succession. "Mia—"

Gracie guffawed. "Sorry, I have a boyfriend."

"Do you like him?"

"A lot."

Mia let her go. "At least I tried."

Stanley ushered Mia toward the door. "Let's go before you embarrass me further."

Mia shot Gracie a grin. "See ya next week!"

꧁꧂

When Ms. Shaw called with an update on First Trust Loans and Investments, Gracie appreciated her even more. The woman was driven and determined. She told Gracie that she had turned the information over to the state Department of Revenue.

"That's the first step. The second is to open an investigation. Which they did today."

Gracie let out a breath and sat down in her office chair. "Okay, then what?"

"Once they investigate, they'll see if they should file charges," Ms. Shaw said. "But I'm sure they will. These guys have been defrauding people for a while. They will want to catch them as soon as possible. But as a backup, I called a friend in the state's Bureau of Enforcement and Investigation."

"So we wait?"

"Yes, and you should prepare to testify if needed."

"I can do that," Gracie said. "And again, thank you. If there is anything I can do for you—"

"Teach me to knit. I'll even pay for a class."

Gracie laughed. "Sure."

"I've been trying to find a way to ask you since you were knitting in my office. My mother used to knit, and I would love to surprise her when I visit again."

"You got it, and no paying for the classes. I can't repay you for what you've done."

"Deal."

After the call, Gracie dressed warmly in knitted hat, cowl, and mittens. She considered standing outside again to wait for Clarence to pick her up. But the December air changed her mind. It had shifted the weather from cold to freezing. She would have to start planning Christmas. A pang pricked her heart. First Christmas without Gran. It would hurt, but she would do her best to find joy in it.

Ada saw her standing by the door and laughed. "You got a boyfriend and a car service. He does know you can drive?"

"I think he likes driving me around."

"I think he likes you a lot."

Gracie looked down at her shoes and fiddled with her mittens. "He told me he loves me."

For a second, Ada was quiet. Gracie looked up at her. She had her hand pressed to her mouth. Then she let out a squeal. "That's so cute." Ada rushed across the room and gave Gracie a huge hug. "I knew he did."

Gracie laughed. "I didn't until he said it."

"That's because you didn't want to believe what you saw." She released Gracie and grasped her shoulders. "Do you love him?"

Gracie grinned. "I do."

Ada let out another squeal, and Gracie hugged her back. But this time when she pulled out of the embrace, Ada had tears in her eyes. "I wish Gran was here. She wanted you to be happy. I wish she could have seen it."

Tears blurred Gracie's vision. "She sorta already approved Clarence. They used to talk about history before I came."

"Well, I have to be a stand-in for Gran and tell you how happy I am for you."

Gracie sniffled. "Are you trying to make me cry harder?"

They hugged until they heard Clarence toot his horn. Gracie wiped the tears from her cheeks. "I'll see you later."

She tried to look like she hadn't just been crying when she got in the car, but it didn't work.

Clarence leaned over to kiss her on the cheek but paused. "Have you been crying?"

"How do you do that?" She sniffled.

"Is everything okay?"

"Yes. Ada and I were talking about how much Gran would have liked you."

He smiled sadly and pulled away from the house. "She did like me. My grandmother introduced me to her as soon as I got to Philly."

Gracie stared at him. "Really? I didn't know that."

"Our grandmothers were too good of friends for her not to." He gave her a quick glance. "I loved Ms. Marian. She was thoughtful and smart like you. I was so sad when she passed."

Gracie gripped her hands in her lap. "I didn't realize you were that close."

"I think they were planning to set us up with each other." He smiled. "Guess they got their wish."

The drive took a little longer than their other trips as they made their way to Temple University. Clarence told her how the Still family had donated many of their records to the college. "It's a massive collection with lots of documents, but they are doing their best to arrange them in some sort of order."

"I would think it would have been dangerous to keep such records."

"It was," Clarence said. "But William Still did it anyway. He actually hid his documents in a cemetery to keep them safe."

"That's pretty smart."

Clarence nodded. "Thanks to his ingenuity, we have detailed records of the workings of the Underground Railroad."

They found a parking space in the college's visitor parking and walked across the campus to the building that housed the records. A receptionist was sitting at a desk in the front hall.

Gracie gave her a smile. "Hi, my name is Gracie McNeil, and I have an appointment with Ms. Quinn."

The woman returned her smile. "Yes. Go right down this hall, turn right, and go all the way to the office at the end. I'll let her know you're here."

Their footsteps echoed loudly in the hall, and Gracie's excitement built with each step. When they turned right, the door at the end of the hall opened, and a tall woman stood in the doorway. "Ms. McNeil. Mr. Evans." When they reached her, she shook their hands. "Nice to meet you."

Ms. Quinn's office was neat, but it was more library than office. The walls were lined with bookcases, and every shelf was full. Two chairs sat in front of a large desk. Behind the desk was a window with a view to the college campus. "Let me start by saying how impressed I am with your work, Mr. Evans. Finding Mr. Still's house was incredible."

Clarence's ears turned pink. "It wasn't just me. A lot of people worked on it."

"But you kept the search going. Good job." She turned her attention to Gracie. "How can I help you?"

"I am doing some research on my grandmother's house and thought there might be some information that would help here in your collection." She told Ms. Quinn about the document Mr. Moore found connecting Caroline Still to her great-great-great grandmother. She didn't tell her about the secret room, but if she was as smart as Mr. Moore, she would figure it out. "I recently inherited the house when my gran died."

Ms. Quinn gave her a sympathetic look. "I'm sorry for your loss."

"Thank you." Gracie swallowed. "I discovered something about the house that suggests it was a part of the Underground Railroad. That, and it's about a half block from William Still's house."

Ms. Quinn's eyes sparkled. "The more we look into the Still records, the more we are amazed at how far the network went. It included all types of people. All ages. All demographics. The neighborhood in Bella Vista had a considerable number of free Blacks involved in the work they did."

"Gracie has another connection to the Stills. Her great-great-great-grandmother served with Caroline Still on the board of The Society for the Betterment of Orphans," Clarence added.

"So all roads lead you to the Stills." Mrs. Quinn stood. "Then I would love to show you some of the records."

As they walked to the records room, Clarence practically hummed with excitement. Ms. Quinn led them into a room that had neat, orderly rows of bookcases. "I think you should probably start with the letters written to and from the Stills, since your great-great-great-grandmother is the connection you know about."

She led Gracie to a microfiche machine. "I'm going to be an expert on using these after this," Gracie said with a laugh.

"Yes, microfiche is a researcher's best friend." Ms. Quinn went back to the door. "Since you have Mr. Evans here, I won't need to tell you how to handle some of the older items. He already knows. Please let me know if you need anything else."

She left and Gracie sat.

Clarence pulled a chair over to sit beside her, excitement in his eyes. "This never gets old."

They focused on searching Caroline Still's letters. After an hour, Gracie was ready to give up.

"Remember," Clarence said, switching places with her to give her eyes a rest, "we only need one clue."

"I don't know how you can do this for so long."

Clarence gave her a sideways glance. "It's interesting and exciting."

Clarence searched for another half an hour. Gracie laid her head on his shoulder. "Anything?"

"Not yet but—" Clarence began and then stopped.

Gracie sat up. "What?"

The screen displayed a letter from Caroline to another committee member. It was a letter detailing the funeral arrangements for Elizabeth's grandmother, Olivia Kingston. It also mentioned how heartbroken Elizabeth was at Olivia's passing.

Gracie leaned closer to the screen. "Wow," she said to Clarence.

"Interesting, no record of her mother, but she mentions her grandmother. The power of grandmothers." He paused. "Wait."

He pulled up the deed list on his phone. "I'll be right back."

Gracie reread the letter on the screen. She had wondered what her ancestors' lives were like. Elizabeth had lost her beloved grandmother, Olivia. Just like her losing Gran.

Clarence returned. "I just called Mr. Moore. I had him look through the property deeds for an Olivia Kingston."

Gracie held her breath, her nerves jittering. "Did he find something?"

Clarence held up his phone. A slightly blurry picture of a microfiche screen. He enlarged it. "Olivia Kingston."

Gracie exhaled hard and looked at the listing. It was a scant entry, but it showed that the original owners of her house were Olivia and Douglas Kingston.

"We found them," she whispered.

Clarence gave her a broad grin. "You did most of it. But think of it. If the room was built when the house was constructed, Olivia and Douglas would have been the ones to do it."

Gracie rushed back to the microfiche boxes on the shelves. "Then let's see if Olivia and Douglas are in the letters."

Excitement charged through her as Clarence searched the files for microfiche dated ten years earlier. He found the box and placed it on the table. "This roll is marked 'Underground Railroad records.' I think this might be the best place to check."

They searched several films but found nothing. Gracie sighed. "Maybe there isn't anything," she said.

"Have hope," Clarence said, eyes on the screen.

"It's okay. We found the most important thing. We can now trace my house's ownership back to Olivia and Douglas."

"And that's a pretty good accomplishment. Most people can't do that." Clarence looked at her. "Do you want to stop?"

She looked at the screen. Her shoulders ached and her eyes felt like they had sand in them. "Let's look at one more film. It's not like I can't come back later."

When she went back to the shelves of films, she studied each of the listings on the spines. One caught her attention. It was marked CHILDREN AND ORPHANS. She considered for a moment before taking it down from the shelf. She brought it to the table where Clarence was. "Maybe we can look at this one. Elizabeth was involved in the care of orphans. Maybe there's a reason she did that. That's a pretty specific concern to get involved in." She thought of the children's knitting class and Mia. She'd started that class because learning to knit as a child had changed her life.

"Sounds good." Clarence returned to his seat, and Gracie carefully loaded the film into the machine.

Neither of them spoke as they skimmed the material. But when

Gracie flipped to the next frame, she gasped.

It was a letter from Olivia Kingston to William Still.

They sat in silence for a moment, shock stealing Gracie's words. They had done it. They had found a direct connection between Olivia, her foremother, and William Still and the Underground Railroad. Undeniable proof.

They read the letter together. Then Gracie leaned against Clarence's shoulder and cried.

CHAPTER THIRTY-ONE

OLIVIA

Olivia looked over at Hope sleeping in her little basket bed and smiled. She had fallen asleep shortly after lunchtime, and Olivia had raced to her sewing table to finish the hem on the dress she was working on. Douglas had cleared Olivia to return to her activities a few days after she arrived home. She had only had a few bouts of dizziness, but they were not frequent. She had gone back to her customers and taking passengers into her room. Fugitives looking for assistance had continued to arrive, and Olivia was glad to return to helping them, even if it took some reordering of her life.

Hope was her first priority. Of course, she had Douglas to help, and with some coordination, they could manage the passengers in their room. Douglas took on more duties, including working as a conductor one night. Milly loved Hope as much as Douglas and Olivia did, so she was always happy to sit with the little girl when Olivia had customers. She and Douglas found that despite the extra responsibility of caring for a child, they could continue their work.

Hope had become a part of their life, a ray of sunshine. She had started to make noises but no words yet. She had also begun to move a lot more, keeping Olivia on her toes and guarding her pins even closer. The child still loved the sound of them all hitting the floor. Only a few days had passed since Beulah died, but it seemed longer to Olivia.

When someone knocked on the door, Olivia opened it to find Mr. Still standing on the doorstep.

"Mr. Still, come in."

He walked into the room, his eyes going to Olivia's sewing table. "This looks like how I left Lucretia this morning." Then he saw Hope sleeping. "Can I speak with you for a moment?"

"Of course," Olivia said.

"I saw Mrs. Brasewell this morning, and she said she can accommodate Hope now," he said, his tone neutral. But the effect the news had on Olivia's heart was not.

She sat down hard in the chair at her sewing table. "She can?"

"Yes. She wants you to bring the child tomorrow and get her settled. She said you and Douglas are welcome to come and visit the child anytime you like."

Visit? "Oh. That would be nice," was all Olivia managed to say.

"I will do everything in my power to see that Hope grows up well and has everything she needs." Mr. Still turned to the door. "Unfortunately, I have to go. I am on my way to a meeting and thought I would relay the message in person."

Olivia rose, numb with shock. "Thank you."

She stayed in the haze of shock the rest of the day. Everything Hope did was more precious to her. Several times when Hope smiled at her, Olivia confused the child by crying in response. She eventually managed to control her emotions a little, but then Douglas arrived home from work.

Douglas. She would have to tell him.

He came through the door and immediately lifted Hope into his arms. "Hello," he said, kissing the child on the forehead. When he came and planted a kiss on Olivia's cheek, he slowed. "Is everything all right?"

Olivia felt her bottom lip tremble. "We need to talk."

They sat, Douglas watching her the whole time. Then he asked, "Are you not feeling well again?"

"I am well." She steadied herself. "Mr. Still visited today. He said that there is space at the orphanage for Hope."

She watched Douglas think through the words. Then he clutched

Hope closer. "An orphanage," he said in a tone that was not quite a question.

"Yes. We can take her tomorrow and visit anytime we like."

He frowned. "An orphanage," he said again. He looked at Hope, who was now trying to put her fingers in his mouth. "But we are the only people she knows."

"Which is why we will have to get her adjusted."

Douglas pressed his lips together, but his expression said everything she was feeling.

Olivia left them and went back to working on the hem, although it turned out to be an exercise in futility. She could not focus her thoughts enough to sew straight.

She should have known this was coming. That one day they would have to give up Hope. She was not theirs, and the agreement was for them to care for her temporarily. But Olivia's feelings were too strong for temporary care.

She and Douglas had been trying to have children for years, but none had come from their trying. Douglas had regularly assured her that it would happen one day, but in her heart, Olivia wondered if it would. They had no children even though they desperately wanted them.

Then Hope arrived.

What if Hope was God's way of sending them a child? If she was the blessing He had sent to them? It could not be a more perfect arrangement. She and Douglas had no children. Hope had no parents. Could they—she paused in her very poor sewing—could they be her parents? Beulah had asked them to be Hope's mama and daddy. The thought seemed too good to be true. She turned and looked at Douglas, who was reading a book to Hope. It would be perfect.

By the time they sat down to dinner, Olivia had managed to find her courage and the words. Douglas said a blessing over the food, his tone bittersweet. Olivia kept her head lowered even after the prayer was finished. She lifted her fork but then put it back down.

She heard Douglas' fork clank against the plate. She looked up and found him staring back at her. Then they were both speaking at the same time.

"I do not want to take Hope to the orphanage," Douglas said.

"We should adopt Hope," Olivia said.

Douglas bolted out of his chair and came to kneel next to Olivia's chair, his eyes full of expectation. "Are you certain?"

"Yes. I cannot bear to think of her going there." She took Douglas' hand. "I know we believe that God will give us children. But what if He already has?"

Douglas' eyes filled with tears. "Then we will adopt her."

Olivia beamed. "I will write a letter to Mr. Still."

They both looked at Hope, who was focused on the mashed potatoes and was wearing a large streak of it on her cheek, oblivious to how her life had just changed for the better.

Olivia went to her sewing table and gathered the needed supplies with a shaky hand and wrote:

> *Dear Mr. Still,*
>
> *I have a matter I would like to discuss with you. Douglas and I would like to adopt Hope. Can you please advise us on how to proceed? We pray that one day after the horrible practice of slavery is outlawed, as we all hope it will be soon, we will be able to officially adopt her. Her arrival at our house for shelter has changed our lives, and we want to change hers.*
>
> *Of course, our work of receiving passengers will have to resume after we have established a routine with Hope. If, however, there is any other assistance Douglas and I can give, please send word to us.*
>
> *A final note. We are considering changing Hope's name to Beulah Hope Kingston in honor of her mother. We want Beulah Hope to always remember what her mother did for her and carry her name with honor.*
>
> *Yours faithfully,*
> *Olivia Kingston*

When she was done, she returned to where Douglas still sat at the table, Hope sleeping in his lap. She read him the letter. He paused for a moment and then said, "It is perfect."

"Are you in agreement with the name change?"

"Yes. Her mother went through great lengths to obtain Hope's freedom."

Tears formed in Olivia's eyes as she looked at Douglas and Hope. Her family.

CHAPTER THIRTY-TWO

GRACIE

$\mathcal{G}$racie stood at the top of the stairs, phone in hand. She took several pictures of the room below.

A roomful of knitters and crocheters.

She and Ada had strung fairy lights around the room, and a few balloons bobbed in the air. A carousel of cupcakes and water bottles sat in the middle of the instruction table. Gracie smiled as she took a candid shot of Mia easily chatting with another knitter. Gracie had been overjoyed to get an email from Stanley asking if Mia could attend the grand opening. Ms. Lila sat in one of the armchairs talking to crocheters she knew from Mother Bethel. Ada had taken over hosting duties. She moved between assisting customers and checking them out at the counter.

Gracie snapped a picture of Ada, thankful again to have her cousin back in her life. When she checked the picture, she saw that the door to the secret room was in the corner of the picture. She took another picture of the door.

Finding that door had changed her life. It began a journey to finding out the house's rich history. Clarence had told her that her house was a shoo-in to be registered as a historic location. It was just waiting for the formality of a vote. She took a picture of Clarence, who stood behind his grandmother's chair with a cup of punch in his hand. Somehow, he must have sensed she was looking at him, because he looked up and blew her a kiss, which she returned.

The event couldn't have gone better. The excitement of having a yarn store in the neighborhood had a line forming on the sidewalk before she even opened the doors. She had had to open up more knitting and crochet classes, and Mia's school had asked her to come and teach some of the teachers. She would be very busy for the next couple of months.

She came down, and Ada met her at the bottom of the stairs. "We already met our sales goal for the day."

Gracie beamed. "Really? This day is almost perfect."

"Almost?" Ada asked.

"The only thing that would have been better is to have Gran here."

Ada put her arm around Gracie. "Because we are here, her memory is here."

Gracie sniffled. "I've already cried enough today."

"This is a happy occasion," Ms. Lila said from behind them. "Only happy tears." She hugged Gracie. "I miss her too."

And then all three of them teared up.

Gracie moved out of Ms. Lila's embrace. "Let's have some cupcakes."

"Yes. I've been waiting for that all day," Ada said, wiping her eyes.

They served the cupcakes on paper plates, and when she handed Clarence one, he leaned closer. "I still need to talk to you about my knitting classes."

Gracie laughed. "We have plenty of time."

He set his plate on the table. "But what if it takes a long time for me to learn?" he asked. He slipped an arm around her waist.

Gracie took a half step, and she was tucked against his chest. "It won't. You're a smart man. I think you'll pick it up quickly."

He moved away, turning to face her. "Then I would like to reserve more time for my classes."

"You have all the time you need," she said with a laugh.

"The rest of our lives?"

She looked up at him, confused. "I don't think it will take—"

Clarence reached into his pocket and produced a small box.

Gracie stared at it for a moment before registering what it was. *The rest of our lives.*

He dropped to one knee and opened the box. The room went quiet. A diamond ring sat nestled in the velvet. "Marry me?"

More tears. Gracie's heart felt full already; now it overflowed. "Yes."

He stood and slipped the ring on her finger as the room erupted with cheers and applause. He kissed her, and then she threw her arms around him. "I hope you don't mind living upstairs from a yarn shop."

He looked down at her. "I want to be wherever you are."

"Good. 'Cause our history continues in this house."

AUTHOR'S NOTE

*W*riting about the Underground Railroad brings both joy and pain. Reading the stories of people taking risks to run to freedom is inspiring—until I remember why they took those risks. There is the pain. The cruelty and inhumanity fugitives fled from. And as a Black woman, knowing that if I were alive at that time, my family and I would have experienced the same cruelty. That's sobering.

Slavery lasted way too long, and too many people suffered. According to the 1860 US Census, over three million people were enslaved by the start of the Civil War.[1] That's roughly the 2020 population of Uruguay or Jamaica. Slavery wasn't abolished until 1865, but many didn't wait. They took flight for the North and freedom.

In his book *The Underground Railroad*, William Still recounted some of the most daring and harrowing acts of bravery. To escape slavery, both men and women would sometimes ship themselves to Philadelphia. Others traveled north in large escape parties for protection. Some parents, like William Still's mother, ran with small children. All to be free.

One of the reasons the Underground Railroad was so effective was because of the secrecy. The Fugitive Slave Act (1793 and 1850) made it illegal to assist enslaved men and women who had escaped their enslavers. Because of this, conductors, stationmasters, and shareholders (people who financially supported the Underground Railroad's efforts), worked in secrecy. Only William Still kept detailed records, and they survived because he had the forethought to hide them where only the dead would see—in a cemetery.

---

[1] Library of Congress, "Africans in America," accessed March 31, 2022, https://www.loc.gov/classroom-materials/immigration/african/africans-in-america/.

In 2018 Philadelphia historians discovered the location of William Still's house. I remember reading the news story and thinking about how amazing that find must have been. Other station houses on the lines that helped people to freedom had been discovered, but none so famous as the Still house. To look at the house before the discovery, one wouldn't think it was anything special. But after, to think that William Still possibly interviewed and moved more than six hundred fugitives through that house boggles the mind.

My story is set in a community named Bella Vista. This community was made up of mostly free Blacks, and in his book *Black Abolitionists*, Benjamin Quarles proved the important role that free Blacks played in the Underground Railroad through not only vigilance committees but by providing shelter and resources to those who ran from the South and arrived in Philadelphia, Ohio, and even Canada. Many of those free Blacks, like William Still's parents, were once enslaved themselves and considered it God's work to help others.

One last note: The villain of this story, Mrs. Johnson. Chilling, but she comes right out of the pages of history. I based Mrs. Johnson's character on a real-life person named Patty Cannon. Patty Cannon is believed to have murdered thirty enslaved and free Blacks. She and her family operated a successful gang of slave catchers and bounty hunters. Historians say she poisoned herself once she was captured. Even more interesting, what is believed to be her skull was on display until 1961 at the Dover Public Library. Her house is a historical location in Delaware.[2]

My hope with this story is to show both the struggle and the survival, the horror and the triumph. I hope that it will be an educational experience as well. That something in this book, from the high mortality rate of Black mothers to the heroism of stationmasters, from family history to knitting, would pique your interest.

Terri J. Haynes

---

[2] "Patty Cannon," Dorchester County Historical Society, Maryland, accessed March 30, 2022, https://www.dorchesterhistory.com/patty-cannon.

ACKNOWLEDGMENTS

To Jesus. You got jokes, but I love You anyway.

To my wonderful family: Brian, I still hold, after twenty-six years of marriage, that you are the best husband God could have picked for me. Your brainstorming skills are unmatched. Thank you for putting up with your wife while she deals with the characters in her head. To my children—Jazmyne, Dartanyon, and Emmanuel. You are three of the funniest, most creative, and weirdest people I know. And I should know, 'cause I raised you. Thank you for understanding that being a writer makes me weird. Love you all.

To Dyara Henderson, thank you so much for mothering me. It's not meddling. It's love. Thank you to my agent, Tamala Hancock Murray. Thank you, Monique Slater, for sharing your real estate knowledge.

Thank you to all my readers for letting me tell you stories. Stick around. I have more.

Terri J. Haynes, a native Baltimorean, is a homeschool mom, writer, prolific knitter, freelance graphic artist, and former army wife (left the army, not the husband). She loves to read, so much so that when she was in elementary school, she masterminded a plan to be locked in a public library armed with only a flashlight to read all the books and a peanut butter and jelly sandwich. As she grew, her love for writing grew as she tried her hand at poetry, articles, speeches, and fiction. She is a storyteller at heart. Her passion is to draw readers into the story world she has created and to bring laughter and joy to their lives.

Terri is a 2010 American Christian Fiction Writers Genesis contest finalist and a 2012 semifinalist. She is also a 2013 Amazon Breakthrough Novel Award Quarterfinalist. Her publishing credits include *Cup of Comfort for Military Families*, Crosswalk.com, *The Secret Place Devotional*, Urbanfaith.com, Vista Devotional, and *Publisher's Weekly*.

Terri holds a bachelor's degree in theology, a master's degree in theological studies, and a certificate in creative writing and graphic design, meeting the minimal requirements for being a geek. She and her husband pastor a church where she serves as executive pastor and worship leader. Terri lives in Maryland with her three wonderful children and her husband, who often beg her not to kill off their favorite characters.

Website: www.terrijhaynes.com
Blog: www.inotherwords.terrijhaynes.com